Charles Dickens 著

汪倜然 譯

A CHRISTMAS CAROL

小氣財神

本書譯文由上海世紀出版股份有限公司譯文出版社授權使用

書　　名：*A Christmas Carol* 小氣財神
作　　者：Charles Dickens
插　　圖：John Leech
譯　　者：汪倜然
責任編輯：張朗欣　黃家麗
封面設計：楊愛文
出　　版：商務印書館 (香港) 有限公司
　　　　　香港筲箕灣耀興道 3 號東滙廣場 8 樓
　　　　　http://www.commercialpress.com.hk
發　　行：香港聯合書刊物流有限公司
　　　　　香港新界大埔汀麗路 36 號中華商務印刷大廈 3 字樓
印　　刷：中華商務彩色印刷有限公司
　　　　　香港新界大埔汀麗路 36 號中華商務印刷大廈
版　　次：2015 年 6 月第 1 版第 1 次印刷
　　　　　© 2015 商務印書館 (香港) 有限公司
　　　　　ISBN 978 962 07 0388 1
　　　　　Printed in Hong Kong

Publisher's Note 出版説明

守財奴史高治以為不斷工作掙錢，就是人生，三幽靈帶他到過去、現在和未來的聖誕，他才發現錯過了很多美好的人和事，讓我們知道要珍惜所有，享受每分每秒。經典故事讀來饒有興味，更啟發讀者對人生的思考。

初、中級英語程度讀者使用本書時，先閱讀英文原文，如遇到理解障礙，則參照中譯作為輔助。在英文原文結束之前或附註解，標註古英語、非現代詞彙拼寫形式及語法；同樣，在譯文結束之前或會附註釋，以助讀者理解原文故事背景。如有餘力，讀者可在閱讀原文部份段落後，查閱相應中譯，觀察同樣詞句在雙語中不同的表達。

讀者亦可藉此書體會如何用優美文字表達深意，進而提升雙語文字修養。此外，故事寓意也值得一再細味：時間一去不復返，我們不能抹去過錯，但生活總會給你另一個機會，這個機會叫明天。

商務印書館 (香港) 有限公司
編輯出版部

Contents　目錄

Stave One

Marley's Ghost

Marley was dead: to begin with. There is no doubt whatever about that. The register of his burial was signed by the clergyman, the clerk, the undertaker, and the chief mourner. Scrooge signed it: and Scrooge's name was good upon 'Change[1], for anything he chose to put his hand to. Old Marley was as dead as a door-nail[2].

Mind! I don't mean to say that I know, of my own knowledge, what there is particularly dead about a door-nail. I might have been inclined, myself, to regard a coffin-nail as the deadest piece of ironmongery in the trade. But the wisdom of our ancestors is in the simile; and my unhallowed hands shall not disturb it, or the Country's done for. You will therefore permit me to repeat, emphatically, that Marley was as dead as a door-nail.

Scrooge knew he was dead? Of course he did. How could it be otherwise? Scrooge and he were partners for I don't know how many years. Scrooge was his sole executor, his sole administrator, his sole assign, his sole residuary legatee, his sole friend and sole mourner. And even Scrooge was not so dreadfully cut up by the sad event, but that he was an excellent man of business on the very day of the funeral, and solemnised it with an undoubted bargain.

The mention of Marley's funeral brings me back to the point I started from. There is no doubt that Marley was dead. This must be distinctly understood, or nothing wonderful can come of the story I am going to relate. If we were not perfectly convinced that Hamlet's Father died before the play began, there would be nothing more remarkable in his taking a stroll at night, in an easterly wind, upon his own ramparts, than there would be in any other middle-aged gentleman rashly turning out after dark in a breezy spot—say Saint Paul's Churchyard for instance—literally to astonish his son's weak mind.

Scrooge never painted out Old Marley's name. There it stood, years afterwards, above the warehouse door: Scrooge and Marley. The firm was known as Scrooge and Marley. Sometimes people new to the business called Scrooge Scrooge, and sometimes Marley, but he answered to both names: it was all the same to him.

Oh! But he was a tight-fisted hand at the grindstone, Scrooge! a[3] squeezing, wrenching, grasping, scraping, clutching, covetous, old sinner! Hard and sharp as flint, from which no steel had ever struck out generous fire; secret, and self-contained, and solitary as an oyster. The cold within him froze his old features, nipped his pointed nose, shrivelled his cheek, stiffened his gait; made his eyes red, his thin lips blue; and spoke out shrewdly in his grating voice. A frosty rime was on his head, and on his eyebrows, and his wiry chin. He carried his own low temperature always about with him; he iced his office in the dog-days; and didn't thaw it one degree at Christmas.

External heat and cold had little influence on Scrooge. No

warmth could warm, no wintry weather chill him. No wind that blew was bitterer than he, no falling snow was more intent upon its purpose, no pelting rain less open to entreaty. Foul weather didn't know where to have him. The heaviest rain, and snow, and hail, and sleet, could boast of the advantage over him in only one respect. They often 'came down' handsomely, and Scrooge never did.

Nobody ever stopped him in the street to say, with gladsome looks, 'My dear Scrooge, how are you? when[4] will you come to see me?' No beggars implored him to bestow a trifle, no children asked him what it was o'clock, no man or woman ever once in all his life inquired the way to such and such a place, of Scrooge. Even the blind men's dogs appeared to know him; and when they saw him coming on, would tug their owners into doorways and up courts; and then would wag their tails as though they said, 'no[5] eye at all is better than an evil eye, dark master!'

But what did Scrooge care? It was the very thing he liked. To edge his way along the crowded paths of life, warning all human sympathy to keep its distance, was what the knowing ones call 'nuts' to Scrooge.

Once upon a time—of all the good days in the year, on Christmas Eve—old Scrooge sat busy in his counting-house. It was cold, bleak, biting weather: foggy withal: and he could hear the people in the court outside, go wheezing up and down, beating their hands upon their breasts, and stamping their feet upon the pavement-stones to warm them. The City clocks had only just gone three, but it was quite dark already: it had not been light all day: and candles were flaring in the windows of the neighbouring offices, like ruddy smears upon the palpable brown air. The fog came pouring in at every chink and keyhole, and was so dense without, that although the court was of the narrowest, the houses opposite were mere phantoms. To see the dingy cloud come drooping down, obscuring everything, one might have thought that Nature lived hard by, and was brewing on a large scale.

The door of Scrooge's counting-house was open that he might keep his eye upon his clerk, who in a dismal little cell beyond, a sort of tank, was copying letters. Scrooge had a very small fire, but the clerk's fire was so very much smaller that it looked like one coal. But he couldn't replenish it, for Scrooge kept the coal-box in his own room; and so surely as the clerk came in with the shovel, the master predicted that it would be necessary for them to part. Wherefore the clerk put on his white comforter, and tried to warm himself at the candle; in which effort, not being a man of strong imagination, he failed.

'A merry[6] Christmas, uncle! God save you!' cried a cheerful voice. It was the voice of Scrooge's nephew, who came upon him so quickly that this was the first intimation he had of his approach.

'Bah!' said Scrooge. 'Humbug!'

He had so heated himself with rapid walking in the fog and frost, this nephew of Scrooge's, that he was all in a glow; his face was ruddy and handsome; his eyes sparkled, and his breath smoked again.

'Christmas a humbug, uncle!' said Scrooge's nephew. 'You don't mean that, I am sure?'

'I do,' said Scrooge. 'Merry Christmas! What right have you to be merry? What reason have you to be merry? You're poor enough.'

'Come, then,' returned the nephew gaily. 'What right have you to be dismal? what[7] reason have you to be morose? You're rich enough.'

Scrooge having no better answer ready on the spur of the moment, said, 'Bah!' again; and followed it up with 'Humbug.'

'Don't be cross, uncle!' said the nephew.

'What else can I be,' returned the uncle, 'when I live in such a world of fools as this? Merry Christmas! Out upon merry Christmas! What's Christmas time to you but a time for paying bills without money; a time for finding yourself a year older, and not an hour richer; a time for balancing your books and having every item in 'em[8] through a round dozen of months presented dead against you? If I could work my will,' said Scrooge, indignantly, 'every idiot who goes about with "Merry Christmas," on his lips, should be boiled with his own pudding, and buried with a stake of holly through his heart. He should!'

'Uncle!' pleaded the nephew.

'Nephew!' returned the uncle sternly, 'keep[9] Christmas in your own way, and let me keep it in mine.'

'Keep it!' repeated Scrooge's nephew. 'But you don't keep it.'

'Let me leave it alone, then,' said Scrooge. 'Much good may it do you! Much good it has ever done you!'

'There are many things from which I might have derived good, by which I have not profited, I dare say,' returned the nephew; 'Christmas among the rest. But I am sure I have always thought of Christmas time, when it has come round—apart from the veneration due to its sacred name and origin, if anything belonging to it can be apart from that—as a good time: a kind, forgiving, charitable, pleasant time: the only time I know of, in the long calendar of the year, when men and women seem by one consent to open their shut-up hearts freely, and to think of people below them as if they really were fellow-passengers to the grave, and not another race of creatures bound on other journeys. And therefore, uncle, though it has never put a scrap of gold or silver in my pocket, I believe that it *has* done me good, and *will* do me good; and I say, God bless it!'

The clerk in the tank involuntarily applauded: becoming immediately sensible of the impropriety, he poked the fire, and extinguished the last frail spark for ever.

'Let me hear another sound from *you*,' said Scrooge, 'and you'll keep your Christmas by losing your situation. You're quite a powerful speaker, sir,' he added, turning to his nephew. 'I wonder you don't go into Parliament.'

'Don't be angry, uncle. Come! Dine with us to-morrow[10].'

Scrooge said that he would see him—yes, indeed he did. He went the whole length of the expression, and said that he would see him in that extremity first.

'But why?' cried Scrooge's nephew. 'Why?'

'Why did you get married?' said Scrooge.

'Because I fell in love.'

'Because you fell in love!' growled Scrooge, as if that were the only one thing in the world more ridiculous than a merry Christmas. 'Good afternoon!'

'Nay, uncle, but you never came to see me before that happened. Why give it as a reason for not coming now?'

'Good afternoon,' said Scrooge.

'I want nothing from you; I ask nothing of you; why cannot we be friends?'

'Good afternoon!' said Scrooge.

'I am sorry, with all my heart, to find you so resolute. We have never had any quarrel, to which I have been a party. But I have made the trial in homage to Christmas, and I'll keep my Christmas humour to the last. So A Merry Christmas, uncle!'

'Good afternoon' said Scrooge.

'And A[11] Happy New Year!'

'Good afternoon!' said Scrooge.

His nephew left the room without an angry word, notwithstanding. He stopped at the outer door to bestow the greetings of the season on the clerk, who, cold as he was, was warmer than Scrooge; for he returned them cordially.

'There's another fellow,' muttered Scrooge, who overheard him: 'my clerk, with fifteen shillings a-week[12], and a wife and family, talking about a merry Christmas. I'll retire to Bedlam.'

This lunatic, in letting Scrooge's nephew out, had let two other people in. They were portly gentlemen, pleasant to behold, and now stood, with their hats off, in Scrooge's office. They had books and papers in their hands, and bowed to him.

'Scrooge and Marley's, I believe,' said one of the gentlemen, referring to his list. 'Have I the pleasure of addressing Mr. Scrooge, or Mr. Marley?'

'Mr. Marley has been dead these seven years,' Scrooge replied. 'He died seven years ago, this very night.'

'We have no doubt his liberality is well represented by his surviving partner,' said the gentleman, presenting his credentials.

It certainly was; for they had been two kindred spirits. At the ominous word 'liberality' Scrooge frowned, and shook his head, and handed the credentials back.

'At this festive season of the year, Mr. Scrooge,' said the gentleman, taking up a pen, 'it is more than usually desirable that we should make some slight provision for the poor and destitute, who suffer greatly at the present time. Many thousands are in want of common necessaries; hundreds of thousands are in want of common comforts, sir.'

'Are there no prisons?' asked Scrooge.

'Plenty of prisons,' said the gentleman, laying down the pen again.

'And the Union workhouses?' demanded Scrooge. 'Are they still in operation?'

'They are. Still,' returned the gentleman, 'I wish I could say they were not.'

'The Treadmill and the Poor Law are in full vigour, then?' said Scrooge.

'Both very busy, sir.'

'Oh! I was afraid, from what you said at first, that something had occurred to stop them in their useful course,' said Scrooge. 'I am very glad to hear it.'

'Under the impression that they scarcely furnish Christian cheer of mind or body to the multitude,' returned the gentleman, 'a few of us are endeavouring to raise a fund to buy the Poor some meat and drink, and means of warmth. We choose this time because it is a time, of all others, when Want is keenly felt, and Abundance rejoices. What shall I put you down for?'

'Nothing!' Scrooge replied.

'You wish to be anonymous?'

'I wish to be left alone,' said Scrooge. 'Since you ask me what I wish, gentlemen, that is my answer. I don't make merry myself at Christmas, and I can't afford to make idle people merry. I help to support the establishments I have mentioned: they cost enough: and those who are badly off must go there.'

'Many can't go there; and many would rather die.'

'If they would rather die,' said Scrooge, 'they had better do it, and decrease the surplus population. Besides—excuse me—I don't know that.'

'But you might know it,' observed the gentleman.

'It's not my business,' Scrooge returned. 'It's enough for a man to understand his own business, and not to interfere with other people's. Mine occupies me constantly. Good afternoon, gentlemen!'

Seeing clearly that it would be useless to pursue their point, the gentlemen withdrew. Scrooge resumed his labours with an improved opinion of himself, and in a more facetious temper than was usual with him.

Meanwhile the fog and darkness thickened so, that people ran about with flaring links, proffering their services to go before horses in carriages, and conduct them on their way. The ancient tower of a church, whose gruff old bell was always peeping slily down at Scrooge out of a gothic window in the wall, became invisible, and struck the hours and quarters in the clouds, with tremulous vibrations afterwards, as if its teeth were chattering in its frozen head up there. The cold became intense. In the main street, at the corner of the court, some labourers were repairing the gas-pipes, and had lighted a great fire in a brazier, round which a party of ragged men and boys were gathered: warming their hands and winking their eyes before the blaze in rapture. The water-plug being left in solitude, its overflowings sullenly congealed, and turned to misanthropic ice. The brightness of the shops where holly sprigs and berries crackled in the lamp-heat of the windows, made pale faces ruddy as they passed. Poulterers' and grocers' trades became a splendid joke: a glorious pageant, with which it was next to impossible to believe that such dull principles as bargain and sale had anything to do. The Lord Mayor, in the stronghold of the mighty Mansion House, gave orders to his fifty cooks and butlers to keep Christmas as a Lord Mayor's household should; and even the little tailor, whom he had fined five shillings on the previous Monday for being drunk and blood-thirsty in the streets, stirred up to-morrow's pudding in his garret, while his lean wife and the baby sallied out to buy the beef.

Foggier yet, and colder! Piercing, searching, biting cold. If the good Saint Dunstan had but nipped the Evil Spirit's nose with a touch of such weather as that, instead of using his familiar weapons, then indeed he would have roared to lusty purpose. The owner of one scant young nose, gnawed and mumbled by the hungry cold as bones are gnawed by dogs, stooped down at Scrooge's keyhole to regale him with a Christmas carol: but at the first sound of—

'God bless you, merry gentleman!

May nothing you dismay!'

Scrooge seized the ruler with such energy of action, that the singer fled in terror, leaving the keyhole to the fog and even more congenial frost.

At length the hour of shutting up the counting-house arrived. With an ill-will Scrooge dismounted from his stool, and tacitly admitted the fact to the expectant clerk in the Tank, who instantly snuffed his candle out, and put on his hat.

'You'll want all day to-morrow, I suppose?' said Scrooge.

'If quite convenient, sir.'

'It's not convenient,' said Scrooge, 'and it's not fair. If I was to stop half-a-crown for it, you'd think yourself ill used[13], I'll be bound?'

The clerk smiled faintly.

'And yet,' said Scrooge, 'you don't think *me* ill used, when I pay a day's wages for no work.'

The clerk observed that it was only once a year.

'A poor excuse for picking a man's pocket every twenty-fifth of December!' said Scrooge, buttoning his great-coat to the chin. 'But I suppose you must have the whole day. Be here all the earlier next morning!'

The clerk promised that he would; and Scrooge walked out with a growl. The office was closed in a twinkling, and the clerk, with the long ends of his white comforter dangling below his waist (for he boasted no great-coat), went down a slide on Cornhill, at the end of a line of boys, twenty times, in honour of its being Christmas-eve[14], and then ran home to Camden Town as hard as he could pelt, to play at blindman's-buff.

Scrooge took his melancholy dinner in his usual melancholy tavern; and having read all the newspapers, and beguiled the rest of the evening with his banker's-book, went home to bed. He lived in chambers which had once belonged to his deceased partner. They were a gloomy suite of rooms, in a lowering pile of building up a yard, where it had so little business to be, that one could scarcely help fancying it must have run there when it was a young house, playing at hide-and-seek with other houses, and have forgotten the way out again. It was old enough now, and dreary enough, for nobody lived in it but Scrooge, the other rooms being all let out as offices. The yard was so dark that even Scrooge, who knew its every stone, was fain to grope with his hands. The fog and frost so hung about the black old gateway of the house, that it seemed as if the Genius of the Weather sat in mournful meditation on the threshold.

Now, it is a fact, that there was nothing at all particular about the knocker on the door, except that it was very large. It is also a fact, that Scrooge had seen it night and morning during his whole residence in that place; also that Scrooge had as little of what is called fancy about him as any man in the City of London, even including—which is a bold word—the corporation, aldermen, and livery. Let it also be borne in mind that Scrooge had not bestowed one thought on Marley, since his last mention of his seven-years'-dead partner that afternoon. And then let any man explain to me, if he can, how it happened that Scrooge, having his key in the lock of the door, saw in the knocker, without its undergoing any intermediate process of change—not a knocker, but Marley's face.

Marley's face. It was not in impenetrable shadow as the other objects in the yard were, but had a dismal light about it, like a bad lobster in a dark cellar. It was not angry or ferocious, but looked at Scrooge as Marley used to look: with ghostly spectacles turned upon its ghostly forehead. The hair was curiously stirred, as if by breath of hot-air; and though the eyes were wide open, they were perfectly motionless. That, and its livid colour, made it horrible; but its horror seemed to be, in spite of the face and beyond its control, rather than a part of its own expression.

As Scrooge looked fixedly at this phenomenon, it was a knocker again.

To say that he was not startled, or that his blood was not conscious of a terrible sensation to which it had been a stranger from infancy, would be untrue. But he put his hand upon the key he had relinquished, turned it sturdily, walked in, and lighted his candle.

He *did* pause, with a moment's irresolution, before he shut the door; and he *did* look cautiously behind it first, as if he half-expected to be terrified with the sight of Marley's pigtail sticking out into the hall. But there was nothing on the back of the door, except the screws and nuts that held the knocker on; so he said, 'Pooh, pooh!' and closed it with a bang.

The sound resounded through the house like thunder. Every room above, and every cask in the wine-merchant's cellars below, appeared to have a separate peal of echoes of its own. Scrooge was not a man to be frightened by echoes. He fastened the door, and walked across the hall, and up the stairs: slowly too: trimming his candle as he went.

You may talk vaguely about driving a coach-and-six up a good old flight of stairs, or through a bad young Act of Parliament; but I mean to say you might have got a hearse up that staircase, and taken it broadwise, with the splinter-bar towards the wall, and the door towards the balustrades: and done it easy. There was plenty of width for that, and room to spare; which is perhaps the reason why Scrooge thought he saw a locomotive hearse going on before him in the gloom. Half a dozen gas-lamps out of the street wouldn't have lighted the entry too well, so you may suppose that it was pretty dark with Scrooge's dip.

Up Scrooge went, not caring a button for that: darkness is cheap, and Scrooge liked it. But, before he shut his heavy door, he walked through his rooms to see that all was right. He had just enough recollection of the face to desire to do that.

Sitting-room[15], bedroom, lumber-room. All as they should be. Nobody under the table, nobody under the sofa; a small fire in the grate; spoon and basin ready; and the little saucepan of gruel (Scrooge had a cold in his head) upon the hob. Nobody under the bed; nobody in the closet; nobody in his dressing-gown, which was hanging up in a suspicious attitude against the wall. Lumber-room as usual. Old fire-guard, old shoes, two fish baskets, washing-stand on three legs, and a poker.

Quite satisfied, he closed his door, and locked himself in; double locked himself in, which was not his custom. Thus secured against surprise, he took off his cravat; put on his dressing-gown and slippers, and his nightcap; and sat down before the fire to take his gruel.

It was a very low fire indeed; nothing on such a bitter night. He was obliged to sit close to it, and brood over it, before he could extract the least sensation of warmth from such a handful of fuel. The fireplace was an old one, built by some Dutch merchant long ago, and paved all round with quaint Dutch tiles, designed to illustrate the Scriptures. There were Cains and Abels; Pharaoh's daughters, Queens of Sheba, Angelic messengers descending through the air on clouds like feather-beds, Abrahams, Belshazzars, Apostles putting off to sea in butter-boats, hundreds of figures to attract his thoughts; and yet that face of Marley, seven years dead, came like the ancient Prophet's rod, and swallowed up the whole. If each smooth tile had been a blank at first, with power to shape some picture on its surface from the disjointed fragments of his thoughts, there would have been a copy of old Marley's head on every one.

'Humbug!' said Scrooge; and walked across the room.

After several turns, he sat down again. As he threw his head back in the chair, his glance happened to rest upon a bell, a disused bell, that hung in the room, and communicated for some purpose now forgotten with a chamber in the highest storey of the building. It was with great astonishment, and with a strange, inexplicable dread, that as he looked, he saw this bell begin to swing. It swung so softly in the outset that it scarcely made a sound; but soon it rang out loudly, and so did every bell in the house.

This might have lasted half a minute, or a minute, but it seemed an hour. The bells ceased as they had begun, together. They were succeeded by a clanking noise, deep down below; as if some person were dragging a heavy chain over the casks in the wine-merchant's cellar. Scrooge then remembered to have heard that ghosts in haunted houses were described as dragging chains.

The cellar-door flew open with a booming sound, and then he heard the noise much louder, on the floors below; then coming up the stairs; then coming straight towards his door.

'It's humbug still!' said Scrooge. 'I won't believe it.'

His colour changed though, when, without a pause, it came on through the heavy door, and passed into the room before his eyes. Upon its coming in, the dying flame leaped up, as though it cried, 'I know him! Marley's Ghost!' and fell again.

The same face: the very same. Marley in his pig-tail, usual waistcoat, tights, and boots; the tassels on the latter bristling, like his pigtail, and his coat-skirts, and the hair upon his head. The chain he drew was clasped about his middle. It was long, and wound about him like a tail; and it was made (for Scrooge observed it closely) of cash-boxes, keys, padlocks, ledgers, deeds,

and heavy purses wrought in steel. His body was transparent: so that Scrooge, observing him, and looking through his waistcoat, could see the two buttons on his coat behind.

Scrooge had often heard it said that Marley had no bowels, but he had never believed it until now.

No, nor did he believe it even now. Though he looked the phantom through and through, and saw it standing before him; though he felt the chilling influence of its death-cold eyes; and marked the very texture of the folded kerchief bound about its head and chin, which wrapper he had not observed before; he was still incredulous, and fought against his senses.

'How now!' said Scrooge, caustic and cold as ever. 'What do you want with me?'

'Much!'—Marley's voice, no doubt about it.

'Who are you?'

'Ask me who I *was*.'

'Who *were* you, then?' said Scrooge, raising his voice. 'You're particular—for a shade.' He was going to say 'to a shade,' but substituted this, as more appropriate.

'In life I was your partner, Jacob Marley.'

'Can you—can you sit down?' asked Scrooge, looking doubtfully at him.

'I can.'

'Do it, then.'

Scrooge asked the question, because he didn't know whether a ghost so transparent might find himself in a condition to take a chair; and felt that in the event of its being impossible, it might involve the necessity of an embarrassing explanation. But the Ghost sat down on the opposite side of the fireplace, as if he were quite used to it.

'You don't believe in me,' observed the Ghost.

'I don't,' said Scrooge.

'What evidence would you have of my reality beyond that of your own senses?'

'I don't know,' said Scrooge.

'Why do you doubt your senses?'

'Because,' said Scrooge, 'a little thing affects them. A slight disorder of the stomach makes them cheats. You may be an undigested bit of beef, a blot of mustard, a crumb of cheese, a fragment of an underdone potato. There's more of gravy than of grave about you, whatever you are!'

Scrooge was not much in the habit of cracking jokes, nor did he feel, in his heart, by any means waggish then. The truth is, that he tried to be smart, as a means of distracting his own attention, and keeping down his terror; for the spectre's voice disturbed the very marrow in his bones.

To sit, staring at those fixed, glazed eyes, in silence for a moment, would play, Scrooge felt, the very deuce with him. There was something very awful, too, in the spectre's being provided with an infernal atmosphere of his own. Scrooge could not feel it himself, but this was clearly the case; for though the Ghost sat perfectly motionless, its hair, and skirts, and tassels, were still agitated as by the hot vapour from an oven.

'You see this toothpick?' said Scrooge, returning quickly to the charge, for the reason just assigned; and wishing, though it were only for a second, to divert the vision's stony gaze from himself.

'I do,' replied the Ghost.

'You are not looking at it,' said Scrooge.

'But I see it,' said the Ghost, 'notwithstanding.'

'Well!' returned Scrooge, 'I have but to swallow this, and be for the rest of my days persecuted by a legion of goblins, all of my own creation. Humbug, I tell you—humbug!'

At this, the spirit raised a frightful cry, and shook its chain with such a dismal and appalling noise, that Scrooge held on tight to his chair, to save himself from falling in a swoon. But how much greater was his horror, when the phantom taking off the bandage round his head, as if it were too warm to wear in-doors[16], its lower jaw dropped down upon its breast!

Scrooge fell upon his knees, and clasped his hands before his face.

'Mercy!' he said. 'Dreadful apparition, why do you trouble me?'

'Man of the worldly mind!' replied the Ghost, 'do[17] you believe in me or not?'

'I do,' said Scrooge. 'I must. But why do spirits walk the earth, and why do they come to me?'

· 'It is required of every man,' the Ghost returned, 'that the spirit within him should walk abroad among his fellow-men, and travel far and wide; and if that spirit goes not forth in life, it is condemned to do so after death. It is doomed to wander through the world—oh, woe is me!—and witness what it cannot share, but might have shared on earth, and turned to happiness!'

Again the spectre raised a cry, and shook its chain and wrung its shadowy hands.

'You are fettered,' said Scrooge, trembling. 'Tell me why?'

'I wear the chain I forged in life,' replied the Ghost. 'I made it link by link, and yard by yard; I girded it on of my own free will, and of my own free will I wore it. Is its pattern strange to *you*?'

Scrooge trembled more and more.

'Or would you know,' pursued the Ghost, 'the weight and length of the strong coil you bear yourself? It was full as heavy and as long as this, seven Christmas Eves ago. You have laboured on it, since. It is a ponderous chain!'

Scrooge glanced about him on the floor, in the expectation of finding himself surrounded by some fifty or sixty fathoms of iron cable, but he could see nothing.

'Jacob!' he said imploringly. 'Old Jacob Marley, tell me more. Speak comfort to me, Jacob.'

'I have none to give,' the Ghost replied. 'It comes from other regions, Ebenezer Scrooge, and is conveyed by other ministers, to other kinds of men. Nor can I tell you what I would. A very little more is all permitted to me. I cannot rest, I cannot stay, I cannot linger anywhere. My spirit never walked beyond our counting-house—mark me!—in life my spirit never roved beyond the narrow limits of our money-changing hole; and weary journeys lie before me!'

It was a habit with Scrooge, whenever he became thoughtful, to put his hands in his breeches pockets. Pondering on what the Ghost had said, he did so now, but without lifting up his eyes, or getting off his knees.

'You must have been very slow about it, Jacob,' Scrooge observed, in a business-like manner, though with humility and deference.

'Slow!' the Ghost repeated.

'Seven years dead,' mused Scrooge. 'And travelling all the time?'

'The whole time,' said the Ghost. 'No rest, no peace. Incessant torture of remorse.'

'You travel fast?' said Scrooge.

'On the wings of the wind,' replied the Ghost.

'You might have got over a great quantity of ground in seven years,' said Scrooge.

The Ghost, on hearing this, set up another cry, and clanked its chain so hideously in the dead silence of the night, that the Ward would have been justified in indicting it for a nuisance.

'Oh! captive, bound, and double-ironed,' cried the phantom, 'not to know that ages of incessant labour by immortal creatures, for this earth must pass into eternity before the good of which it is susceptible is all developed. Not to know that any Christian spirit working kindly in its little sphere, whatever it may be, will find its mortal life too short for its vast means of usefulness. Not to know that no space of regret can make amends for one life's opportunities misused! Yet such was I! Oh, such was I!'

'But you were always a good man of business, Jacob,' faltered Scrooge, who now began to apply this to himself.

'Business!' cried the Ghost, wringing its hands again. 'Mankind was my business. The common welfare was my business; charity, mercy, forbearance, and benevolence were, all, my business. The dealings of my trade were but a drop of water in the comprehensive ocean of my business!'

It held up its chain at arm's length, as if that were the cause of all its unavailing grief, and flung it heavily upon the ground again.

'At this time of the rolling year,' the spectre said, 'I suffer most. Why did I walk through crowds of fellow-beings with my eyes turned down, and never raise them to that blessed Star which led the Wise Men to a poor abode? Were there no poor homes to which its light would have conducted *me!*'

Scrooge was very much dismayed to hear the spectre going on

at this rate, and began to quake exceedingly.

'Hear me!' cried the Ghost. 'My time is nearly gone.'

'I will,' said Scrooge. 'But don't be hard upon me! Don't be flowery, Jacob! Pray!'

'How it is that I appear before you in a shape that you can see, I may not tell. I have sat invisible beside you many and many a day.'

It was not an agreeable idea. Scrooge shivered, and wiped the perspiration from his brow.

'That is no light part of my penance,' pursued the Ghost. 'I am here to-night to warn you that you have yet a chance and hope of escaping my fate. A chance and hope of my procuring, Ebenezer.'

'You were always a good friend to me,' said Scrooge. 'Thank'ee[18]!'

'You will be haunted,' resumed the Ghost, 'by Three Spirits.'

Scrooge's countenance fell almost as low as the Ghost's had done.

'Is that the chance and hope you mentioned, Jacob?' he demanded, in a faltering voice.

'It is.'

'I—I think I'd rather not,' said Scrooge.

'Without their visits,' said the Ghost, 'you cannot hope to shun the path I tread. Expect the first to-morrow, when the bell tolls one.'

'Couldn't I take 'em all at once, and have it over, Jacob?' hinted Scrooge.

'Expect the second on the next night at the same hour. The third upon the next night when the last stroke of twelve has ceased to vibrate. Look to see me no more; and look that, for your own sake, you remember what has passed between us!'

When it had said these words, the spectre took its wrapper from the table, and bound it round its head, as before. Scrooge knew this, by the smart sound its teeth made, when the jaws were brought together by the bandage. He ventured to raise his eyes again, and found his supernatural visitor confronting him in an erect attitude, with its chain wound over and about its arm.

The apparition walked backward from him; and at every step it took, the window raised itself a little, so that when the spectre reached it, it was wide open. It beckoned Scrooge to approach, which he did. When they were within two paces of each other, Marley's Ghost held up its hand, warning him to come no nearer. Scrooge stopped.

Not so much in obedience as in surprise and fear: for on the raising of the hand, he became sensible of confused noises in the air; incoherent sounds of lamentation and regret; wailings inexpressibly sorrowful and self-accusatory. The spectre, after listening for a moment, joined in the mournful dirge; and floated out upon the bleak, dark night.

Scrooge followed to the window: desperate in his curiosity. He looked out.

The air was filled with phantoms, wandering hither and thither in restless haste, and moaning as they went. Every one of them wore chains like Marley's Ghost; some few (they might be guilty governments) were linked together; none were free. Many had been personally known to Scrooge in their lives. He had been quite familiar with one old ghost in a white waistcoat, with a monstrous iron safe attached to its ankle, who cried piteously at being unable to assist a wretched woman with an infant, whom it saw below, upon a door-step. The misery with them all was, clearly, that they sought to interfere, for good, in human matters, and had lost the power for ever.

Whether these creatures faded into mist, or mist enshrouded them, he could not tell. But they and their spirit voices faded together; and the night became as it had been when he walked home.

Scrooge closed the window, and examined the door by which the Ghost had entered. It was double-locked, as he had locked it with his own hands, and the bolts were undisturbed. He tried to say 'Humbug!' but stopped at the first syllable. And being, from the emotion he had undergone, or the fatigues of the day, or his

glimpse of the Invisible World, or the dull conversation of the Ghost, or the lateness of the hour, much in need of repose, went straight to bed, without undressing, and fell asleep upon the instant.

Stave Two

The First of the Three Sprits

When Scrooge awoke, it was so dark, that, looking out of bed, he could scarcely distinguish the transparent window from the opaque walls of his chamber. He was endeavouring to pierce the darkness with his ferret eyes, when the chimes of a neighbouring church struck the four quarters. So he listened for the hour.

To his great astonishment, the heavy bell went on from six to seven, and from seven to eight, and regularly up to twelve; then stopped. Twelve! It was past two when he went to bed. The clock was wrong. An icicle must have got into the works. Twelve!

He touched the spring of his repeater, to correct this most preposterous clock. Its rapid little pulse beat twelve; and stopped.

'Why, it isn't possible,' said Scrooge, 'that I can have slept through a whole day and far into another night. It isn't possible that anything has happened to the sun, and this is twelve at noon!'

The idea being an alarming one, he scrambled out of bed, and groped his way to the window. He was obliged to rub the frost off with the sleeve of his dressing-gown before he could see anything;

and could see very little then. All he could make out was, that it was still very foggy and extremely cold, and that there was no noise of people running to and fro, and making a great stir, as there unquestionably would have been if night had beaten off bright day, and taken possession of the world. This was a great relief, because 'three days after sight of this First of Exchange pay to Mr. Ebenezer Scrooge or his order,' and so forth, would have become a mere United States' security if there were no days to count by.

Scrooge went to bed again, and thought, and thought, and thought it over and over, and could make nothing of it. The more he thought, the more perplexed he was; and the more he endeavoured not to think, the more he thought. Marley's Ghost bothered him exceedingly. Every time he resolved within himself, after mature inquiry, that it was all a dream, his mind flew back again, like a strong spring released, to its first position, and presented the same problem to be worked all through, 'Was it a dream or not?'

Scrooge lay in this state until the chime had gone three-quarters more, when he remembered, on a sudden, that the Ghost had warned him of a visitation when the bell tolled one. He resolved to lie awake until the hour was passed; and, considering that he could no more go to sleep than go to Heaven, this was perhaps the wisest resolution in his power.

The quarter was so long, that he was more than once convinced he must have sunk into a doze unconsciously, and missed the clock. At length it broke upon his listening ear.

'Ding, dong!'

'A quarter past,' said Scrooge, counting.

'Ding, dong!'

'Half past!' said Scrooge.

'Ding, dong!'

'A quarter to it,' said Scrooge.

'Ding, dong!'

'The hour itself,' said Scrooge triumphantly, 'and nothing else!'

He spoke before the hour bell sounded, which it now did with a deep, dull, hollow, melancholy One. Light flashed up in the room upon the instant, and the curtains of his bed were drawn.

The curtains of his bed were drawn aside, I tell you, by a hand. Not the curtains at his feet, nor the curtains at his back, but those to which his face was addressed. The curtains of his bed were drawn aside; and Scrooge, starting up into a half-recumbent attitude, found himself face to face with the unearthly visitor who drew them: as close to it as I am now to you, and I am standing in the spirit at your elbow.

It was a strange figure—like a child: yet not so like a child as like an old man, viewed through some supernatural medium, which gave him the appearance of having receded from the view, and being diminished to a child's proportions. Its hair, which hung about its neck and down its back, was white as if with age; and yet the face had not a wrinkle in it, and the tenderest bloom was on the skin. The arms were very long and muscular; the hands the same, as if its hold were of uncommon strength. Its legs and feet, most delicately formed, were, like those upper members, bare. It wore a tunic of the purest white; and round its waist was bound a lustrous belt, the sheen of which was beautiful. It held a branch of fresh green holly in its hand: and, in singular contradiction of that wintry emblem, had its dress trimmed with summer flowers. But the strangest thing about it was, that from the crown of its head there sprung a bright clear jet of light, by which all this was visible; and which was doubtless the occasion of its using, in its duller moments, a great extinguisher for a cap, which it now held under its arm.

Even this, though, when Scrooge looked at it with increasing steadiness, was *not* its strangest quality. For as its belt sparkled and glittered now in one part and now in another, and what was light one instant, at another time was dark, so the figure itself fluctuated in its distinctness: being now a thing with one arm, now with one leg, now with twenty legs, now a pair of legs without a head, now a head without a body: of which dissolving parts, no outline would be visible in the dense gloom wherein they melted away. And in the very wonder of this, it would be itself again; distinct and clear as ever.

'Are you the Spirit, sir, whose coming was foretold to me?' asked Scrooge.

'I am!'

The voice was soft and gentle. Singularly low, as if instead of being so close beside him, it were at a distance.

'Who, and what are you?' Scrooge demanded.

'I am the Ghost of Christmas Past.'

'Long Past?' inquired Scrooge; observant of its dwarfish stature.

'No. Your past.'

Perhaps Scrooge could not have told anybody why, if anybody could have asked him; but he had a special desire to see the Spirit in his cap; and begged him to be covered.

'What!' exclaimed the Ghost, 'would you so soon put out, with worldly hands, the light I give? Is it not enough that you are one of those whose passions made this cap, and force me through whole trains of years to wear it low upon my brow!'

Scrooge reverently disclaimed all intention to offend, or any knowledge of having wilfully 'bonneted' the Spirit at any period of his life. He then made bold to inquire what business brought him there.

'Your welfare!' said the Ghost.

Scrooge expressed himself much obliged, but could not help thinking that a night of unbroken rest would have been more conducive to that end. The Spirit must have heard him thinking for it said immediately:

'Your reclamation, then. Take heed!'

It put out its strong hand as it spoke, and clasped him gently by the arm.

'Rise! and[19] walk with me!'

It would have been in vain for Scrooge to plead that the weather and the hour were not adapted to pedestrian purposes; that bed was warm, and the thermometer a long way below freezing; that he was clad but lightly in his slippers, dressing-gown, and nightcap; and that he had a cold upon him at that time. The grasp, though gentle as a woman's hand, was not to be resisted. He rose: but finding that the Spirit made towards the window, clasped its robe in supplication.

'I am a mortal,' Scrooge remonstrated, 'and liable to fall.'

'Bear but a touch of my hand *there*,' said the Spirit, laying it upon his heart, 'and you shall be upheld in more than this!'

As the words were spoken, they passed through the wall, and stood upon an open country road, with fields on either hand. The city had entirely vanished. Not a vestige of it was to be seen. The darkness and the mist had vanished with it, for it was a clear, cold, winter day, with the snow upon the ground.

'Good Heaven!' said Scrooge, clasping his hands together, as he looked about him. 'I was bred in this place. I was a boy here!'

The Spirit gazed upon him mildly. Its gentle touch, though it had been light and instantaneous, appeared still present to the old man's sense of feeling. He was conscious of a thousand odours floating in the air, each one connected with a thousand thoughts, and hopes, and joys, and cares long, long forgotten!

'Your lip is trembling,' said the Ghost. 'And what is that upon your cheek?'

Scrooge muttered, with an unusual catching in his voice, that it was a pimple; and begged the Ghost to lead him where he would.

'You recollect the way?' inquired the Spirit.

'Remember it!' cried Scrooge with fervour—'I could walk it blindfold.'

'Strange to have forgotten it for so many years!' observed the Ghost. 'Let us go on.'

They walked along the road, Scrooge recognising every gate, and post, and tree, until a little market-town appeared in the distance, with its bridge, its church, and winding river. Some shaggy ponies now were seen trotting towards them with boys upon their backs, who called to other boys in country gigs and carts, driven by farmers. All these boys were in great spirits, and shouted to each other, until the broad fields were so full of merry music, that the crisp air laughed to hear it.

'These are but shadows of the things that have been,' said the Ghost. 'They have no consciousness of us.'

The jocund travellers came on; and as they came, Scrooge knew and named them every one. Why was he rejoiced beyond all bounds to see them! Why did his cold eye glisten, and his heart leap up as they went past! Why was he filled with gladness when he heard them give each other Merry Christmas, as they parted at cross-roads and bye-ways for their several homes! What was merry Christmas to Scrooge? Out upon merry Christmas! What good had it ever done to him?

'The school is not quite deserted,' said the Ghost. 'A solitary child, neglected by his friends, is left there still.'

Scrooge said he knew it. And he sobbed.

They left the high-road, by a well-remembered lane, and soon approached a mansion of dull red brick, with a little weathercock-surmounted cupola on the roof, and a bell hanging in it. It was a large house, but one of broken fortunes; for the spacious offices were little used, their walls were damp and mossy, their windows broken, and their gates decayed. Fowls clucked and strutted in the stables; and the coach-houses and sheds were over-run with grass. Nor was it more retentive of its ancient state, within; for entering the dreary hall, and glancing through the open doors of many rooms, they found them poorly furnished, cold, and vast. There was an earthly savour in the air, a chilly bareness in the place, which associated itself somehow with too much getting up by candle-light[20], and not too much to eat.

They went, the Ghost and Scrooge, across the hall, to a door at the back of the house. It opened before them, and disclosed a long, bare, melancholy room, made barer still by lines of plain deal forms and desks. At one of these a lonely boy was reading near a feeble fire; and Scrooge sat down upon a form, and wept to see his poor forgotten self as he had used to be.

Not a latent echo in the house, not a squeak and scuffle from the mice behind the panelling, not a drip from the half-thawed water-spout in the dull yard behind, not a sigh among the leafless boughs of one despondent poplar, not the idle swinging of an empty store-house[21] door, no, not a clicking in the fire, but fell upon the heart of Scrooge with softening influence, and gave a freer passage to his tears.

The Spirit touched him on the arm, and pointed to his younger self, intent upon his reading. Suddenly a man, in foreign garments: wonderfully real and distinct to look at: stood outside the window, with an axe stuck in his belt, and leading an ass laden with wood by the bridle.

'Why, it's Ali Baba!' Scrooge exclaimed in ecstasy. 'It's dear old honest Ali Baba! Yes, yes, I know. One Christmas time, when yonder solitary child was left here all alone, he *did* come, for the first time, just like that. Poor boy! And Valentine,' said Scrooge, 'and his wild brother, Orson; there they go! And what's his name, who was put down in his drawers, asleep, at the gate of Damascus; don't you see him? And the Sultan's Groom turned upside-down by the Genii; there he is upon his head! Serve him right. I'm glad of it. What business had *he* to be married to the Princess!'

To hear Scrooge expending all the earnestness of his nature on such subjects, in a most extraordinary voice between laughing and crying; and to see his heightened and excited face; would have been a surprise to his business friends in the city, indeed.

'There's the Parrot!' cried Scrooge. 'Green body and yellow tail, with a thing like a lettuce growing out of the top of his head; there he is! Poor Robin Crusoe, he called him, when he came home again after sailing round the island. "Poor Robin Crusoe, where have you been, Robin Crusoe?" The man thought he was dreaming, but he wasn't. It was the Parrot, you know. There goes Friday, running for his life to the little creek! Halloa! Hoop! Halloo!'

Then, with a rapidity of transition very foreign to his usual character, he said, in pity for his former self, 'Poor boy!' and cried again.

'I wish,' Scrooge muttered, putting his hand in his pocket, and looking about him, after drying his eyes with his cuff: 'but it's too late now.'

'What is the matter?' asked the Spirit.

'Nothing,' said Scrooge. 'Nothing. There was a boy singing a Christmas Carol at my door last night. I should like to have given him something: that's all.'

The Ghost smiled thoughtfully, and waved its hand: saying as it did so, 'Let us see another Christmas!'

Scrooge's former self grew larger at the words, and the room became a little darker and more dirty[22]. The panels shrunk, the windows cracked; fragments of plaster fell out of the ceiling, and the naked laths were shown instead; but how all this was brought about, Scrooge knew no more than you do. He only knew that it was quite correct: that everything had happened so; that there he was, alone again, when all the other boys had gone home for the jolly holidays.

He was not reading now, but walking up and down despairingly. Scrooge looked at the Ghost, and with a mournful shaking of his head, glanced anxiously towards the door.

It opened; and a little girl, much younger than the boy, came darting in, and putting her arms about his neck, and often kissing him, addressed him as her 'Dear, dear brother.'

'I have come to bring you home, dear brother!' said the child, clapping her tiny hands, and bending down to laugh. 'To bring you home, home, home!'

'Home, little Fan?' returned the boy.

'Yes!' said the child, brimful of glee. 'Home for good and all. Home, for ever and ever. Father is so much kinder than he used to be, that home's like Heaven! He spoke so gently to me one dear night when I was going to bed, that I was not afraid to ask him once more if you might come home; and he said Yes, you should; and sent me in a coach to bring you. And you're to be a man!' said the child, opening her eyes, 'and are never to come back here; but first, we're to be together all the Christmas long, and have the merriest time in all the world.'

'You are quite a woman, little Fan!' exclaimed the boy.

She clapped her hands and laughed, and tried to touch his head; but being too little, laughed again, and stood on tiptoe to embrace him. Then she began to drag him, in her childish eagerness, towards the door; and he, nothing loath to go, accompanied her.

A terrible voice in the hall cried, 'Bring down Master Scrooge's box, there!' and in the hall appeared the schoolmaster himself, who glared on Master Scrooge with a ferocious condescension, and threw him into a dreadful state of mind by shaking hands with him. He then conveyed him and his sister into the veriest old well of a shivering best-parlour that ever was seen, where the maps upon the wall, and the celestial and terrestrial globes in the windows were waxy with cold. Here he produced a decanter of curiously light wine, and a block of curiously heavy cake, and administered instalments of those dainties to the young people: at the same time, sending out a meagre servant to offer a glass of 'something' to the postboy, who answered that he thanked the gentleman, but if it was the same tap as he had tasted before, he had rather not. Master Scrooge's trunk being by this time tied on to the top of the chaise, the children bade the schoolmaster good-bye right willingly; and getting into it, drove gaily down the garden-sweep: the quick wheels dashing the hoar-frost and snow from off the dark leaves of the evergreens like spray.

'Always a delicate creature, whom a breath might have withered,' said the Ghost. 'But she had a large heart!'

'So she had,' cried Scrooge. 'You're right. I will not gainsay it, Spirit. God forbid!'

'She died a woman,' said the Ghost, 'and had, as I think, children.'

'One child,' Scrooge returned.

'True,' said the Ghost. 'Your nephew!'

Scrooge seemed uneasy in his mind; and answered briefly, 'Yes.'

Although they had but that moment left the school behind them, they were now in the busy thoroughfares of a city, where shadowy passengers passed and repassed; where shadowy carts and coaches battled for the way, and all the strife and tumult of a real city were. It was made plain enough, by the dressing of the shops, that here too it was Christmas time again; but it was evening, and the streets were lighted up.

The Ghost stopped at a certain warehouse door, and asked Scrooge if he knew it.

'Know it!' said Scrooge. 'Was I apprenticed here?'

They went in. At sight of an old gentleman in a Welsh wig, sitting behind such a high desk, that if he had been two inches taller he must have knocked his head against the ceiling, Scrooge cried in great excitement:

'Why, it's old Fezziwig! Bless his heart; it's Fezziwig alive again!'

Old Fezziwig laid down his pen, and looked up at the clock, which pointed to the hour of seven. He rubbed his hands; adjusted his capacious waistcoat; laughed all over himself, from his shoes to his organ of benevolence; and called out in a comfortable, oily, rich, fat, jovial voice:

'Yo ho, there! Ebenezer! Dick!'

Scrooge's former self, now grown a young man, came briskly in, accompanied by his fellow-'prentice[23].

'Dick Wilkins, to be sure!' said Scrooge to the Ghost. 'Bless me, yes. There he is. He was very much attached to me, was Dick. Poor Dick! Dear, dear!'

'Yo ho, my boys!' said Fezziwig. 'No more work to-night. Christmas-eve, Dick. Christmas, Ebenezer! Let's have the shutters up,' cried old Fezziwig, with a sharp clap of his hands, 'before a man can say, Jack Robinson!'

You wouldn't believe how those two fellows went at it! They charged into the street with the shutters—one, two, three—had 'em up in their places—four, five, six—barred 'em and pinned 'em— seven, eight, nine—and came back before you could have got to twelve, panting like race-horses.

'Hilli-ho!' cried old Fezziwig, skipping down from the high desk, with wonderful agility. 'Clear away, my lads, and let's have lots of room here! Hilli-ho, Dick! Chirrup, Ebenezer!'

Clear away! There was nothing they wouldn't have cleared away, or couldn't have cleared away, with old Fezziwig looking on. It was done in a minute. Every movable was packed off, as if it were dismissed from public life for evermore; the floor was swept and watered, the lamps were trimmed, fuel was heaped upon the fire; and the warehouse was as snug, and warm, and dry, and bright a ball-room as you would desire to see upon a winter's night.

In came a fiddler with a music-book, and went up to the lofty desk, and made an orchestra of it, and tuned like fifty stomach-aches. In came Mrs. Fezziwig, one vast substantial smile. In came the three Miss Fezziwigs, beaming and lovable. In came the six young followers whose hearts they broke. In came all the young men and women employed in the business. In came the housemaid, with her cousin, the baker. In came the cook, with her brother's particular friend, the milkman. In came the boy from over the way, who was suspected of not having board enough from his master; trying to hide himself behind the girl from next door but one, who was proved to have had her ears pulled by her mistress. In they all came, one after another; some shyly, some boldly, some gracefully, some awkwardly, some pushing, some pulling; in they all came, anyhow and everyhow. Away they all went, twenty couples at once, hands half round and back again the other way; down the middle and up again; round and round in various stages of affectionate grouping; old top couple always turning up in the wrong place; new top couple starting off again, as soon as they got there; all top couples at last, and not a bottom one to help them. When this result was brought about, old Fezziwig, clapping his hands to stop the dance, cried out, 'Well done!' and the fiddler plunged his hot face into a pot of porter, especially provided for that purpose. But scorning rest upon his reappearance, he instantly began again, though there were no dancers yet, as if the other fiddler had been carried home, exhausted, on a shutter; and he were a bran-new man resolved to beat him out of sight, or perish.

There were more dances, and there were forfeits, and more

dances, and there was cake, and there was negus, and there was a great piece of Cold Roast, and there was a great piece of Cold Boiled, and there were mince-pies, and plenty of beer. But the great effect of the evening came after the Roast and Boiled, when the fiddler (an artful dog, mind! The sort of man who knew his business better than you or I could have told it him[24]!) struck up 'Sir Roger de Coverley.' Then old Fezziwig stood out to dance with Mrs. Fezziwig. Top couple, too; with a good stiff piece of work cut out for them; three or four and twenty pair[25] of partners; people who were not to be trifled with; people who *would* dance, and had no notion of walking.

But if they had been twice as many—ah, four times: old Fezziwig would have been a match for them, and so would Mrs. Fezziwig. As to *her*, she was worthy to be his partner in every sense of the term. If that's not high praise, tell me higher, and I'll use it. A positive light appeared to issue from Fezziwig's calves. They shone in every part of the dance like moons. You couldn't have predicted, at any given time, what would become of 'em next. And when old Fezziwig and Mrs. Fezziwig had gone all through the dance; advance and retire, hold hands with your partner, bow and curtsy, corkscrew, thread-the-needle, and back again to your place; Fezziwig 'cut'—cut so deftly, that he appeared to wink with his legs, and came upon his feet again without a stagger.

When the clock struck eleven, this domestic ball broke up. Mr. and Mrs. Fezziwig took their stations, one on either side the door, and shaking hands with every person individually as he or she went out, wished him or her a Merry Christmas. When everybody had retired but the two 'prentices, they did the same to them; and thus the cheerful voices died away, and the lads were left to their beds; which were under a counter in the back-shop.

During the whole of this time Scrooge had acted like a man out of his wits. His heart and soul were in the scene, and with his former self. He corroborated everything, remembered everything, enjoyed everything, and underwent the strangest agitation. It was not until now, when the bright faces of his former self and Dick were turned from them, that he remembered the Ghost, and became conscious that it was looking full upon him, while the light upon its head burnt very clear.

'A small matter,' said the Ghost, 'to make these silly folks so full of gratitude.'

'Small!' echoed Scrooge.

The Spirit signed to him to listen to the two apprentices, who were pouring out their hearts in praise of Fezziwig; and when he had done so, said:

'Why! Is it not? He has spent but a few pounds of your mortal money: three or four, perhaps. Is that so much that he deserves this praise?'

'It isn't that,' said Scrooge, heated by the remark, and speaking unconsciously like his former, not his latter, self. 'It isn't that, Spirit. He has the power to render us happy or unhappy; to make our service light or burdensome; a pleasure or a toil. Say that his power lies in words and looks; in things so slight and insignificant that it is impossible to add and count 'em up: what then? The happiness he gives, is quite as great as if it cost a fortune.'

He felt the Spirit's glance, and stopped.

'What is the matter?' asked the Ghost.

'Nothing particular,' said Scrooge.

'Something, I think?' the Ghost insisted.

'No,' said Scrooge, 'no. I should like to be able to say a word or two to my clerk just now! That's all.'

His former self turned down the lamps as he gave utterance to the wish; and Scrooge and the Ghost again stood side by side in the open air.

'My time grows short,' observed the Spirit. 'Quick!'

This was not addressed to Scrooge, or to any one whom he could see, but it produced an immediate effect. For again Scrooge saw himself. He was older now; a man in the prime of life. His face had not the harsh and rigid lines of later years; but it had begun to wear the signs of care and avarice. There was an eager, greedy, restless motion in the eye, which showed the passion that had taken root, and where the shadow of the growing tree would fall.

He was not alone, but sat by the side of a fair young girl in a mourning-dress: in whose eyes there were tears, which sparkled in the light that shone out of the Ghost of Christmas Past.

'It matters little,' she said softly. 'To you, very little. Another idol has displaced me; and, if it can cheer and comfort you in time to come, as I would have tried to do, I have no just cause to grieve.'

'What Idol has displaced you?' he rejoined.

'A golden one.'

'This is the even-handed dealing of the world!' he said. 'There is nothing on which it is so hard as poverty; and there is nothing it professes to condemn with such severity as the pursuit of wealth!'

'You fear the world too much,' she answered, gently. 'All your other hopes have merged into the hope of being beyond the chance of its sordid reproach. I have seen your nobler aspirations fall off one by one, until the master-passion, Gain, engrosses you. Have I not?'

'What then?' he retorted. 'Even if I have grown so much wiser, what then? I am not changed towards you.'

She shook her head.

'Am I?'

'Our contract is an old one. It was made when we were both poor and content to be so, until, in good season, we could improve our worldly fortune by our patient industry. You *are* changed. When it was made, you were another man.'

'I was a boy,' he said impatiently.

'Your own feeling tells you that you were not what you are,' she returned. 'I am. That which promised happiness when we were one in heart, is fraught with misery now that we are two. How often and how keenly I have thought of this, I will not say. It is enough that I *have* thought of it, and can release you.'

'Have I ever sought release?'

'In words. No. Never.'

'In what, then?'

'In a changed nature; in an altered spirit; in another atmosphere of life; another Hope as its great end. In everything that made my love of any worth or value in your sight. If this had never been between us,' said the girl, looking mildly, but with steadiness, upon him; 'tell me, would you seek me out and try to win me now? Ah, no!'

He seemed to yield to the justice of this supposition, in spite of himself. But he said, with a struggle, 'You think not.'

'I would gladly think otherwise if I could,' she answered. 'Heaven knows! When *I* have learned a Truth like this, I know how strong and irresistible it must be. But if you were free to-day[26], to-morrow, yesterday, can even I believe that you would choose a dowerless girl—you who, in your very confidence with her, weigh everything by Gain: or, choosing her, if for a moment you were false enough to your one guiding principle to do so, do I not know that your repentance and regret would surely follow? I do; and I release you. With a full heart, for the love of him you once were.'

He was about to speak; but with her head turned from him, she resumed.

'You may—the memory of what is past half makes me hope you will—have pain in this. A very, very brief time, and you will dismiss the recollection of it, gladly, as an unprofitable dream, from which it happened well that you awoke. May you be happy in the life you have chosen!'

She left him, and they parted.

'Spirit!' said Scrooge, 'show[27] me no more! Conduct me home. Why do you delight to torture me?'

'One shadow more!' exclaimed the Ghost.

'No more!' cried Scrooge. 'No more. I don't wish to see it. Show me no more!'

But the relentless Ghost pinioned him in both his arms, and forced him to observe what happened next.

They were in another scene and place: a room, not very large or handsome, but full of comfort. Near to the winter fire sat a beautiful young girl, so like that last that Scrooge believed it was the same, until he saw *her*, now a comely matron, sitting opposite her daughter. The noise in this room was perfectly tumultuous, for there were more children there, than Scrooge in his agitated state of mind could count; and, unlike the celebrated herd in the poem, they were not forty children conducting themselves like one, but every child was conducting itself like forty. The consequences were uproarious beyond belief; but no one seemed to care; on the contrary, the mother and daughter laughed heartily, and enjoyed it very much; and the latter, soon beginning to mingle in the sports, got pillaged by the young brigands most ruthlessly. What would I not have given to be one of them! Though I never could have been so rude, no, no! I wouldn't for the wealth of all the world have crushed that braided hair, and torn it down; and for the precious little shoe, I wouldn't have plucked it off, God bless my soul! to save my life. As to measuring her waist in sport, as they did, bold young brood, I couldn't have done it; I should have expected my arm to have grown round it for a punishment, and never come straight again. And yet I should have dearly liked, I own, to have touched her lips; to have questioned her, that she might have opened them; to have looked upon the lashes of her downcast eyes, and never raised a blush; to have let loose waves of hair, an inch of which would be a keepsake beyond price: in short, I should have liked, I do confess, to have had the lightest license of a child, and yet to have been man enough to know its value.

But now a knocking at the door was heard, and such a rush immediately ensued that she with laughing face and plundered dress was borne towards it in the centre of a flushed and boisterous group, just in time to greet the father, who came home attended by a man laden with Christmas toys and presents. Then the shouting and the struggling, and the onslaught that was made on the defenceless porter! The scaling him with chairs for ladders, to dive into his pockets, despoil him of brown-paper parcels, hold on tight by his cravat, hug him round the neck, pommel his back, and kick his legs in irrepressible affection! The shouts of wonder and delight with which the development of every package was received! The terrible announcement that the baby had been taken in the act of putting a doll's frying pan into his mouth, and was more than suspected of having swallowed a fictitious turkey, glued on a wooden platter! The immense relief of finding this a false alarm! The joy, and gratitude, and ecstasy! They are all indescribable alike. It is enough that by degrees the children and their emotions got out of the parlour and by one stair at a time, up to the top of the house, where they went to bed, and so subsided.

And now Scrooge looked on more attentively than ever, when the master of the house, having his daughter leaning fondly on him, sat down with her and her mother at his own fireside; and when he thought that such another creature, quite as graceful and as full of promise, might have called him father, and been a spring-time in the haggard winter of his life, his sight grew very dim indeed.

'Belle,' said the husband, turning to his wife with a smile, 'I saw an old friend of yours this afternoon.'

'Who was it?'

'Guess!'

'How can I? Tut, don't I know?' she added in the same breath, laughing as he laughed. 'Mr. Scrooge.'

'Mr. Scrooge it was. I passed his office window; and as it was not shut up, and he had a candle inside, I could scarcely help seeing him. His partner lies upon the point of death, I hear; and there he sat alone. Quite alone in the world, I do believe.'

'Spirit!' said Scrooge in a broken voice, 'remove[28] me from this place.'

'I told you these were shadows of the things that have been,' said the Ghost. 'That they are what they are, do not blame me!'

'Remove me!' Scrooge exclaimed. 'I cannot bear it!'

He turned upon the Ghost, and seeing that it looked upon him with a face, in which in some strange way there were fragments of all the faces it had shown him, wrestled with it.

'Leave me! Take me back! Haunt me no longer!'

In the struggle, if that can be called a struggle in which the Ghost with no visible resistance on its own part was undisturbed by any effort of its adversary, Scrooge observed that its light was burning high and bright; and dimly connecting that with its influence over him, he seized the extinguisher-cap, and by a sudden action pressed it down upon its head.

The Spirit dropped beneath it, so that the extinguisher covered its whole form; but, though Scrooge pressed it down with all his force, he could not hide the light, which streamed from under it, in an unbroken flood upon the ground.

He was conscious of being exhausted, and overcome by an irresistible drowsiness; and, further, of being in his own bedroom. He gave the cap a parting squeeze, in which his hand relaxed; and had barely time to reel to bed, before he sank into a heavy sleep.

Stave Three

The Second of
the Three Spirits

Awaking in the middle of a prodigiously tough snore, and sitting up in bed to get his thoughts together, Scrooge had no occasion to be told that the bell was again upon the stroke of One. He felt that he was restored to consciousness in the right nick of time, for the especial[29] purpose of holding a conference with the second messenger despatched to him through Jacob Marley's intervention. But, finding that he turned uncomfortably cold when he began to wonder which of his curtains this new spectre would draw back, he put them every one aside with his own hands; and lying down again, established a sharp look-out all round the bed. For he wished to challenge the Spirit on the moment of its appearance, and did not wish to be taken by surprise and made nervous.

Gentlemen of the free-and-easy sort, who plume themselves on being acquainted with a move or two, and being usually equal to the time-of-day, express the wide range of their capacity for adventure by observing that they are good for anything from pitch-and-toss to manslaughter; between which opposite extremes, no doubt, there lies a tolerably wide and comprehensive range of subjects. Without venturing for Scrooge quite as hardily as this, I don't mind calling on you to believe that he was ready for a good broad field of strange appearances, and that nothing between a baby and a rhinoceros would have astonished him very much.

Now, being prepared for almost anything, he was not by any means prepared for nothing; and, consequently, when the bell struck One, and no shape appeared, he was taken with a violent fit of trembling. Five minutes, ten minutes, a quarter of an hour went by, yet nothing came. All this time, he lay upon his bed, the very core and centre of a blaze of ruddy light, which streamed upon it when the clock proclaimed the hour; and which being only light, was more alarming than a dozen ghosts, as he was powerless to make out what it meant, or would be at; and was sometimes apprehensive that he might be at that very moment an interesting case of spontaneous combustion, without having the consolation of knowing it. At last, however, he began to think—as you or I would have thought at first; for it is always the person not in the predicament who knows what ought to have been done in it, and would unquestionably have done it too—at last, I say, he began to think that the source and secret of this ghostly light might be in the adjoining room: from whence, on further tracing it, it seemed to shine. This idea taking full possession of his mind, he got up softly and shuffled in his slippers to the door.

The moment Scrooge's hand was on the lock, a strange voice called him by his name, and bade him enter. He obeyed.

It was his own room. There was no doubt about that. But it had undergone a surprising transformation. The walls and ceiling were so hung with living green, that it looked a perfect grove, from every part of which, bright gleaming berries glistened. The crisp leaves of holly, mistletoe, and ivy reflected back the light, as if so many little mirrors had been scattered there; and such a mighty blaze went roaring up the chimney, as that dull petrification of a hearth had never known in Scrooge's time, or Marley's, or for many and many a winter season gone. Heaped up on the floor, to form a kind of throne, were turkeys, geese, game, poultry, brawn, great joints of meat, sucking-pigs, long wreaths of sausages, mince-pies, plum-puddings, barrels of oysters, red-hot chestnuts, cherry-cheeked apples, juicy oranges, luscious pears, immense twelfth-cakes, and seething bowls of punch, that made the chamber dim with their delicious steam. In easy state upon this couch there sat a jolly Giant, glorious to see; who bore a glowing torch, in shape not unlike Plenty's horn, and held it up, high up, to shed its light on Scrooge, as he came peeping round the door.

'Come in!' exclaimed the Ghost. 'Come in! and know me better, man!'

Scrooge entered timidly, and hung his head before this Spirit. He was not the dogged Scrooge he had been; and though the Spirit's eyes were clear and kind, he did not like to meet them.

'I am the Ghost of Christmas Present,' said the Spirit. 'Look upon me!'

Scrooge reverently did so. It was clothed in one simple deep green robe, or mantle, bordered with white fur. This garment hung so loosely on the figure, that its capacious breast was bare, as if disdaining to be warded or concealed by any artifice. Its feet, observable beneath the ample folds of the garment, were also bare; and on its head it wore no other covering than a holly wreath, set here and there with shining icicles. Its dark brown curls were long

and free: free as its genial face, its sparkling eye, its open hand, its cheery voice, its unconstrained demeanour, and its joyful air. Girded round its middle was an antique scabbard; but no sword was in it, and the ancient sheath was eaten up with rust.

'You have never seen the like of me before!' exclaimed the Spirit.

'Never,' Scrooge made answer to it.

'Have never walked forth with the younger members of my family; meaning (for I am very young) my elder brothers born in these later years?' pursued the Phantom.

'I don't think I have,' said Scrooge. 'I am afraid I have not. Have you had many brothers, Spirit?'

'More than eighteen hundred,' said the Ghost.

'A tremendous family to provide for!' muttered Scrooge.

The Ghost of Christmas Present rose.

'Spirit,' said Scrooge submissively, 'conduct me where you will. I went forth last night on compulsion, and I learnt a lesson which is working now. To-night, if you have aught to teach me, let me profit by it.'

'Touch my robe!'

Scrooge did as he was told, and held it fast.

Holly, mistletoe, red berries, ivy, turkeys, geese, game, poultry, brawn, meat, pigs, sausages, oysters, pies, puddings, fruit, and punch, all vanished instantly. So did the room, the fire, the ruddy glow, the hour of night, and they stood in the city streets on Christmas morning, where (for the weather was severe) the people made a rough, but brisk and not unpleasant kind of music, in scraping the snow from the pavement in front of their dwellings, and from the tops of their houses: whence it was mad delight to the boys to see it come plumping down into the road below, and splitting into artificial little snow-storms.

The house fronts looked black enough, and the windows blacker, contrasting with the smooth white sheet of snow upon the roofs, and with the dirtier snow upon the ground; which last deposit had been ploughed up in deep furrows by the heavy wheels of carts and wagons; furrows that crossed and re-crossed each other hundreds of times where the great streets branched off, and made intricate channels, hard to trace, in the thick yellow mud and icy water. The sky was gloomy, and the shortest streets were choked up with a dingy mist, half thawed, half frozen, whose heavier particles descended in a shower of sooty atoms, as if all the chimneys in Great Britain had, by one consent, caught fire, and were blazing away to their dear hearts' content. There was nothing very cheerful in the climate or the town, and yet was there an air of cheerfulness abroad that the clearest summer air and brightest summer sun might have endeavoured to diffuse in vain.

For the people who were shovelling away on the housetops were jovial and full of glee; calling out to one another from the parapets, and now and then exchanging a facetious snowball— better-natured missile far than many a wordy jest—laughing heartily if it went right, and not less heartily if it went wrong. The poulterers' shops were still half open, and the fruiterers' were radiant in their glory. There were great, round, pot-bellied baskets of chestnuts, shaped like the waistcoats of jolly old gentlemen, lolling at the doors, and tumbling out into the street in their apoplectic opulence. There were ruddy, brown-faced, broad-girthed Spanish onions, shining in the fatness of their growth like Spanish Friars; and winking from their shelves in wanton slyness at the girls as they went by, and glanced demurely at the hung-up mistletoe. There were pears and apples, clustered high in blooming pyramids; there were bunches of grapes, made in the shopkeepers' benevolence to dangle from conspicuous hooks, that people's mouths might water gratis as they passed; there were piles of filberts, mossy and brown, recalling, in their fragrance, ancient walks among the woods, and pleasant shufflings ankle deep through withered leaves; there were Norfolk Biffins, squab and swarthy, setting off the yellow of the oranges and lemons, and, in the great compactness of their juicy persons, urgently entreating and beseeching to be carried home in paper bags and eaten after dinner. The very gold and silver fish, set forth among these choice fruits in a bowl, though members of a dull and stagnant-blooded race, appeared to know that there was something going on; and, to a fish, went gasping round and round their little world in slow and passionless excitement.

The Grocers'! oh[30], the Grocers'! nearly[31] closed, with perhaps two shutters down, or one; but through those gaps such glimpses! It was not alone that the scales descending on the counter made a merry sound, or that the twine and roller parted company so briskly, or that the canisters were rattled up and down like juggling tricks, or even that the blended scents of tea and coffee were so grateful to the nose, or even that the raisins were so plentiful and rare, the almonds so extremely white, the sticks of cinnamon so long and straight, the other spices so delicious, the candied fruits so caked and spotted with molten sugar as to make the coldest lookers-on feel faint and subsequently bilious. Nor was it that the figs were moist and pulpy, or that the French plums blushed in modest tartness from their highly-decorated boxes, or that everything was good to eat and in its Christmas dress: but the customers were all so hurried and so eager in the hopeful promise of the day, that they tumbled up against each other at the door, clashing their wicker baskets wildly, and left their purchases upon the counter, and came running back to fetch them, and committed hundreds of the like mistakes in the best humour possible; while the Grocer and his people were so frank and fresh that the polished hearts with which they fastened their aprons behind might have been their own, worn outside for general inspection, and for Christmas daws to peck at if they chose.

But soon the steeples called good people all, to church and chapel, and away they came, flocking through the streets in their best clothes, and with their gayest faces. And at the same time there emerged from scores of bye streets, lanes, and nameless turnings, innumerable people, carrying their dinners to the bakers' shops. The sight of these poor revellers appeared to interest the Spirit very much, for he stood with Scrooge beside him in a baker's doorway, and taking off the covers as their bearers passed, sprinkled incense on their dinners from his torch. And it was a very uncommon kind of torch, for once or twice when there were angry words between some dinner-carriers who had jostled each other, he shed a few drops of water on them from it, and their good-humour was restored directly. For they said, it was a shame to quarrel upon Christmas Day. And so it was! God love it, so it was!

In time the bells ceased, and the bakers were shut up; and yet there was a genial shadowing forth of all these dinners, and the progress of their cooking, in the thawed blotch of wet above each baker's oven; where the pavement smoked as if its stones were cooking too.

'Is there a peculiar flavour in what you sprinkle from your

torch?' asked Scrooge.

'There is. My own.'

'Would it apply to any kind of dinner on this day?' asked Scrooge.

'To any kindly given. To a poor one most.'

'Why to a poor one most?' asked Scrooge.

'Because it needs it most.'

'Spirit!' said Scrooge after a moment's thought, 'I wonder you, of all the beings in the many worlds about us, should desire to cramp these people's opportunities of innocent enjoyment.'

'I!' cried the Spirit.

'You would deprive them of their means of dining every seventh day, often the only day on which they can be said to dine at all,' said Scrooge. 'Wouldn't you?'

'I!' cried the Spirit.

'You seek to close these places on the Seventh Day?' said Scrooge. 'And it comes to the same thing.'

'*I* seek!' exclaimed the Spirit.

'Forgive me if I am wrong. It has been done in your name, or at least in that of your family, ' said Scrooge.

'There are some upon this earth of yours,' returned the Spirit, 'who lay claim to know us, and who do their deeds of passion, pride, ill-will, hatred, envy, bigotry, and selfishness in our name, who are as strange to us and all our kith and kin, as if they had never lived. Remember that, and charge their doings on themselves, not us.'

Scrooge promised that he would; and they went on, invisible, as they had been before, into the suburbs of the town. It was a remarkable quality of the Ghost (which Scrooge had observed at the baker's) that notwithstanding his gigantic size, he could accommodate himself to any place with ease; and that he stood beneath a low roof quite as gracefully and like a supernatural creature, as it was possible he could have done in any lofty hall.

And perhaps it was the pleasure the good Spirit had in showing off this power of his, or else it was his own kind, generous, hearty nature, and his sympathy with all poor men, that led him straight to Scrooge's clerk's; for there he went, and took Scrooge with him, holding to his robe; and on the threshold of the door the Spirit smiled, and stopped to bless Bob Cratchit's dwelling with the sprinkling of his torch. Think of that! Bob had but fifteen 'Bob' a-week himself; he pocketed on Saturdays but fifteen copies of his Christian name; and yet the Ghost of Christmas Present blessed his four-roomed house!

Then up rose Mrs. Cratchit, Cratchit's wife, dressed out but poorly in a twice-turned gown, but brave in ribbons, which are cheap and make a goodly show for sixpence; and she laid the cloth, assisted by Belinda Cratchit, second of her daughters, also brave in ribbons; while Master Peter Cratchit plunged a fork into the saucepan of potatoes, and getting the corners of his monstrous shirt-collar (Bob's private property, conferred upon his son and heir in honour of the day) into his mouth, rejoiced to find himself so gallantly attired, and yearned to show his linen in the fashionable Parks. And now two smaller Cratchits, boy and girl, came tearing in, screaming that outside the baker's they had smelt the goose, and known it for their own; and basking in luxurious thoughts of sage and onion, these young Cratchits danced about the table, and exalted Master Peter Cratchit to the skies, while he (not proud, although his collars nearly choked him) blew the fire, until the slow potatoes bubbling up, knocked loudly at the saucepan-lid to be let out and peeled.

'What has ever got your precious father then,' said Mrs. Cratchit. 'And your brother, Tiny Tim; and Martha warn't[32] as late last Christmas day by half-an-hour!'

'Here's Martha, mother!' said a girl, appearing as she spoke.

'Here's Martha, mother!' cried the two young Cratchits. 'Hurrah! There's *such* a goose, Martha!'

'Why, bless your heart alive, my dear, how late you are!' said Mrs. Cratchit, kissing her a dozen times, and taking off her shawl and bonnet for her with officious zeal.

'We'd a deal of work to finish up last night,' replied the girl, 'and had to clear away this morning, mother!'

'Well! Never mind so long as you are[33] come,' said Mrs. Cratchit. 'Sit ye[34] down before the fire, my dear, and have a warm, Lord bless ye!'

'No, no! There's father coming,' cried the two young Cratchits, who were everywhere at once. 'Hide, Martha, hide!'

So Martha hid herself, and in came little Bob, the father, with at least three feet of comforter exclusive of the fringe, hanging down before him; and his thread-bare clothes darned up and brushed to look seasonable; and Tiny Tim upon his shoulder. Alas for Tiny Tim, he bore a little crutch, and had his limbs supported by an iron frame!

'Why, where's our Martha?' cried Bob Cratchit, looking round.

'Not coming,' said Mrs. Cratchit.

'Not coming!' said Bob, with a sudden declension in his high spirits; for he had been Tim's blood horse all the way from church, and had come home rampant. 'Not coming upon Christmas day!'

Martha didn't like to see him disappointed, if it were only in joke; so she came out prematurely from behind the closet door, and ran into his arms, while the two young Cratchits hustled Tiny Tim, and bore him off into the wash-house, that he might hear the pudding singing in the copper.

'And how did little Tim behave?' asked Mrs. Cratchit, when she had rallied Bob on his credulity and Bob had hugged his daughter to his heart's content.

'As good as gold,' said Bob, 'and better. Somehow he gets thoughtful sitting by himself so much, and thinks the strangest things you ever heard. He told me, coming home, that he hoped the people saw him in the church, because he was a cripple, and it might be pleasant to them to remember upon Christmas Day, who made lame beggars walk and blind men see.'

Bob's voice was tremulous when he told them this, and trembled more when he said that Tiny Tim was growing strong and hearty.

His active little crutch was heard upon the floor, and back came Tiny Tim before another word was spoken, escorted by his brother and sister to his stool beside the fire; and while Bob, turning up his cuffs—as if, poor fellow, they were capable of being made more shabby—compounded some hot mixture in a jug with gin and lemons, and stirred it round and round and put it on the hob to simmer; Master Peter, and the two ubiquitous young Cratchits went to fetch the goose, with which they soon returned in high procession.

Such a bustle ensued that you might have thought a goose the rarest of all birds; a feathered phenomenon, to which a black swan was a matter of course; and in truth it was something very like it in that house. Mrs. Cratchit made the gravy (ready beforehand in a little saucepan) hissing hot; Master Peter mashed the potatoes with incredible vigour; Miss Belinda sweetened up the apple-sauce; Martha dusted the hot plates; Bob took Tiny Tim beside him in a tiny corner at the table; the two young Cratchits set chairs for everybody, not forgetting themselves, and mounting guard upon their posts, crammed spoons into their mouths, lest they should shriek for goose before their turn came to be helped. At last the dishes were set on, and grace was said. It was succeeded by a breathless pause, as Mrs. Cratchit, looking slowly all along the carving-knife, prepared to plunge it in the breast; but when she did, and when the long expected gush of stuffing issued forth, one murmur of delight arose all round the board, and even Tiny Tim, excited by the two young Cratchits, beat on the table with the handle of his knife, and feebly cried Hurrah!

There never was such a goose. Bob said he didn't believe there ever was such a goose cooked. Its tenderness and flavour, size and cheapness, were the themes of universal admiration. Eked out by the apple-sauce and mashed potatoes, it was a sufficient dinner for the whole family; indeed, as Mrs. Cratchit said with great delight (surveying one small atom of a bone upon the dish), they hadn't ate it all at last! Yet every one had had enough, and the youngest Cratchits, in particular, were steeped in sage and onion to the eyebrows! But now, the plates being changed by Miss Belinda, Mrs. Cratchit left the room alone—too nervous to bear witnesses—to take the pudding up, and bring it in.

Suppose it should not be done enough! Suppose it should break in turning out! Suppose somebody should have got over the wall of the back-yard[35] and stolen it, while they were merry with the goose: a supposition at which the two young Cratchits became livid! All sorts of horrors were supposed.

Hallo! A great deal of steam! The pudding was out of the copper. A smell like a washing-day! That was the cloth. A smell like an eating-house, and a pastry cook's next door to each other, with a laundress's next door to that! That was the pudding. In half a minute Mrs. Cratchit entered: flushed, but smiling proudly: with the pudding, like a speckled cannon-ball, so hard and firm, blazing in half of half-a-quartern of ignited brandy, and bedight with Christmas holly stuck into the top.

Oh, a wonderful pudding! Bob Cratchit said, and calmly too, that he regarded it as the greatest success achieved by Mrs. Cratchit since their marriage. Mrs. Cratchit said that now the weight was off her mind, she would confess she had her doubts about the quantity of flour. Everybody had something to say about it, but nobody said or thought it was at all a small pudding for a large family. It would have been flat heresy to do so. Any Cratchit would have blushed to hint at such a thing.

At last the dinner was all done, the cloth was cleared, the hearth swept, and the fire made up. The compound in the jug being tasted, and considered perfect, apples and oranges were put upon the table, and a shovel-full of chestnuts on the fire. Then all the Cratchit family drew round the hearth, in what Bob Cratchit called a circle, meaning half a one; and at Bob Cratchit's elbow stood the family display of glass; two tumblers, and a custard-cup without a handle.

These held the hot stuff from the jug, however, as well as golden goblets would have done; and Bob served it out with beaming looks, while the chestnuts on the fire sputtered and cracked noisily. Then Bob proposed:

'A merry Christmas to us all, my dears. God bless us!'

Which all the family re-echoed.

'God bless us every one!' said Tiny Tim, the last of all.

He sat very close to his father's side, upon his little stool. Bob held his withered little hand in his, as if he loved the child, and wished to keep him by his side, and dreaded that he might be taken from him.

'Spirit,' said Scrooge with an interest he had never felt before, 'tell me if Tiny Tim will live.'

'I see a vacant seat,' replied the Ghost, 'in the poor chimney corner, and a crutch without an owner, carefully preserved. If these shadows remain unaltered by the Future, the child will die.'

'No, no,' said Scrooge. 'Oh, no, kind Spirit! say[36] he will be spared.'

'If these shadows remain unaltered by the Future none other of my race,' returned the Ghost, 'will find him here. What then? If he be like to die, he had better do it, and decrease the surplus population.'

Scrooge hung his head to hear his own words quoted by the Spirit, and was overcome with penitence and grief.

'Man,' said the Ghost, 'if man you be in heart, not adamant, forbear that wicked cant until you have discovered What the surplus is, and Where it is. Will you decide what men shall live, what men shall die? It may be, that in the sight of Heaven, you are more worthless and less fit to live than millions like this poor man's child. Oh God! to hear the insect on the leaf pronouncing on the too much life among his hungry brothers in the dust!'

Scrooge bent before the Ghost's rebuke, and, trembling cast his eyes upon the ground. But he raised them speedily, on hearing his own name.

'Mr. Scrooge!' said Bob; 'I'll give you Mr. Scrooge, the Founder of the Feast!'

'The Founder of the Feast, indeed!' cried Mrs. Cratchit, reddening. 'I wish I had him here. I'd give him a piece of my mind to feast upon, and I hope he'd have a good appetite for it.'

'My dear,' said Bob, 'the children; Christmas Day.'

'It should be Christmas Day, I am sure,' said she, 'on which one drinks the health of such an odious, stingy, hard, unfeeling man as Mr. Scrooge. You know he is, Robert! Nobody knows it better than you do, poor fellow!'

'My dear,' was Bob's mild answer. 'Christmas Day.'

'I'll drink his health for your sake and the Day's,' said Mrs. Cratchit, 'not for his. Long life to him! A merry Christmas and a happy new year[37]! —he'll be very merry and very happy, I have no doubt!'

The children drank the toast after her. It was the first of their proceedings which had no heartiness in it. Tiny Tim drank it last of all, but he didn't care twopence for it. Scrooge was the Ogre of the family. The mention of his name cast a dark shadow on the party, which was not dispelled for full five minutes.

After it had passed away they were ten times merrier than before, from the mere relief of Scrooge the Baleful being done with. Bob Cratchit told them how he had a situation in his eye for Master Peter, which would bring in, if obtained, full five-and-sixpence weekly. The two young Cratchits laughed tremendously at the idea of Peter's being a man of business; and Peter himself looked thoughtfully at the fire from between his collars, as if he were deliberating what particular investments he should favour when he came into the receipt of that bewildering income. Martha, who was a poor apprentice at a milliner's, then told them what kind of work she had to do, and how many hours she worked at a stretch, and how she meant to lie a-bed to-morrow morning for a good long rest; to-morrow being a holiday she passed at home. Also how she had seen a countess and a lord some days before, and how the lord 'was much about as tall as Peter'; at which Peter pulled up his collars so high that you couldn't have seen his head if you had been there. All this time the chestnuts and the jug went round and round; and bye and bye they had a song, about a lost child travelling in the snow, from Tiny Tim; who had a plaintive little voice, and sang it very well indeed.

There was nothing of high mark in this. They were not a handsome family; they were not well dressed; their shoes were far from being water-proof; their clothes were scanty; and Peter might have known, and very likely did, the inside of a pawnbroker's. But they were happy, grateful, pleased with one another, and contented with the time; and when they faded, and looked happier yet in the bright sprinklings of the Spirit's torch at parting, Scrooge had his eye upon them, and especially on Tiny Tim, until the last.

By this time it was getting dark, and snowing pretty heavily; and as Scrooge and the Spirit went along the streets, the brightness of the roaring fires in kitchens, parlours, and all sorts of rooms, was wonderful. Here, the flickering of the blaze showed preparations for a cosy dinner, with hot plates baking through and through before the fire, and deep red curtains, ready to be drawn, to shut out cold and darkness. There, all the children of the house were running out into the snow to meet their married sisters, brothers, cousins, uncles, aunts, and be the first to greet them. Here, again, were shadows on the window-blind of guests assembling; and there a group of handsome girls, all hooded and fur-booted, and all chattering at once, tripped lightly off to some near neighbour's house; where, woe upon the single man who saw them enter— artful witches: well they knew it—in a glow!

But, if you had judged from the numbers of people on their way to friendly gatherings, you might have thought that no one was at home to give them welcome when they got there, instead of every house expecting company, and piling up its fires half-chimney high. Blessings on it, how the Ghost exulted! How it bared its breadth of breast, and opened its capacious palm, and floated on, outpouring, with a generous hand, its bright and harmless mirth on everything within its reach! The very lamplighter, who ran on before dotting the dusky street with specks of light, and who was dressed to spend the evening somewhere, laughed out loudly as the Spirit passed, though little kenned the lamplighter that he had any company but Christmas.

And now, without a word of warning from the Ghost, they stood upon a bleak and desert moor, where monstrous masses of rude stone were cast about, as though it were the burial-place or giants; and water spread itself wheresoever it listed—or would have done so, but for the frost that held it prisoner; and nothing grew but moss and furze, and coarse, rank grass. Down in the west the setting sun had left a streak of fiery red, which glared upon the desolation for an instant, like a sullen eye, and frowning lower, lower, lower yet, was lost in the thick gloom of darkest night.

'What place is this?' asked Scrooge.

'A place where Miners live, who labour in the bowels of the earth,' returned the Spirit. 'But they know me. See!'

A light shone from the window of a hut, and swiftly they advanced towards it. Passing through the wall of mud and stone, they found a cheerful company assembled round a glowing fire. An old, old man and woman, with their children and their children's children, and another generation beyond that, all decked out gaily in their holiday attire. The old man, in a voice that seldom rose above the howling of the wind upon the barren waste, was singing them a Christmas song; it had been a very old song when he was a boy; and from time to time they all joined in the chorus. So surely as they raised their voices, the old man got quite blithe and loud; and so surely as they stopped, his vigour sang[38] again.

The Spirit did not tarry here, but bade Scrooge hold his robe, and passing on above the moor, sped whither? Not to sea? To sea. To Scrooge's horror, looking back, he saw the last of the land, a frightful range of rocks, behind them; and his ears were deafened by the thundering of water, as it rolled, and roared, and raged among the dreadful caverns it had worn, and fiercely tried to undermine the earth.

Built upon a dismal reef of sunken rocks, some league or so from shore, on which the waters chafed and dashed, the wild year through, there stood a solitary lighthouse. Great heaps of sea-weed[39] clung to its base, and storm-birds—born of the wind one might suppose, as sea-weed of the water—rose and fell about it, like the waves they skimmed.

But, even here, two men who watched the light had made a fire, that through the loophole in the thick stone wall shed out a ray of brightness on the awful sea. Joining their horny hands over the rough table at which they sat, they wished each other Merry Christmas in their can of grog; and one of them, the elder, too, with his face all damaged and scarred with hard weather, as the figure-head of an old ship might be: struck up a sturdy song that was like a Gale in itself.

Again the Ghost sped on, above the black and heaving sea— on, on—until, being far away, as he told Scrooge, from any shore, they lighted on a ship. They stood beside the helmsman at the wheel, the look-out in the bow, the officers who had the watch; dark, ghostly figures in their several stations; but every man among them hummed a Christmas tune, or had a Christmas thought, or spoke below his breath to his companion of some bygone Christmas Day, with homeward hopes belonging to it. And every man on board, waking or sleeping, good or bad, had had a kinder word for another on that day than on any day in the year; and had shared to some extent in its festivities; and had remembered those he cared for at a distance, and had known that they delighted to remember him.

It was a great surprise to Scrooge, while listening to the moaning of the wind, and thinking what a solemn thing it was to move on through the lonely darkness over an unknown abyss, whose depths were secrets as profound as Death: it was a great surprise to Scrooge, while thus engaged, to hear a hearty laugh. It was a much greater surprise to Scrooge to recognise it as his own nephew's, and to find himself in a bright, dry, gleaming room, with the Spirit standing smiling by his side, and looking at that same nephew with approving affability!

'Ha, ha!' laughed Scrooge's nephew. 'Ha, ha, ha!'

If you should happen, by any unlikely chance, to know a man more blest in a laugh than Scrooge's nephew, all I can say is, I should like to know him too. Introduce him to me, and I'll cultivate his acquaintance.

It is a fair, even-handed, noble adjustment of things, that while there is infection in disease and sorrow, there is nothing in the world so irresistibly contagious as laughter and good-humour. When Scrooge's nephew laughed in this way: holding his sides, rolling his head, and twisting his face into the most extravagant contortions, Scrooge's niece, by marriage, laughed as heartily as he. And their assembled friends being not a bit behindhand, roared out lustily.

'Ha, ha! Ha, ha, ha, ha!'

'He said that Christmas was a humbug, as I live!' cried Scrooge's nephew. 'He believed it, too!'

'More shame for him, Fred!' said Scrooge's niece, indignantly. Bless those women; they never do anything by halves. They are always in earnest.

She was very pretty: exceedingly pretty. With a dimpled, surprised-looking, capital face; a ripe little mouth, that seemed made to be kissed—as no doubt it was; all kinds of good little dots about her chin, that melted into one another when she laughed; and the sunniest pair of eyes you ever saw in any little creature's head. Altogether she was what you would have called provoking, you know; but satisfactory too. Oh, perfectly satisfactory!

'He's a comical old fellow,' said Scrooge's nephew, 'that's the truth: and not so pleasant as he might be. However, his offences carry their own punishment, and I have nothing to say against him.'

'I'm sure he is very rich, Fred,' hinted Scrooge's niece. 'At least, you always tell *me* so.'

'What of that, my dear!' said Scrooge's nephew. 'His wealth

is of no use to him. He don't do any good with it. He don't make himself comfortable with it. He hasn't the satisfaction of thinking—ha, ha, ha!—that he is ever going to benefit US with it.'

'I have no patience with him,' observed Scrooge's niece. Scrooge's niece's sisters, and all the other ladies, expressed the same opinion.

'Oh, I have!' said Scrooge's nephew. 'I am sorry for him; I couldn't be angry with him if I tried. Who suffers by his ill whims! Himself, always. Here, he takes it into his head to dislike us, and he won't come and dine with us. What's the consequence? He don't lose much of a dinner.'

'Indeed, I think he loses a very good dinner,' interrupted Scrooge's niece. Everybody else said the same, and they must be allowed to have been competent judges, because they had just had dinner; and with the dessert upon the table, were clustered round the fire, by lamplight.

'Well! I am very glad to hear it,' said Scrooge's nephew, 'because I haven't any great faith in these young housekeepers. What do *you* say, Topper?'

Topper had clearly got his eye upon one of Scrooge's niece's sisters, for he answered that a bachelor was a wretched outcast, who had no right to express an opinion on the subject. Whereat Scrooge's niece's sister—the plump one with the lace tucker: not the one with the roses—blushed.

'Do go on, Fred,' said Scrooge's niece, clapping her hands. 'He never finishes what he begins to say! He is such a ridiculous fellow!'

Scrooge's nephew revelled in another laugh, and as it was impossible to keep the infection off; though the plump sister tried hard to do it with aromatic vinegar; his example was unanimously followed.

'I was going to say,' said Scrooge's nephew, 'that the consequence of his taking a dislike to us, and not making merry with us, is, as I think, that he loses some pleasant moments, which could do him no harm. I am sure he loses pleasanter companions than he can find in his own thoughts, either in his mouldy old office, or his dusty chambers. I mean to give him the same chance every year, whether he likes it or not, for I pity him. He may rail at Christmas till he dies, but he can't help thinking better of it— I defy him—if he finds me going there, in good temper, year after year, and saying, Uncle Scrooge, how are you? If it only puts him in the vein to leave his poor clerk fifty pounds, *that's* something; and I think I shook him, yesterday.'

It was their turn to laugh now, at the notion of his shaking Scrooge. But being thoroughly good-natured, and not much caring what they laughed at, so that they laughed at any rate, he encouraged them in their merriment, and passed the bottle, joyously.

After tea they had some music. For they were a musical family, and knew what they were about, when they sung a Glee or Catch, I can assure you: especially Topper, who could growl away in the bass like a good one, and never swell the large veins in his forehead, or get red in the face over it. Scrooge's niece played well upon the harp; and played among other tunes a simple little air (a mere nothing: you might learn to whistle it in two minutes), which had been familiar to the child who fetched Scrooge from the boarding-school, as he had been reminded by the Ghost of Christmas Past. When this strain of music sounded, all the things that Ghost had shown him, came upon his mind; he softened more and more; and thought that if he could have listened to it often, years ago, he might have cultivated the kindnesses of life for his own happiness with his own hands, without resorting to the sexton's spade that buried Jacob Marley.

But they didn't devote the whole evening to music. After a while they played at forfeits; for it is good to be children sometimes, and never better than at Christmas, when its mighty Founder was a child himself. Stop! There was first a game at blind-man's buff. Of course there was. And I no more believe Topper was really blind than I believe he had eyes in his boots. My opinion is, that it was a done thing between him and Scrooge's nephew; and that the Ghost of Christmas Present knew it. The way he went after that plump sister in the lace tucker, was an outrage on the credulity of human nature. Knocking down the fire-irons, tumbling over the chairs, bumping against the piano, smothering himself among the curtains, wherever she went, there went he. He always knew where the plump sister was. He wouldn't catch anybody else. If you had fallen up against him, as some of them did, and stood there; he would have made a feint of endeavouring to seize you, which would have been an affront to your understanding; and would instantly have sidled off in the direction of the plump sister. She often cried out that it wasn't fair; and it really was not. But when at last, he caught her; when, in spite of all her silken rustlings, and her rapid flutterings past him, he got her into a corner whence there was no escape; then his conduct was the most execrable. For his pretending not to know her; his pretending that it was necessary to touch her head-dress, and further to assure himself of her identity by pressing a certain ring upon her finger, and a certain chain about her neck; was vile, monstrous! No doubt she told him her opinion of it, when, another blind-man being in office, they were so very confidential together behind the curtains.

Scrooge's niece was not one of the blind-man's buff party, but was made comfortable with a large chair and a footstool, in a snug corner, where the Ghost and Scrooge were close behind her. But she joined in the forfeits, and loved her love to admiration with all the letters of the alphabet. Likewise at the game of How, When, and Where, she was very great, and to the secret joy of Scrooge's nephew, beat her sisters hollow: though they were sharp girls too, as Topper could have told you. There might have been twenty people there, young and old, but they all played, and so did Scrooge; for wholly forgetting in the interest he had in what was going on, that his voice made no sound in their ears, he sometimes came out with his guess quite loud, and very often guessed quite right, too, for the sharpest needle, best Whitechapel, warranted not to cut in the eye, was not sharper than Scrooge: blunt as he took it in his head to be.

The Ghost was greatly pleased to find him in this mood, and looked upon him with such favour that he begged like a boy to be allowed to stay until the guests departed. But this the Spirit said could not be done.

'Here is a new game,' said Scrooge. 'One half hour, Spirit, only one!'

It was a game called Yes and No, where Scrooge's nephew had to think of something, and the rest must find out what; he only answering to their questions yes or no as the case was. The brisk fire of questioning to which he was exposed, elicited from him that he was thinking of an animal, a live animal, rather a disagreeable animal, a savage animal, an animal that growled and grunted sometimes, and talked sometimes, and lived in London, and walked about the streets, and wasn't made a show of, and wasn't led by anybody, and didn't live in a menagerie, and was never killed in a market, and was not a horse, or an ass, or a cow, or a bull, or a tiger, or a dog, or a pig, or a cat, or a bear. At every fresh question that was put to him, this nephew burst into a fresh roar of laughter; and was so inexpressibly tickled, that he was obliged to get up off the sofa and stamp. At last the plump sister, falling into a similar state, cried out:

'I have found it out! I know what it is, Fred! I know what it is!'

'What is it?' cried Fred.

'It's your uncle Scro-o-o-o-oge!'

Which it certainly was. Admiration was the universal sentiment, though some objected that the reply to 'Is it a bear?' ought to have been 'Yes;' inasmuch as an answer in the negative was sufficient to have diverted their thoughts from Mr. Scrooge, supposing they had ever had any tendency that way.

'He has given us plenty of merriment, I am sure,' said Fred, 'and it would be ungrateful not to drink his health. Here is a glass of mulled wine ready to our hand at the moment; and I say "Uncle Scrooge!" '

'Well! Uncle Scrooge!' they cried.

'A merry Christmas and a Happy New Year to the old man, whatever he is!' said Scrooge's nephew. 'He wouldn't take it from me, but may he have it, nevertheless. Uncle Scrooge!'

Uncle Scrooge had imperceptibly become so gay and light of heart, that he would have pledged the unconscious company in return, and thanked them in an inaudible speech, if the Ghost had given him time. But the whole scene passed off in the breath of the last word spoken by his nephew; and he and the Spirit were again upon their travels.

Much they saw, and far they went, and many homes they visited, but always with a happy end. The Spirit stood beside sick beds, and they were cheerful; on foreign lands, and they were close at home; by struggling men, and they were patient in their greater hope; by poverty, and it was rich. In alms-house, hospital, and jail, in misery's every refuge, where vain man in his little brief authority had not made fast the door, and barred the Spirit out, he left his blessing, and taught Scrooge his precepts.

It was a long night, if it were only a night; but Scrooge had his doubts of this, because the Christmas Holidays appeared to be condensed into the space of time they passed together. It was strange, too, that while Scrooge remained unaltered in his outward form, the Ghost grew older, clearly older. Scrooge had observed this change, but never spoke of it, until they left a children's Twelfth Night party, when, looking at the Spirit as they stood together in an open place, he noticed that its hair was grey.

'Are spirits' lives so short?' asked Scrooge.

'My life upon this globe, is very brief,' replied the Ghost. 'It ends to-night.'

'To-night!' cried Scrooge.

'To-night at midnight. Hark! The time is drawing near.'

The chimes were ringing the three quarters past eleven at that moment.

'Forgive me if I am not justified in what I ask,' said Scrooge, looking intently at the Spirit's robe, 'but I see something strange, and not belonging to yourself, protruding from your skirts. Is it a foot or a claw!'

'It might be a claw, for the flesh there is upon it,' was the Spirit's sorrowful reply. 'Look here.'

From the foldings of its robe, it brought two children; wretched, abject, frightful, hideous, miserable. They knelt down at its feet, and clung upon the outside of its garment.

'Oh, Man! look[40] here! Look, look, down here!' exclaimed the Ghost.

They were a boy and girl. Yellow, meagre, ragged, scowling, wolfish; but prostrate, too, in their humility. Where graceful youth should have filled their features out, and touched them with its freshest tints, a stale and shrivelled hand, like that of age, had pinched, and twisted them, and pulled them into shreds. Where angels might have sat enthroned, devils lurked; and glared out menacing. No change, no degradation, no perversion of humanity, in any grade, through all the mysteries of wonderful creation, has monsters half so horrible and dread.

Scrooge started back, appalled. Having them shown to him in this way, he tried to say they were fine children, but the words choked themselves, rather than be parties to a lie of such enormous magnitude.

'Spirit! are[41] they yours?' Scrooge could say no more.

'They are Man's,' said the Spirit, looking down upon them. 'And they cling to me, appealing from their fathers. This boy is Ignorance. This girl is Want. Beware of them both, and all of their degree, but most of all beware this boy, for on his brow I see that written which is Doom, unless the writing be erased. Deny it!' cried the Spirit, stretching out its hand towards the city. 'Slander those who tell it ye! Admit it for your factious purposes, and make it worse! And bide the end!'

'Have they no refuge or resource?' cried Scrooge.

'Are there no prisons?' said the Spirit, turning on him for the last time with his own words. 'Are there no workhouses?'

The bell struck twelve.

Scrooge looked about him for the Ghost, and saw it not. As the last stroke ceased to vibrate, he remembered the prediction of old Jacob Marley, and lifting up his eyes, beheld a solemn Phantom, draped and hooded, coming, like a mist along the ground, towards him.

Stave Four

The Last of the Spirits

The Phantom slowly, gravely, silently, approached. When it came near him, Scrooge bent down upon his knee; for in the very air through which this Spirit moved it seemed to scatter gloom and mystery.

It was shrouded in a deep black garment, which concealed its head, its face, its form, and left nothing of it visible save one outstretched hand. But for this it would have been difficult to detach its figure from the night, and separate it from the darkness by which it was surrounded.

He felt that it was tall and stately when it came beside him, and that its mysterious presence filled him with a solemn dread. He knew no more, for the Spirit neither spoke nor moved.

'I am in the presence of the Ghost of Christmas Yet to Come?' said Scrooge.

The Spirit answered not, but pointed onward with its hand.

'You are about to show me shadows of the things that have not happened, but will happen in the time before us,' Scrooge pursued. 'Is that so, Spirit?'

The upper portion of the garment was contracted for an instant in its folds, as if the Spirit had inclined its head. That was the only answer he received.

Although well used to ghostly company by this time, Scrooge feared the silent shape so much that his legs trembled beneath him, and he found that he could hardly stand when he prepared to follow it. The Spirit paused a moment, as observing his condition, and giving him time to recover.

But Scrooge was all the worse for this. It thrilled him with a vague uncertain horror, to know that behind the dusky shroud, there were ghostly eyes intently fixed upon him, while he, though he stretched his own to the utmost, could see nothing but a spectral hand and one great heap of black.

'Ghost of the Future!' he exclaimed, 'I fear you more than any Spectre I have seen. But as I know your purpose is to do me good, and as I hope to live to be another man from what I was, I am prepared to bear you company, and do it with a thankful heart. Will you not speak to me?'

It gave him no reply. The hand was pointed straight before them.

'Lead on!' said Scrooge. 'Lead on! The night is waning fast, and it is precious time to me, I know. Lead on, Spirit!'

The phantom moved away as it had come towards him. Scrooge followed in the shadow of its dress, which bore him up, he thought, and carried him along.

They scarcely seemed to enter the city; for the City rather seemed to spring up about them, and encompass them of its own act. But there they were, in the heart of it; on 'Change, amongst the merchants; who hurried up and down, and chinked the money in their pockets, and conversed in groups, and looked at their watches, and trifled thoughtfully with their great gold seals; and so forth, as Scrooge had seen them often.

The Spirit stopped beside one little knot of business men. Observing that the hand was pointed to them, Scrooge advanced to listen to their talk.

'No,' said a great fat man with a monstrous chin, 'I don't know much about it, either way. I only know he's dead.'

'When did he die?' inquired another.

'Last night, I believe.'

'Why, what was the matter with him?' asked a third, taking a vast quantity of snuff out of a very large snuff-box. 'I thought he'd never die.'

'God knows,' said the first, with a yawn.

'What has he done with his money?' asked a red-faced gentleman with a pendulous excrescence on the end of his nose, that shook like the gills of a turkey-cock.

'I haven't heard,' said the man with the large chin, yawning again. 'Left it to his Company, perhaps. He hasn't left it to *me*. That's all I know.'

This pleasantry was received with a general laugh.

'It's likely to be a very cheap funeral,' said the same speaker; 'for upon my life I don't know of anybody to go to it. Suppose we make up a party and volunteer?'

'I don't mind going if a lunch is provided,' observed the gentleman with the excrescence on his nose. 'But I must be fed, if I make one.'

Another laugh.

'Well, I am the most disinterested among you, after all,' said the first speaker, 'for I never wear black gloves, and I never eat lunch. But I'll offer to go, if anybody else will. When I come to think of it, I'm not at all sure that I wasn't his most particular friend; for we used to stop and speak whenever we met. Bye, bye!'

Speakers and listeners strolled away, and mixed with other groups. Scrooge knew the men, and looked towards the Spirit for an explanation.

The Phantom glided on into a street. Its finger pointed to two persons meeting. Scrooge listened again, thinking that the explanation might lie here.

He knew these men, also, perfectly. They were men of business: very wealthy, and of great importance. He had made a point always of standing well in their esteem: in a business point of view, that is; strictly in a business point of view.

'How are you?' said one.

'How are you?' returned the other.

'Well!' said the first. 'Old Scratch has got his own at last, hey?'

'So I am told,' returned the second. 'Cold, isn't it?'

'Seasonable for Christmas time. You are not a skater, I suppose?'

'No. No. Something else to think of. Good morning!'

Not another word. That was their meeting, their conversation, and their parting.

Scrooge was at first inclined to be surprised that the Spirit should attach importance to conversations apparently so trivial; but, feeling assured that they must have some hidden purpose, he set himself to consider what it was likely to be. They could scarcely be supposed to have any bearing on the death of Jacob, his old partner, for that was Past, and this Ghost's province was the Future. Nor could he think of any one immediately connected with himself, to whom he could apply them. But nothing doubting that to whomsoever they applied they had some latent moral for his own improvement, he resolved to treasure up every word he heard, and everything he saw; and especially to observe the shadow of himself when it appeared. For he had an expectation that the conduct of his future self would give him the clue he missed, and would render the solution of these riddles easy.

He looked about in that very place for his own image; but another man stood in his accustomed corner, and though the clock pointed to his usual time of day for being there, he saw no likeness of himself among the multitudes that poured in through the Porch. It gave him little surprise, however; for he had been revolving in his mind a change of life, and thought and hoped he saw his new-born resolutions carried out in this.

Quiet and dark, beside him stood the Phantom, with its outstretched hand. When he roused himself from his thoughtful quest, he fancied from the turn of the hand, and its situation in reference to himself, that the Unseen Eyes were looking at him keenly. It made him shudder, and feel very cold.

They left the busy scene, and went into an obscure part of the town, where Scrooge had never penetrated before although he recognised its situation, and its bad repute. The ways were foul and narrow; the shops and houses wretched; the people half-naked, drunken, slipshod, ugly. Alleys and archways, like so many cesspools, disgorged their offences of smell, and dirt, and life, upon the straggling streets; and the whole quarter reeked with crime, with filth, and misery.

Far in this den of infamous resort, there was a low-browed, beetling shop, below a pent-house[42] roof, where iron, old rags, bottles, bones, and greasy offal, were bought. Upon the floor within, were piled up heaps of rusty keys, nails, chains, hinges, files, scales, weights, and refuse iron of all kinds. Secrets that few would like to scrutinise were bred and hidden in mountains of unseemly rags, masses of corrupted fat, and sepulchres of bones. Sitting in among the wares he dealt in, by a charcoal-stove, made of old bricks, was a grey-haired rascal, nearly seventy years of age; who had screened himself from the cold air without, by a frousy curtaining of miscellaneous tatters, hung upon a line; and smoked his pipe in all the luxury of calm retirement.

Scrooge and the Phantom came into the presence of this man, just as a woman with a heavy bundle slunk into the shop. But she had scarcely entered, when another woman, similarly laden, came in too; and she was closely followed by a man in faded black, who was no less startled by the sight of them, than they had been upon the recognition of each other. After a short period of blank astonishment, in which the old man with the pipe had joined them, they all three burst into a laugh.

'Let the charwoman alone to be the first!' cried she who had entered first. 'Let the laundress alone to be the second; and let the undertaker's man alone to be the third. Look here, old Joe, here's a chance! If we haven't all three met here without meaning it.'

'You couldn't have met in a better place,' said old Joe, removing his pipe from his mouth. 'Come into the parlour. You were made free of it long ago, you know; and the other two an't[43] strangers. Stop till I shut the door of the shop. Ah! How it skreeks! There an't such a rusty bit of metal in the place as its own hinges, I believe; and I'm sure there's no such old bones here, as mine. Ha! ha[44]! We're all suitable to our calling, we're well matched. Come into the parlour. Come into the parlour.'

The parlour was the space behind the screen of rags. The old man raked the fire together with an old stair-rod, and having trimmed his smoky lamp (for it was night), with the stem of his pipe, put it into his mouth again.

While he did this, the woman who had already spoken threw her bundle on the floor and sat down in a flaunting manner on a stool; crossing her elbows on her knees, and looking with a bold defiance at the other two.

'What odds then! What odds, Mrs. Dilber?' said the woman. 'Every person has a right to take care of themselves. *He* always did!'

'That's true, indeed!' said the laundress. 'No man more so.'

'Why then, don't stand staring as if you was afraid, woman; who's the wiser? We're not going to pick holes in each other's coats, I suppose?'

'No, indeed!' said Mrs. Dilber and the man together. 'We should hope not.'

'Very well, then!' cried the woman. 'That's enough. Who's the worse for the loss of a few things like these? Not a dead man, I suppose.'

'No, indeed,' said Mrs. Dilber, laughing.

'If he wanted to keep 'em after he was dead, a wicked old screw,' pursued the woman, 'why wasn't he natural in his lifetime? If he had been, he'd have had somebody to look after him when he was struck with Death, instead of lying gasping out his last there, alone by himself.'

'It's the truest word that ever was spoke,' said Mrs. Dilber, 'It's a judgment on him.'

'I wish it was a little heavier one,' replied the woman; 'and it should have been, you may depend upon it, if I could have laid my hands on anything else. Open that bundle, old Joe, and let me know the value of it. Speak out plain. I'm not afraid to be the first, nor afraid for them to see it. We knew pretty well that we were helping ourselves, before we met here, I believe. It's no sin. Open the bundle, Joe.'

But the gallantry of her friends would not allow of this; and the man in faded black, mounting the breach first, produced *his* plunder. It was not extensive. A seal or two, a pencil-case[45], a pair of sleeve-buttons, and a brooch of no great value, were all. They were severally examined and appraised by old Joe, who chalked the sums he was disposed to give for each, upon the wall, and added them up into a total when he found that there was nothing more to come.

'That's your account,' said Joe, 'and I wouldn't give another six-pence, if I was to be boiled for not doing it. Who's next?'

Mrs. Dilber was next. Sheets and towels, a little wearing apparel, two old-fashioned silver teaspoons, a pair of sugar-tongs, and a few boots. Her account was stated on the wall in the same manner.

'I always give too much to ladies. It's a weakness of mine, and that's the way I ruin myself,' said old Joe. 'That's your account. If you asked me for another penny, and made it an open question, I'd repent of being so liberal, and knock off half-a-crown.'

'And now undo *my* bundle, Joe,' said the first woman.

Joe went down on his knees for the greater convenience of opening it, and having unfastened a great many knots, dragged out a large heavy roll of some dark stuff.

'What do you call this?' said Joe. 'Bed-curtain!'

'Ah!' returned the woman, laughing and leaning forward on

her crossed arms. 'Bed-curtains!'

'You don't mean to say you took 'em down, rings and all, with him lying there?' said Joe.

'Yes, I do,' replied the woman. 'Why not?'

'You were born to make your fortune,' said Joe, 'and you'll certainly do it.'

'I certainly shan't hold my hand, when I can get anything in it by reaching it out, for the sake of such a man as He was, I promise you, Joe,' returned the woman coolly. 'Don't drop that oil upon the blankets, now.'

'His blankets?' asked Joe.

'Whose else's do you think?' replied the woman. 'He isn't likely to take cold without 'em, I dare say.'

'I hope he didn't die of anything catching? Eh?' said old Joe, stopping in his work, and looking up.

'Don't you be afraid of that,' returned the woman. 'I an't so fond of his company that I'd loiter about him for such things, if he did. Ah! You may look through that shirt till your eyes ache; but you won't find a hole in it, nor a thread-bare place. It's the best he had, and a fine one too. They'd have wasted it, if it hadn't been for me.'

'What do you call wasting of it?' asked old Joe.

'Putting it on him to be buried in, to be sure,' replied the woman with a laugh. 'Somebody was fool enough to do it, but I took it off again. If calico an't good enough for such a purpose, it isn't good enough for anything. It's quite as becoming to the body. He can't look uglier than he did in that one.'

Scrooge listened to this dialogue in horror. As they sat group-ed about their spoil, in the scanty light afforded by the old man's lamp, he viewed them with a detestation and disgust, which could hardly have been greater, though they had been obscene demons, marketing the corpse itself.

'Ha, ha!' laughed the same woman when old Joe, producing a flannel bag with money in it, told out their several gains upon the ground. 'This is the end of it, you see! He frightened every one away from him when he was alive, to profit us when he was dead! Ha, ha, ha!'

'Spirit!' said Scrooge, shuddering from head to foot. 'I see, I see. The case of this unhappy man might be my own. My life tends that way now. Merciful Heaven, what is this!'

He recoiled in terror, for the scene had changed, and now he almost touched a bed: a bare, uncurtained bed: on which, beneath a ragged sheet, there lay a something covered up, which, though it was dumb, announced itself in awful language.

The room was very dark, too dark to be observed with any accuracy, though Scrooge glanced round it in obedience to a secret impulse, anxious to know what kind of room it was. A pale light, rising in the outer air, fell straight upon the bed; and on it, plundered and bereft, unwatched, unwept, uncared for, was the body of this man.

Scrooge glanced towards the Phantom. Its steady hand was pointed to the head. The cover was so carelessly adjusted that the slightest raising of it, the motion of a finger upon Scrooge's part, would have disclosed the face. He thought of it, felt how easy it would be to do, and longed to do it; but had no more power to withdraw the veil than to dismiss the spectre at his side.

Oh, cold, cold, rigid, dreadful Death, set up thine[46] altar here, and dress it with such terrors as thou[47] hast[48] at thy[49] command:

for this is thy dominion! But of the loved, revered, and honoured head, thou canst[50] not turn one hair to thy dread purposes, or make one feature odious. It is not that the hand is heavy and will fall down when released; it is not that the heart and pulse are still; but that the hand WAS open, generous, and true; the heart brave, warm, and tender; and the pulse a man's. Strike, Shadow, strike! And see his good deeds springing from the wound, to sow the world with life immortal!

No voice pronounced these words in Scrooge's ears, and yet he heard them when he looked upon the bed. He thought, if this man could be raised up now, what would be his foremost thoughts? Avarice, hard dealing, griping cares? They have brought him to a rich end, truly!

He lay, in the dark empty house, with not a man, a woman, or a child, to say he was kind to me in this or that, and for the memory of one kind word I will be kind to him. A cat was tearing at the door, and there was a sound of gnawing rats beneath the hearth-stone[51]. What *they* wanted in the room of death, and why they were so restless and disturbed, Scrooge did not dare to think.

'Spirit!' he said, 'this is a fearful place. In leaving it, I shall not leave its lesson, trust me. Let us go!'

Still the Ghost pointed with an unmoved finger to the head.

'I understand you,' Scrooge returned, 'and I would do it, if I could. But I have not the power, Spirit. I have not the power.'

Again it seemed to look upon him.

'If there is any person in the town, who feels emotion caused by this man's death,' said Scrooge quite agonised, 'show that person to me, Spirit! I beseech you!'

The Phantom spread its dark robe before him for a moment,

like a wing; and withdrawing it, revealed a room by daylight, where a mother and her children were.

She was expecting someone, and with anxious eagerness; for she walked up and down the room; started at every sound, looked out from the window, glanced at the clock; tried, but in vain, to work with her needle, and could hardly bear the voices of her children in their play.

At length the long-expected knock was heard. She hurried to the door, and met her husband; a man whose face was care-worn[50] and depressed, though he was young. There was a remarkable expression in it now; a kind of serious delight of which he felt ashamed, and which he struggled to repress.

He sat down to the dinner that had been hoarding for him by the fire; and when she asked him faintly what news (which was not until after a long silence), he appeared embarrassed how to answer.

'Is it good,' she said, 'or bad?' —to help him.

'Bad,' he answered.

'We are quite ruined?'

'No. There is hope yet, Caroline.'

'If *he* relents,' she said, amazed, 'there is! Nothing is past hope, if such a miracle has happened.'

'He is past relenting,' said her husband. 'He is dead.'

She was a mild and patient creature if her face spoke truth; but she was thankful in her soul to hear it, and she said so, with clasped hands. She prayed forgiveness the next moment, and was sorry; but the first was the emotion of her heart.

'What the half-drunken woman whom I told you of last night, said to me, when I tried to see him and obtain a week's delay; and what I thought was a mere excuse to avoid me; turns out to have been quite true. He was not only very ill, but dying, then.'

'To whom will our debt be transferred?'

'I don't know. But before that time we shall be ready with the money; and even though we were not, it would be bad fortune indeed to find so merciless a creditor in his successor. We may sleep to-night with light hearts, Caroline!'

Yes. Soften it as they would, their hearts were lighter. The children's faces, hushed and clustered round to hear what they so little understood, were brighter; and it was a happier house for this man's death! The only emotion that the Ghost could show him, caused by the event, was one of pleasure.

'Let me see some tenderness connected with a death,' said Scrooge; 'or that dark chamber, Spirit, which we left just now, will be for ever present to me.'

The Ghost conducted him through several streets familiar to his feet; and, as they went along, Scrooge looked here and there to find himself, but nowhere was he to be seen. They entered poor Bob Cratchit's house, the dwelling he had visited before; and found the mother and the children seated round the fire.

Quiet. Very quiet. The noisy little Cratchits were as still as statues in one corner, and sat looking up at Peter, who had a book before him. The mother and her daughters were engaged in sewing. But surely they were very quiet!

"And He took a child, and set him in the midst of them."

Where had Scrooge heard those words? He had not dreamed them. The boy must have read them out, as he and the Spirit crossed the threshold. Why did he not go on?

The mother laid her work upon the table, and put her hand up to her face.

'The colour hurts my eyes,' she said.

The colour? Ah, poor Tiny Tim!

'They're better now again,' said Cratchit's wife. 'It makes them weak by candle-light; and I wouldn't show weak eyes to your father when he comes home, for the world. It must be near his time.'

'Past it rather,' Peter answered, shutting up his book. 'But I think he's walked a little slower than he used, these few last evenings, mother.'

They were very quiet again. At last she said, and in a steady, cheerful voice, that only faltered once:

'I have known him walk with—I have known him walk with Tiny Tim upon his shoulder, very fast indeed.'

'And so have I,' cried Peter. 'Often.'

'And so have I!' exclaimed another. So had all.

'But he was very light to carry,' she resumed, intent upon her work, 'and his father loved him so, that it was no trouble—no trouble. And there is your father at the door!'

She hurried out to meet him; and little Bob in his comforter— he had need of it, poor fellow—came in. His tea was ready for him on the hob, and they all tried who should help him to it most. Then the two young Cratchits got upon his knees and laid, each child a little cheek, against his face, as if they said, 'Don't mind it, father. Don't be grieved!'

Bob was very cheerful with them, and spoke pleasantly to all the family. He looked at the work upon the table, and praised the industry and speed of Mrs. Cratchit and the girls. They would be done long before Sunday, he said.

'Sunday! You went to-day, then, Robert?' said his wife.

'Yes, my dear,' returned Bob. 'I wish you could have gone. It would have done you good to see how green a place it is. But you'll see it often. I promised him that I would walk there on a Sunday. My little, little child!' cried Bob. 'My little child!'

He broke down all at once. He couldn't help it. If he could have helped it, he and his child would have been farther apart perhaps than they were.

He left the room, and went up stairs into the room above, which was lighted cheerfully, and hung with Christmas. There was a chair set close beside the child, and there were signs of some one having been there, lately. Poor Bob sat down in it, and when he had thought a little and composed himself, he kissed the little face. He was reconciled to what had happened, and went down again quite happy.

They drew about the fire, and talked, the girls and mother working still. Bob told them of the extraordinary kindness of Mr. Scrooge's nephew, whom he had scarcely seen but once, and who, meeting him in the street that day, and seeing that he looked a little—'just a little down you know' said Bob, inquired what had happened to distress him. 'On which,' said Bob, 'for he is the pleasantest-spoken gentleman you ever heard, I told him. "I am heartily sorry for it, Mr. Cratchit," he said, "and heartily sorry for your good wife." By the bye, how he ever knew *that* I don't know.'

'Knew what, my dear?'

'Why, that you were a good wife,' replied Bob.

'Everybody knows that!' said Peter.

'Very well observed, my boy!' cried Bob. 'I hope they do. "Heartily sorry," he said, "for your good wife. If I can be of service to you in any way," he said, giving me his card, "that's where I live. Pray come to me." Now, it wasn't,' cried Bob, 'for the sake of anything he might be able to do for us, so much as for his kind way, that this was quite delightful. It really seemed as if he had known our Tiny Tim, and felt with us.'

'I'm sure he's a good soul!' said Mrs. Cratchit.

'You would be surer of it, my dear,' returned Bob, 'if you saw and spoke to him. I shouldn't be at all surprised, mark what I say, if he got Peter a better situation.'

'Only hear that, Peter,' said Mrs. Cratchit.

'And then,' cried one of the girls, 'Peter will be keeping company with some one, and setting up for himself.'

'Get along with you!' retorted Peter, grinning.

'It's just as likely as not,' said Bob, 'one of these days; though there's plenty of time for that, my dear. But however and whenever we part from one another, I am sure we shall none of us forget poor Tiny Tim—shall we—or this first parting that there was among us?'

'Never, father!' cried they all.

'And I know,' said Bob, 'I know, my dears, that when we recollect how patient and how mild he was, although he was a little, little child, we shall not quarrel easily among ourselves, and forget poor Tiny Tim in doing it.'

'No, never, father!' they all cried again.

'I am very happy,' said little Bob, 'I am very happy!'

Mrs. Cratchit kissed him, his daughters kissed him, the two young Cratchits kissed him, and Peter and himself shook hands. Spirit of Tiny Tim, thy childish essence was from God!

'Spectre,' said Scrooge, 'something informs me that our parting moment is at hand. I know it, but I know not how. Tell me what man that was whom we saw lying dead?'

The Ghost of Christmas Yet To Come conveyed him, as before— though at a different time, he thought: indeed, there seemed no order in these latter visions, save that they were in the Future— into the resorts of business men, but showed him not himself. Indeed, the Spirit did not stay for anything, but went straight on, as to the end just now desired, until besought by Scrooge to tarry for a moment.

'This court,' said Scrooge, 'through which we hurry now, is where my place of occupation is, and has been for a length of time. I see the house. Let me behold what I shall be in days to come.'

The Spirit stopped; the hand was pointed elsewhere.

'The house is yonder,' Scrooge exclaimed. 'Why do you point away?'

The inexorable finger underwent no change.

Scrooge hastened to the window of his office, and looked in. It was an office still, but not his. The furniture was not the same, and the figure in the chair was not himself. The Phantom pointed as before.

He joined it once again, and, wondering why and whither he had gone, accompanied it until they reached an iron gate. He paused to look round before entering.

A churchyard. Here, then, the wretched man whose name he had now to learn, lay underneath the ground. It was a worthy place. Walled in by houses; overrun by grass and weeds, the growth of vegetation's death, not life; choked up with too much burying; fat with repleted appetite. A worthy place!

The Spirit stood among the graves, and pointed down to One.

He advanced towards it trembling. The Phantom was exactly as it had been, but he dreaded that he saw new meaning in its solemn shape.

'Before I draw nearer to that stone to which you point,' said Scrooge, 'answer me one question. Are these the shadows of the things that Will be, or are they shadows of the things that May be, only?'

Still the Ghost pointed downward to the grave by which it stood.

'Men's courses will foreshadow certain ends, to which, if persevered in, they must lead,' said Scrooge. 'But if the courses be departed from, the ends will change. Say it is thus with what you show me!'

The Spirit was immovable as ever.

Scrooge crept towards it, trembling as he went; and, following the finger, read upon the stone of the neglected grave his own name, **EBENEZER SCROOGE**.

'Am I that man who lay upon the bed?' he cried, upon his knees.

The finger pointed from the grave to him, and back again.

'No, Spirit! Oh, no, no!'

The finger still was there.

'Spirit!' he cried, tight clutching at its robe, 'hear[53] me! I am not the man I was. I will not be the man I must have been but for this intercourse. Why show me this, if I am past all hope?'

For the first time the hand appeared to shake.

'Good Spirit,' he pursued, as down upon the ground he fell before it: 'Your nature intercedes for me, and pities me. Assure me that I yet may change these shadows you have shown me, by an

altered life!'

The kind hand trembled.

'I will honour Christmas in my heart, and try to keep it all the year. I will live in the Past, the Present, and the Future. The Spirits of all Three shall strive within me. I will not shut out the lessons that they teach. Oh, tell me I may sponge away the writing on this stone!'

In his agony, he caught the spectral hand. It sought to free itself, but he was strong in his entreaty, and detained it. The Spirit, stronger yet, repulsed him.

Holding up his hands in a last prayer to have his fate reversed, he saw an alteration in the Phantom's hood and dress. It shrunk, collapsed, and dwindled down into a bedpost.

Stave Five

The End of It

Yes! and the bedpost was his own. The bed was his own, the room was his own. Best and happiest of all, the Time before him was his own, to make amends in!

'I will live in the Past, the Present, and the Future!' Scrooge repeated, as he scrambled out of bed. 'The Spirits of all Three shall strive within me. Oh Jacob Marley! Heaven, and the Christmas Time be praised for this! I say it on my knees, old Jacob; on my knees!'

He was so fluttered and so glowing with his good intentions, that his broken voice would scarcely answer to his call. He had been sobbing violently in his conflict with the Spirit, and his face was wet with tears.

'They are not torn down,' cried Scrooge, folding one of his bed-curtains in his arms, 'they are not torn down, rings and all. They are here: I am here: the shadows of the things that would have been, may be dispelled. They will be. I know they will!'

His hands were busy with his garments all this time: turning them inside out, putting them on upside down, tearing them, mislaying them, making them parties to every kind of extravagance.

'I don't know what to do!' cried Scrooge, laughing and crying in the same breath; and making a perfect Laocoön of himself with his stockings. 'I am as light as a feather, I am as happy as an angel, I am as merry as a school-boy, I am as giddy as a drunken man. A merry Christmas to everybody! A happy New Year to all the world! Hallo here! Whoop! Hallo!'

He had frisked into the sitting-room, and was now standing there: perfectly winded.

'There's the saucepan that the gruel was in!' cried Scrooge, starting off again, and frisking round the fire-place[54]. 'There's the door, by which the Ghost of Jacob Marley entered! There's the corner where the Ghost of Christmas Present, sat! There's the window where I saw the wandering Spirits! It's all right, it's all true, it all happened. Ha, ha, ha!'

Really, for a man who had been out of practice for so many years, it was a splendid laugh, a most illustrious laugh. The father of a long, long line of brilliant laughs!

'I don't know what day of the month it is!' said Scrooge. 'I don't know how long I have been among the Spirits. I don't know anything. I'm quite a baby. Never mind. I don't care. I'd rather be a baby. Hallo! Whoop! Hallo here!'

He was checked in his transports by the churches ringing out the lustiest peals he had ever heard. Clash, clash, hammer, ding, dong, bell. Bell, dong, ding, hammer, clang, clash! Oh, glorious, glorious!

Running to the window, he opened it, and put out his head. No fog, no mist; clear, bright, jovial, stirring, cold; cold, piping for the blood to dance to; Golden sunlight; Heavenly sky; sweet fresh air; merry bells. Oh, glorious. Glorious!

'What's to-day?' cried Scrooge, calling downward to a boy in Sunday clothes, who perhaps had loitered in to look about him.

'EH?' returned the boy with all his might of wonder.

'What's to-day, my fine fellow?' said Scrooge.

'To-day!' replied the boy. 'Why, CHRISTMAS DAY.'

'It's Christmas Day!' said Scrooge to himself. 'I haven't missed it. The Spirits have done it all in one night. They can do anything they like. Of course they can. Of course they can. Hallo, my fine fellow!'

'Hallo!' returned the boy.

'Do you know the Poulterer's, in the next street but one, at the corner?' Scrooge inquired.

'I should hope I did,' replied the lad.

'An intelligent boy!' said Scrooge. 'A remarkable boy! Do you know whether they've sold the prize Turkey that was hanging up there? Not the little prize Turkey: the big one?'

'What, the one as big as me?' returned the boy.

'What a delightful boy!' said Scrooge. 'It's a pleasure to talk to him. Yes, my buck!'

'It's hanging there now,' replied the boy.

'Is it?' said Scrooge. 'Go and buy it.'

'Walk-ER!' exclaimed the boy.

'No, no,' said Scrooge, 'I am in earnest. Go and buy it, and tell 'em to bring it here, that I may give them the directions where to take it. Come back with the man, and I'll give you a shilling. Come back with him in less than five minutes, and I'll give you half-a-crown!'

The boy was off like a shot. He must have had a steady hand at a trigger who could have got a shot off half so fast.

'I'll send it to Bob Cratchit's!' whispered Scrooge, rubbing his hands, and splitting with a laugh. 'He shan't know who sends it. It's twice the size of Tiny Tim. Joe Miller never made such a joke as sending it to Bob's will be!'

The hand in which he wrote the address was not a steady one, but write it he did, somehow, and went down stairs to open the street door, ready for the coming of the poulterer's man. As he stood there, waiting his arrival, the knocker caught his eye.

'I shall love it, as long as I live!' cried Scrooge, patting it with his hand. 'I scarcely ever looked at it before. What an honest expression it has in its face! It's a wonderful knocker!—Here's the Turkey! Hallo! Whoop! How are you! Merry Christmas!'

It *was* a Turkey! He never could have stood upon his legs, that bird. He would have snapped 'em short off in a minute, like sticks of sealing-wax.

'Why, it's impossible to carry that to Camden Town,' said Scrooge. 'You must have a cab.'

The chuckle with which he said this, and the chuckle with which he paid for the Turkey, and the chuckle with which he paid for the cab, and the chuckle with which he recompensed the boy, were only to be exceeded by the chuckle with which he sat down breathless in his chair again, and chuckled till he cried.

Shaving was not an easy task, for his hand continued to shake very much; and shaving requires attention, even when you don't dance while you are at it. But if he had cut the end of his nose off, he would have put a piece of sticking-plaster[55] over it, and been quite satisfied.

He dressed himself 'all in his best,' and at last got out into the streets. The people were by this time pouring forth, as he had seen them with the Ghost of Christmas Present; and walking with his hands behind him, Scrooge regarded every one with a delighted smile. He looked so irresistibly pleasant, in a word, that three or four good-humoured fellows said, 'Good morning, sir! A merry Christmas to you!' And Scrooge said often afterwards, that of all the blithe sounds he had ever heard, those were the blithest in his ears.

He had not gone far, when coming on towards him he beheld the portly gentleman, who had walked into his counting-house the day before and said, 'Scrooge and Marley's, I believe?' It sent a pang across his heart to think how this old gentleman would look upon him when they met; but he knew what path lay straight before him, and he took it.

'My dear sir,' said Scrooge, quickening his pace, and taking the old gentleman by both his hands, 'How do you do? I hope you succeeded yesterday. It was very kind of you. A merry Christmas to you, sir!'

'Mr. Scrooge?'

'Yes,' said Scrooge. 'That is my name, and I fear it may not be pleasant to you. Allow me to ask your pardon. And will you have the goodness'— here Scrooge whispered in his ear.

'Lord bless me!' cried the gentleman, as if his breath were gone. 'My dear Mr. Scrooge, are you serious?'

'If you please,' said Scrooge. 'Not a farthing less. A great many back-payments are included in it, I assure you. Will you do me that favour?'

'My dear sir,' said the other, shaking hands with him, 'I don't know what to say to such munif—'

'Don't say anything, please,' retorted Scrooge. 'Come and see me. Will you come and see me?'

'I will!' cried the old gentleman. And it was clear he meant to do it.

'Thank'ee,' said Scrooge. 'I am much obliged to you. I thank you fifty times. Bless you!'

He went to church, and walked about the streets, and watched the people hurrying to and fro, and patted the children on the head, and questioned beggars, and looked down into the kitchens of houses, and up to the windows; and found that everything could yield him pleasure. He had never dreamed that any walk— that anything—could give him so much happiness. In the afternoon, he turned his steps towards his nephew's house.

He passed the door a dozen times, before he had the courage to go up and knock. But he made a dash, and did it:

'Is your master at home, my dear?' said Scrooge to the girl. Nice girl! Very.

'Yes sir.'

'Where is he, my love?' said Scrooge.

'He's in the dining-room, sir, along with mistress. I'll show you up stairs, if you please.'

'Thank'ee. He knows me,' said Scrooge, with his hand already on the dining-room lock. 'I'll go in here, my dear.'

He turned it gently, and sidled his face in, round the door. They were looking at the table (which was spread out in great array); for these young housekeepers are always nervous on such points, and like to see that everything is right.

'Fred!' said Scrooge.

Dear heart alive, how his niece by marriage started! Scrooge had forgotten, for the moment, about her sitting in the corner with the footstool, or he wouldn't have done it, on any account.

'Why bless my soul!' cried Fred, 'who's[56] that?'

'It's I[57]. Your uncle Scrooge. I have come to dinner. Will you let me in, Fred?'

Let him in! It is a mercy he didn't shake his arm off. He was at home in five minutes. Nothing could be heartier. His niece looked just the same. So did Topper when *he* came. So did the plump sister, when *she* came. So did every one when *they* came. Wonderful party, wonderful games, wonderful unanimity, won-der-ful happiness!

But he was early at the office next morning. Oh, he was early there. If he could only be there first, and catch Bob Cratchit coming late! That was the thing he had set his heart upon.

And he did it; yes, he did! The clock struck nine. No Bob. A quarter past. No Bob. He was full eighteen minutes and a half, behind his time. Scrooge sat with his door wide open, that he might see him come into the Tank.

His hat was off, before he opened the door; his comforter too. He was on his stool in a jiffy; driving away with his pen, as if he were trying to overtake nine o'clock.

'Hallo!' growled Scrooge, in his accustomed voice as near as he could feign it. 'What do you mean by coming here at this time of day?'

'I am very sorry, sir,' said Bob. 'I *am* behind my time.'

'You are!' repeated Scrooge. 'Yes. I think you are. Step this way, sir, if you please.'

'It's only once a year, sir,' pleaded Bob, appearing from the Tank. 'It shall not be repeated. I was making rather merry yesterday, sir.'

'Now, I'll tell you what, my friend,' said Scrooge. 'I am not going to stand this sort of thing any longer. And therefore,' he continued, leaping from his stool, and giving Bob such a dig in the waistcoat that he staggered back into the Tank again: 'and therefore I am about to raise your salary!'

Bob trembled, and got a little nearer to the ruler. He had a momentary idea of knocking Scrooge down with it; holding him; and calling to the people in the court for help and a strait-waistcoat.

'A merry Christmas, Bob!' said Scrooge, with an earnestness that could not be mistaken, as he clapped him on the back. 'A merrier Christmas, Bob, my good fellow, than I have given you, for many a year! I'll raise your salary, and endeavour to assist your struggling family, and we will discuss your affairs this very afternoon, over a Christmas bowl of smoking bishop, Bob! Make up the fires, and buy another coal-scuttle before you dot another i, Bob Cratchit!'

Scrooge was better than his word. He did it all, and infinitely more; and to Tiny Tim, who did NOT die, he was a second father. He became as good a friend, as good a master, and as good a man, as the good old city knew, or any other good old city, town, or borough, in the good old world. Some people laughed to see the alteration in him, but he let them laugh, and little heeded them; for he was wise enough to know that nothing ever happened on this globe, for good, at which some people did not have their fill of laughter in the outset; and knowing that such as these would be blind anyway, he thought it quite as well that they should wrinkle up their eyes in grins, as have the malady in less attractive forms. His own heart laughed: and that was quite enough for him.

He had no further intercourse with Spirits, but lived upon the Total Abstinence Principle, ever afterwards; and it was always said of him, that he knew how to keep Christmas well, if any man alive possessed the knowledge. May that be truly said of us, and all of us! And so, as Tiny Tim observed, God bless Us, Every One!

THE END

Notes

1 Exchange
2 doornail
3 A
4 When
5 No
6 Merry
7 What
8 them
9 Keep
10 tomorrow
11 a
12 a week
13 ill-used
14 Christmas Eve
15 Sitting room
16 indoors
17 Do
18 Thank you
19 And

20 candlelight
21 storehouse
22 dirtier
23 fellow-apprentice
24 ...told it to him
25 pairs
26 today
27 Show
28 Remove
29 special
30 Oh
31 Nearly
32 wasn't
33 have
34 you
35 backyard
36 Say
37 Happy New Year
38 sank

39 seaweed
40 Look
41 Are
42 penthouse
43 are not
44 Ha
45 pencil case
46 your
47 you
48 have
49 your
50 can
51 hearthstone
52 careworn
53 Hear
54 fireplace
55 sticking plaster
56 Who's
57 me

小氣財神

Preface to the Chinese Translation
中文譯本序

　　我在這本關於鬼的小書裏，竭力想召來一個"意念之鬼"，它決不致使我的讀者們對於他們自己，對於彼此之間，對於這季節，或是對於我，感到不愉快。願這隻鬼愉快地出沒於他們的屋裏，而沒有人想要去驅除它！

　　一八四三年十二月這是狄更斯寫的第一篇聖誕故事，也是他最著名的作品之一。這一年他目睹天寒歲暮，平民生活困苦，為喚起對於平民的同情，他創作了這篇小說，在聖誕節前出版。法國作家莫洛亞在他的《英國名人研究》的狄更斯篇中，開頭寫道："當狄更斯的死訊傳到英國、美國、加拿大和澳洲的家庭中時，人們就像死掉了親人一樣。一個小孩問道：'如果狄更斯先生死了，聖誕老人是不是也會死呢？'"可見本書影響之大。

汪倜然

馬利的鬼魂

話說馬利死了。千真萬確地死了。在他安葬的登記簿上有牧師、辦事員、殯儀承辦人和主要送殯人的簽名。史高治在上面簽了名。而史高治的這姓氏在交易所裏是很吃得開的，不管他高興着手做甚麼事情都行。老馬利已經像一顆門釘似的死死的。

請注意！我的意思並不是說，我憑自己的知識，知道一顆門釘會死到甚麼程度。我自己倒還是想把一顆棺材釘當作五金業買賣中最死絕的東西。但是門釘這個比喻表現了我們祖先的智慧，我不應該用我這雙不敬神明的手來竄改它，否則我們的祖國就要滅亡了。因此，請各位准許我再強調：馬利已經像一顆門釘似的死死的了。

史高治是否知道馬利死了呢？他當然是知道的。他怎麼會不知道呢？史高治跟他合夥做生意已不知道有多少年了。史高治是他唯一的遺囑執行人、唯一的財產管理人、唯一的財產受讓人、唯一的財產繼承人、唯一的朋友和唯一的送殯人。史高治並沒有因為這喪事而極度悲傷，在老馬利落葬那一天仍然是一位出色的生意人，做了一筆挺划算的交易來舉行這次葬禮。

談到馬利的葬禮，我又要從頭說起。毫無疑問，馬利已經死了。這件事情一定要知道得一清二楚，否則，我下面要說的故事就一點也不稀奇了。正好像我們若不是深信哈姆雷特的父親是在戲開場以前就死掉的，那麼，他夜裏冒着東風漫步在自己的城牆上，也就跟任何別的中年紳士在天黑以後魯莽地出現在一個風颼颼的地方——比方說聖保羅大教堂的墳場吧——來嚇唬他那個懦怯的兒子，一樣不足為奇了。

史高治始終沒有把老馬利的姓氏塗掉。好些年以後，貨倉的大門頂上還是這數個字："史高治與馬利"。這家商行就叫做"史高治與馬利"。剛做這行買賣的人，有時候把史高治叫作史高治，有時候把他叫作馬利，但不管叫哪個姓氏他都回應。對於他，這反正都是一樣。

噢，史高治這人真是一個吝嗇鬼！一個巧取豪奪、能搜善刮、貪得無厭的老黑心！又硬又厲害，像一塊打火石，隨便哪種鋼從它上面都打不出甚麼星火來；行跡隱秘、沉默寡言、孤孤單單的，像一隻蠔。他心中的冷酷，令他那蒼老的五官凍結了起來，尖鼻子凍壞了、臉頰乾癟了，步伐也僵硬了；也令他的眼睛發紅、薄薄的嘴唇發青；他說話尖酸刻薄、聲音尖銳刺耳。他頭髮已經白得像霜一樣，一雙眉毛和瘦削結實的下巴也都是這樣。他總是帶着自己一身的寒氣，人走到哪兒，就帶到哪兒；在大熱天裏，他調低空調，使自己的辦公室冰凍起來；即使到了聖誕節，還是不讓氣溫上升一度來解凍。

外面轉冷變熱，對於史高治絲毫不起作用。無論怎樣炎熱都不能使他溫暖，無論怎樣酷寒也不能夠使他發冷。風颳得怎樣兇，也比不上他的心那樣狠；雪下得怎樣猛，也比不上他求財之心那樣迫切；雨下得怎樣大，也比不上他從來不聽人懇求那樣無情。惡劣的天氣也不知道怎樣才能征服他。即使猛烈的雨、雪、冰雹和凍雨也只有一點可以自誇勝過他。它們常常"出手"很大方，而史高治卻是從來不會這樣的。

　　在街上，從來沒有人迎上他，用一種高興的神情對他説："親愛的史高治，你好嗎？你甚麼時候來看看我？"沒有哪一個乞丐會請求他施捨一個小錢，沒有哪一個小孩會問他現在是何時。在史高治的一生中，從來沒有一個男人或女人問過他路。連瞎子養的狗似乎都認得他，一看見他走過來，就趕快拖着牠們的主人躲到門洞裏，或者跑進院子裏去；接着牠們還會搖搖尾巴，彷彿在説："失明的主人啊，生着一雙兇惡的眼睛，還不如沒有眼睛的好！"

　　但是史高治才不在乎這一切呢！這正是他想要的。對史高治來説，在擁擠不堪的人生道路上，側着身體一路擠過去，同時叫人世間的同情心都對他遠而避之，這正是那些明眼人所説的"正中下懷"之事。

　　話説從前有一次——偏偏是在一年之中的這個最好的節日，聖誕節的前夕——老史高治坐在他的賬房裏忙着。天氣陰寒砭骨，而且有霧；他聽得見外面院子裏人們喘着氣在走來走去，用手拍着胸部，用腳在石板地上跺着取暖。城裏鐘樓上的大鐘剛剛敲過三時，但是天色已經很黑了。——這一整天就沒有怎麼亮過

——附近那些辦公室的窗裏，蠟燭都已經在燃燒着，彷彿給這觸摸得到的棕色空氣抹上了一些紅色。霧從每一道隙縫和每一個鑰匙孔裏湧進來；在外面，霧濃得連對面的屋（雖然只隔着一個極其狹小的院子）看起來也好像幻影一樣了。看見這片陰暗的雲霧低垂下來，遮蔽住一切東西，人們不禁要以為大自然就住在附近，正在那裏大規模地醞釀着氣候的劇變。

史高治賬房的門是開着的，因為這樣他才可以時刻留意他的辦事員，那人坐在外面那間像一個水槽似的陰森的小房間裏，正在抄寫信件。史高治屋裏生着一爐很小的火，可是辦事員的那爐火比他的還要小得多，看起來就像是只燒着一塊煤。他可沒法加點煤上去，因為史高治把煤箱放在他自己的房間裏；只要這辦事員拿了煤鍬進去，老闆就準要預告說，他們看來非分別不可了。於是辦事員只可披上了白圍巾，嘗試在蠟燭上面取暖；可惜他並不是一個想像力很強的人，他這番努力失敗了。

"祝聖誕快樂，舅舅！上帝保佑你！"一把快活的聲音說。說話的人是史高治的外甥，因為他來得這麼突然，史高治聽見他的聲音，才知道他來了。

"呸！"史高治說。"胡鬧！"

史高治的這位外甥，因為是冒着霧霜匆匆趕來，走得很熱，所以滿面紅光，臉蛋又紅潤又漂亮；他的眼睛閃閃發亮，他的呼吸又冒起熱氣來了。

"聖誕節真胡鬧，舅舅！"史高治的外甥說。"你的意思不會真是這樣吧，我相信！"

"我的意思就是這樣，"史高治說。"聖誕快樂！你有甚麼權利值得快樂？你有甚麼理由值得快樂？你已經夠窮了。"

"那，"他的外甥快活地回答說。"你有甚麼權利值得不快活？你有甚麼理由值得悶悶不樂？你已經夠富有了。"

史高治一時想不出甚麼好的回答來，就又說了聲"呸！"接着又是一聲"胡鬧！"。

"別生氣，舅舅！"外甥說。

"我不生氣可以怎樣呢，"舅舅回答說，"我就生活在這麼一個滿是傻瓜的世界裏！快樂的聖誕節！滾它的聖誕快樂！對你而言，聖誕節不過是一個沒有錢還賬的時節；一個發現自己大了一歲，可是隨着時光流逝並不多一點錢的時節；一個年底結賬，結果發現整整十二個月裏筆筆賬都是虧空的時節；除此以外，還有甚麼意義？如果我的願望能夠實現的話，"史高治憤怒地說，"凡是跑來跑去把'聖誕快樂'掛在嘴上的笨蛋，都應該把他跟自己的布丁一起煮熟了，再給他當胸插上一根冬青樹枝，埋掉了他。他本應如此！"

"舅舅！"外甥懇求道。

"外甥！"舅舅嚴厲地回答，"你照你自己的方式去過聖誕節，讓我照我自己的方式來過聖誕節吧。"

"過節！"史高治的外甥重複了一遍。"但是你並不過節呢。"

"那麼，就讓我不過節吧，"史高治說。"但願這個節日會給你許多好處！它到底給過你多少好處！"

"有許多事情，我本來可以從中得到好處，可是我並沒有去撈取好處，我敢說，"他外甥回答。"聖誕節就是其中一例。但是我確信，我每逢這個節日到來的時候——且不說它那神聖的名字和起源所引起的崇敬，如果任何屬於聖誕節的事情可以撇開這種崇敬不談的話——我總是把它當作一個好日子，一個友好、寬恕、慈善、快樂的日子；據我所知，在漫長的一年之中，只有在這時節，男男女女才似乎不約而同地把他們那緊閉的心房敞開，把那些比他們卑微的人真的看作是一起走向墳墓的旅伴，而不是走向其他路程的另一種生物。因此，舅舅，聖誕節雖則從來沒把絲毫金銀放進我的口袋，我還是相信它的確給了我好處，而且以後還會給我好處；所以我說，上帝保佑它！"

"水槽"裏的那個辦事員禁不住喝起彩來。他立刻感覺到這是不當的舉動，就去撥弄那爐火，卻把最後一顆微弱的星火都弄熄了。

"我如果聽見你再哼一聲，"史高治說，"那你就丟了你的飯碗，去過你的聖誕節吧！你真是一位很有力的演說家，先生，"他接着轉身向着他的外甥說。"我奇怪的是，你怎麼不進國會去。"

"不要生氣，舅舅。來吧！明天來跟我們一起吃飯。"

史高治說他寧願先看見他外甥……是的，他的確是這樣說的。他把這句咒人的話都說了出口，說是他寧願先看見他外甥死難臨頭。

"這是為甚麼呢？"史高治的外甥叫道。"為甚麼呢？"

"你為甚麼結了婚？"史高治說。

"因為我當初戀愛了。"

"因為你當初戀愛了！"史高治咆哮着說，彷彿這是世界上唯一比快樂的聖誕節更荒唐可笑的事情。"再見！"

"不，舅舅，即使在我結婚以前，你也從沒有來看過我呀，為何現在要把這件事作為不來的理由呢？"

"再見，"史高治說。

"我不需要你給我任何東西；我不向你要求任何東西；我們為甚麼不能友好相處呢？"

"再見，"史高治說。

"看見你這樣堅決，我心裏實在覺得難過。在我們兩人的爭吵裏，我從來不是一個參與者。我如今作這次嘗試，是為了向聖誕節表示敬意，所以我一定要把我的聖誕節歡樂心情保持到底。我還是要祝你聖誕快樂，舅舅！"

"再見！"史高治說。

"並祝新年快樂！"

"再見！"史高治說。

然而他外甥還是不說一句生氣的話，就離開了這房間。他在外面門口停了一下，向那辦事員致以節日的祝賀，而那人雖則身上寒冷，心裏卻比史高治溫暖得多，因為他滿腔熱誠地回答他的祝賀。

"又一個這樣的人，"史高治偷聽到他的答話，嘀咕道，"我這個辦事員，一個禮拜賺十五個先令，有老婆和一家人，卻還在說甚麼聖誕快樂。我真要躲進瘋人院去了。"

這個瘋子讓史高治的外甥出去時，同時讓另外兩個人進來。他們都是肥頭胖耳的紳士，看起來親切友好；這時他們都脫下了帽，站在史高治的辦公室裏。他們手裏拿着簿冊和一些紙張，向他鞠躬致意。

"是史高治與馬利商行吧，我相信，"紳士中的一個説，參看着他手中的那張表。"請問您是史高治先生，還是馬利先生？"

"馬利先生已經死去七年，"史高治回答。"他是七年前去世的，就在今天這樣的聖誕夜。"

"我們深信，這位健在的合夥老闆的慷慨之心一定不下於他的，"這位紳士説，一面拿出證明文件來。

這倒確實如此；因為他們一直就是兩個性格相同的人。一聽見"慷慨"這個不祥的字眼，史高治就眉頭一皺，搖搖頭，把證明書還給了他。

"逢到一年之中的這個節日，史高治先生，"這紳士説，拿起一枝筆來，"我們就格外需要替那些窮苦人，稍微提供一點補助物品，因為他們目前正在水深火熱之中。成千上萬的人缺乏日用必需品；數十萬人缺乏生活福利上所需的東西，先生。"

"難道沒有監獄嗎？"史高治問。

"監獄多得很，"那紳士説，又把筆放下來。

"還有聯合救濟院呢？"史高治問。"現在還辦不辦？"

"都辦的。可是，"這紳士回答，"我也想説一聲，它們都不辦了。"

"那麼，踏車[1]和濟貧法[2]現在還都在發揮充份的影響力嗎？"史高治説。

"兩者都不斷運作着，先生。"

"哦！我起初聽了你的話，還生怕發生了甚麼事情，使它們不能夠進行這種有益的工作，"史高治説。"現在聽你這樣説，我就放心了。"

"我們因為意識到，它們對於大眾幾乎無法提供甚麼基督教式的、精神上和肉體上的愉快，"那紳士答道，"我們這數個人才正在努力想籌集一筆錢來給窮人們買一點肉、酒以及禦寒的東西。我們選擇這個時節，是因為這時節窮人們最感到困苦拮据，而有錢人最興高采烈。我給您寫上多少？"

"甚麼也不要寫！"史高治回答。

"您是想要匿名？"

"我想要不受騷擾，"史高治說。"既然你問我想要甚麼，先生們，這就是我的答覆。我自己在聖誕節不尋歡作樂，我也沒那麼多錢來讓懶漢們尋歡作樂。我幫着維持剛才我提到過的那數個機構，它們要的錢已經夠多的了；那些景況不好的人都應該到那裏去。"

"有許多人不能到那裏去；還有許多人寧死也不肯去。"

"如果他們寧願死的話，"史高治說。"他們還是死掉的好，同時還可以減少過剩的人口。況且——對不起——我不了解這種事情。"

"但你也許是了解的，"那位紳士說。

"那不關我的事，"史高治回答。"一個人管好他自己的事情，別去干涉別人的事情，也就足夠了。我自己的事情一直使我夠忙的。再見，先生們！"

這兩個紳士清楚地看出，再說下去也還是沒有結果的，就告辭了。史高治繼續做他的事情，對於自己更加滿意了，而且情緒也比往常輕鬆了。

這時候，霧更濃了，夜色也更黑了，有些人拿着耀眼的火把跑來跑去，為人們照明。他們走在馬車的馬匹前面，給這些馬車帶路。已經看不見禮拜堂古老的鐘樓了，裏面有一個聲音粗糲的老鐘，老是從牆上一個哥德式的窗裏偷偷地向下看着史高治，它在雲端裏報時和報刻，敲過以後發出一陣顫抖的尾音，彷彿它的頭伸在高空裏，給凍壞了，牙齒在打顫。寒氣更酷烈了。在大街上，院子的轉角處，有數個工人正在修理煤氣管，在火盆裏生起了熊熊的一大堆火，一群衣衫襤褸的大人和小孩圍在這火盆的周圍，暖和他們的手，興高采烈地衝着火光眨眼。水龍頭呢，因為這時沒人去理睬它了，它那溢出的水憤懣地凍結起來，變成厭恨人類的冰塊。店鋪裏燈火明亮，人們經過時，蒼白的臉給照得紅彤彤的。冬青樹的枝條和紅果，給櫥窗裏的燈光烘得嗶剝作響。家禽鋪和雜貨店裏的生意成為一種絕妙的賞心樂事，一種壯麗的慶祝大典，人們簡直無法相信，那種乏味的討價還價和廉價出售的原則會跟它有甚麼相干。市長大人在他那高大府邸的壁壘裏，命令他的五十名廚師和管家把聖誕節過得像市長府邸應當過的那樣。連那小裁縫，上星期一因為喝醉了酒在街上打架，被市長罰款五先令，這時也在他的閣樓裏攪着明天要吃的布丁；他那瘦小的老婆呢，帶着寶寶上街去買牛肉了。

霧更加濃了，天更加冷了，冷得徹骨切膚，無孔不入。如果仁慈的聖鄧斯丹[3]不用他那慣用的武器，而用一點這樣的寒氣來鉗住惡魔的鼻子，這惡魔也一定會有強烈的理由大聲叫嚷！有個鼻子瘦削的小孩子，給這餓慌了的寒風咬住了咀嚼着，像狗啃骨頭似的，這時正蹲下身來，湊着史高治門上的鑰匙孔，獻唱一首聖誕歌[4]；但是史高治一聽見歌的開端：

上帝保佑你，快樂的先生！

願你一切如意，無憂無慮！

他就馬上抓起直尺，動作極其迅猛，嚇得那唱歌的人慌忙逃走，讓迷霧以及與之臭味相投的寒氣鑽進鑰匙孔去。

最後，賬房關門的時候到了。史高治才不樂意地從圓橙上爬下來，對那在"水槽"裏等待下班的辦事員默認時間已經到了，那辦事員便立刻剪熄了蠟燭，戴上了帽。

"我看你明天想歇一整天吧？"史高治説。

"如果方便的話，先生。"

"不方便，"史高治説，"而且也不公平。如果我因為這個緣故，扣掉你半個克朗，你不就要以為自己吃虧了嗎？這我可以保證。"

辦事員勉強地笑笑。

"然而，"史高治説，"我付了一天的工資，沒有人替我工作，你倒不認為我吃虧了。"

辦事員説，這只不過是一年一次而已。

"每逢十二月二十五日，就要取走別人一筆錢，這實在不成藉口！"史高治説着，把大衣直扣到下巴。"但是我看你是非要一整天不可的。後天早晨可要來得早些！"

辦事員答應他一定早些來，史高治就抱怨一聲，走了出去。一眨眼，賬房的門關上了，辦事員便圍上白圍巾，圍巾兩頭一直掛到腰下面（因為他沒有大衣可以誇耀），他跑到康希爾街結了冰發滑的人行道上，跟在一長行小孩的末尾，溜了二十遍，以慶祝這個聖誕節前夕，然後用最快的速度，跑回到卡姆登鎮自己家裏，去玩捉迷藏遊戲。

史高治呢，在他慣常去的那家淒涼的小客店裏，吃了他那頓淒涼的晚餐；他把所有的報紙全讀過了，並且把晚上其餘的時間消磨在他的銀行賬目上之後，才回家去睡覺。他所住的這數個房間，從前是屬於他那已故的合夥人的。這是一套陰暗的房間，在院子後面一幢陰鬱的建築內。這幢屋跟這個院子毫不相干，人們不禁會想像：它一定是在它還是新屋的時候，跟別的屋玩捉迷藏，跑到那裏去了，就此忘掉出來的路。它現在已經老得很了，而且悽慘得很，除了史高治之外，沒有別人住在裏頭，別的房間都租出去作為辦公室了。院子裏黑得很，史高治雖然連那裏的每一塊石頭都很熟悉，也不得不用手摸索着走。在那漆黑古老的大門上，霜厚霧濃，看起來好像氣候之神就坐在門檻上靜默誌哀。

事實上，說起門上的那個門環，它除了很大之外，並沒有甚麼特別的地方。而且，這也是事實，在史高治居住在這地方的整個時期裏，他每天早晚都看見這個門環；何況他也像倫敦城裏的任何人一樣——說句大膽的話，甚至連市府當局、高級市政官和那些穿制服的人[5]在內——是一個很少有所謂幻想的人。此外我們還要記住，史高治自從那天下午提到他那死去了七年的合夥人以來，還沒有再想起馬利。那麼，如果有哪一位能夠解釋箇中道理的，就請他來解釋給我聽吧：怎麼這樣，當史高治把他的鑰匙插入門上的鎖孔時，這期間那門環本身一點也沒有發生過變化，然而史高治看見的卻不是一個門環，而竟是馬利的臉。

馬利的臉。它不像院子裏其他的東西那樣，籠罩在深不可測的陰影裏頭，而是帶着一種慘淡的亮光，好像黑暗地窖裏的一隻腐爛的龍蝦。那張臉既不在生氣，也並不猙獰可怕，只是對史高治看着，像馬利生前看他那樣，一副鬼相的眼鏡架在他鬼相的額角上。頭髮在古怪地飄動着，彷彿是被呼吸或熱氣吹拂着；而且，兩隻眼睛雖然是張大着的，卻一動也不動。這種神情，再加上它那青灰的膚色，使它猙獰可怕；但它的可怕，與其說是它自身表情的一部份，還不如說是它自己無法控制的臉相。

當史高治緊盯着這怪現象看時，它又變成一個門環了。

如果說史高治並不驚慌，或者說他的血脈裏並沒有產生自出娘胎以來從未有過的恐怖之感，那未免不符事實。可是他把手又擱在他剛才放開的鑰匙上，用力把它轉了一下，就開門進去，把蠟燭點起來。

他的確站住了，躊躇了片刻，才關上大門。他也的確先小心地對門背後望望，彷彿他多少在期待會看見馬利的辮子伸進大廳，使他自己大吃一驚。但是門背後甚麼東西都沒有，只有那釘住門環的螺釘和螺帽，因此他說了兩聲"呸，呸！"就嘭的一聲把門關上了。

關門聲像打雷似的在全屋裏產生了回響。樓上的每一個房間和下面酒商地窖裏的每一個酒桶，都似乎各自發出一陣轟隆隆的回音。史高治並不是一個會被回音嚇住的人。他關好門，走過大廳，走上樓去，還是慢吞吞地邊走邊修剪着燭芯。

你也許會含混地談到：駕一部六匹馬的大馬車，駛上一道古老的樓梯，或者衝破國會裏新通過的一道不好的法案[6]；但是我的意思是說，你大可以把一輛柩車駛上這道樓梯，而且是橫着上去，車輛的橫木對着牆壁，車後的門對着欄杆，而且可以輕易地做到這一點。那樓梯的寬度足夠讓人這樣做，而且有多餘位置；也許就是因為這個緣故，史高治才自以為看見一輛機動柩車，在幽暗中在他面前行駛着。外面街上的六七盞煤氣燈都不會把這條過道照得很亮，因此你可想而知，單靠史高治的一支小蠟燭頭，這裏當然是很暗的。

史高治還是往上走，絲毫不理會這一點。黑暗不用費錢，所以史高治喜歡黑暗。但是他在把他那扇沉重的房門關上以前，先在數個房間裏走了一遍，看看一切是否都正常。他還相當記得那張臉，所以要這樣做。

客廳、臥室、雜物室，都依然如故。枱底下沒有人；沙發底下沒有人；壁爐裏生着一堆小火；湯瓢和餐盆都已準備好；一小鍋燕麥粥（史高治的頭着了點涼）擱在爐邊的保溫鐵架上。牀鋪底下沒有人；壁櫥裏沒有人；他的晨衣掛在牆上，模樣頗為可疑，但是裏面也沒有人。雜物室跟平時一樣。一塊舊爐柵、數雙舊鞋、兩個魚簍、一個三隻腳的臉盆架以及一根撥火棍。

對一切都覺得放心之後，他便關上房門，把自己反鎖在裏面；用雙重鎖把自己反鎖在裏面，這可是一反他向來的習慣的。這樣部署妥當，不會有遭受突然襲擊的危險了，他才解下領巾，穿上晨衣和拖鞋，戴上睡帽，在壁爐前坐下來，吃他的燕麥粥。

壁爐裏的火確實非常微弱；在這麼一個寒冷的夜間，這點火起不了甚麼作用。他只可以靠近壁爐坐着，並且俯身在爐火上，才能從這一點點燃料上得到極細微的溫暖。這壁爐是個古老的東西，是很久以前一個荷蘭商人造的，周圍砌着古色古香的荷蘭瓷磚，上面的圖畫描繪了《聖經》中的一些故事。磚上有該隱和亞伯、法老的女兒們、示巴女王、駕着鴨絨墊般的雲朵從空中下降的天使們、亞伯拉罕、伯沙撒、乘着牛油碟般的船隻出海的使徒們，一共有數百個人物來吸引他的注意力；然而死了七年的馬利的臉，卻像古先知的杖據似的出現，把其他人物全都吞沒了。如果每一塊光滑的瓷磚起初都是空白的，卻有法力把他思想中雜亂無章的片段拼成一幅圖畫的話，那麼，每一塊磚上都會有一幅老馬利的頭。

"胡鬧！"史高治說，一面朝房間的另一頭走去。

繞了數圈之後，他又坐下來。當他把頭朝後靠在椅背上時，他的目光湊巧落到一個鈴上，這個鈴掛在房間裏，已經不用了，它是跟屋裏頂樓樓上的一個房間連接着的，至於當初用來做甚麼，如今已被人忘記了。看着看着，他看見這個鈴搖擺起來，不禁大為驚詫，並產生了一種奇異的、莫名其妙的恐懼。起初，這鈴搖擺得非常輕微，可說是一點聲音也沒有；但是不久響聲就大起來了，屋裏的每一個鈴也都響了起來。

這樣大約響了有半分鐘，或者一分鐘，但是好像有一個小時之久。鈴聲一齊停止了，正像剛才一齊響起來一樣。接着是一陣從下面深處發出的鐺銀銀的聲音，彷彿有人在酒商的地窖裏把一根沉重的鏈條從一個個酒桶上面拖過去。史高治這時候才想起聽人說過，在凶宅裏的鬼是拖着鏈條的。

地窖的門嘭的一聲打開了，於是他聽見下面地板上的聲音更加大了；接着響到樓梯上來了；接着一直響到他房門口來了。

"這還是胡鬧！"史高治說。"我不相信。"

然而，它片刻不停地穿過那道厚重的門，一直跑到房間裏來了，史高治親眼目睹之下，臉色都變白了。它一進來，那快要熄滅的火焰就躍了起來，好像在叫道，"我認識他，那是馬利的鬼魂！"說完火光又熄滅了。

還是這張臉，一模一樣。馬利留着辮子，穿着平時常穿的背心、緊身衣褲和皮靴；靴上的流蘇倒豎着，像他的辮子、他的上裝下擺以及他的頭髮一樣。他拖着的那根鏈條繞在他的腰際。鏈條很長，像一條尾巴似的纏在他身上；它是由（因為史高治看得很仔細）一些銀箱、鑰匙、掛鎖、賬簿、契據和鋼製的錢袋等組成的。他的身體是透明的，因此史高治在注視他時，能夠透過他的背心，看見他上裝背後的兩顆鈕扣。

史高治常常聽到別人說，馬利是沒有肚腸心肺的，他以前一直不相信，但是現在親眼看見了。

不，即使到現在，他還是不相信。他雖然對着這幻象看了又看，而且眼見它站在自己面前；雖然感到它那死亡般冰冷的眼睛陰氣襲人，而且注意到那條圍住他腦袋和下巴的圍巾是甚麼質料（這條圍巾他以前從沒看見過），他還是不相信，還是疑心自己看錯了。

"怎麼了！"史高治說，仍然是又尖刻又冷酷。"你找我有甚麼事？"

"事情多着呢！"——毫無疑問，這是馬利的聲音。

"你是誰？"

"你該問我從前是誰。"

"那麼，你從前是誰？"史高治提高嗓子問。"你真愛挑剔，鬼透了。"

"我生前是你的合夥人，雅各‧馬利。"

"你能不能夠——能不能夠坐下來？"史高治問，滿腹狐疑地看着他。

"我能夠。"

"那麼，坐下來吧。"

史高治問這句話，是因為他不知道像這樣一個通體透明的鬼能不能坐到椅上；他以為，這鬼如果不可能坐下的話，那就免不了要作一番艦尬的解釋。但是這隻鬼已經在壁爐的對面那邊坐下了，彷彿它慣常都是這樣做的。

"你不相信我，"鬼說。

"我不相信，"史高治說。

"除了你自己的感覺之外，你要有甚麼證據才能相信我真的在這兒呢？"

"我不知道，"史高治說。

"你為甚麼懷疑你自己的感覺？"

"因為，"史高治說，"只要有一點地方不對頭，感覺就會失常的。譬如說胃裏稍微有點不舒服，感覺就會靠不住。你也許是一小塊未消化的牛肉、一攤芥末、一片乾芝士的碎、一塊沒有煮熟的馬鈴薯。不管你是甚麼東西，你身上的油的成份總比遊魂的成份多！"

史高治是不太習慣說笑話的，而且那時候他也一點也沒有想開玩笑的心思。其實，他是想裝得精明些，以便轉移他自己的注意力，同時抑制他的恐懼心理，因為那隻鬼的聲音使他從骨髓裏感到惶恐不安。

　　史高治覺得，這樣一直默不作聲地坐着注視這雙呆滯而無神的眼睛，實在是叫他受不了。何況，非常可怕的是，這幽靈本身就帶着一種地獄般的氣氛。史高治自己感覺不到這股氣氛，但情況明顯是這樣；因為那隻鬼雖然坐在那裏一動不動，可是他的頭髮、衣擺和流蘇，都照樣在飄動着，好像被爐灶裏的熱氣激盪着似的。

　　"你看見這根牙籤沒有？"史高治說；他為了剛才提到的那個原因，很快地又來發動攻勢了，只希望能把這幽靈的鐵石般的凝視轉移到他自身以外的東西上去，即使是一秒鐘也好。

　　"我看得見，"鬼回答說。

　　"你並沒有看它呢，"史高治說。

　　"可是，"這鬼說，"我還是看得見它的。"

　　"好吧！"史高治回答說。"我只要把這根牙籤吞下肚去，我這後半世就會一直受到我自己想像中的一大批幽靈所迫害。胡鬧，我告訴你！胡鬧！"

　　那鬼聽到這裏，發出一聲可怕的叫喊，並且搖動他的鏈條，發出一陣那麼悽涼可怕的聲音，嚇得史高治緊緊抓住了椅子，以免暈倒。但是更使他驚駭的是，只見這幽靈把頭上的圍巾解了下來（好像在室內圍着太熱似的），它的下巴竟一直垂到了胸前！

　　史高治雙膝跪下，緊握雙手遮住了臉。

　　"饒了我吧！"他說。"可怕的陰魂，你為甚麼要來纏我？"

　　"凡夫俗子啊！"鬼回答說，"你現在相信不相信我？"

　　"我相信了，"史高治說。"我不能不相信。但是幽靈們為甚麼要到人間來走動，而且為甚麼要來找我呢？”

“每個人，”那鬼回答說，“都應當使自己內在的心靈到人們之間去活動，到四處旅行；如果在世的時候他的心靈不到外面去，那麼死後就要罰它這樣做。它將注定要到全世界去流浪——咳，好苦啊！——而且要親眼看到許多他在世時本來可以分享得到、並且從中得到幸福的事物，現在他卻沒有資格分享了。”

這鬼魂又發出一聲號叫，搖動它的鏈條，搓着一雙鬼手。

“你給上了鎖鏈，”史高治發着抖說。“告訴我這是為了甚麼？”

“我身上纏着的鎖鏈是我在世時自己鍛造的，”鬼回答說。“我一環一環，一碼一碼地把它打成；我自願把它繞在身上，自願佩戴着它。你是不是從未見過這個式樣？”

史高治抖得更厲害了。

“或者，你知道嗎，”這鬼接下去說，“你自己身上纏着的那條結實的鎖鏈有多重多長嗎？在七個聖誕夜以前，它就已經足足有這樣重，這樣長了。從那時候起，你還在辛辛苦苦地製造它。現在它是一條奇重無比的鎖鏈！”

史高治看看周圍的地板，以為會發現自己被五六十英呎長的鐵索包圍着；但是他甚麼也沒有看見。

“雅各，”他懇求着，“老雅各·馬利啊，你再對我說多點。說點安慰的話給我聽聽，雅各！”

“我沒有甚麼安慰的話可以跟你說，”這鬼回答說。“這種話是從別的地域來的，埃伯尼澤·史高治，這是要由別的使者們帶來，傳達給另外數種人聽的。我也不能把我想說的話告訴你。准許我跟你説的只有很短的數句話了。我不能休息，不能停住，不能在任何地方逗留。我的靈魂從來沒有走到我們賬房的外面去過——注意聽我的話！——我在世時，我的心靈從來沒有漫遊到我們那狹窄的兌換處窗口的外面去過；如今疲勞的旅程正展開在我面前！"

史高治有這樣一個習慣：每逢有心事的時候，總要把雙手插進褲袋裏。他現在思量着那鬼所説的話，手也就這樣做了，不過他的眼睛並不向上看，也沒有站起來。

"你一定是走得很慢的，雅各，"史高治一本正經地説，然而是帶着謙卑和恭敬的樣子的。

"慢！"鬼重複説了這個字。

"死了已經七年了，"史高治思量着説。"這時期中一直在旅行嗎？"

"整整七年了，"那鬼説。"沒有休息，沒有安寧。在不斷的悔恨中受盡苦楚。"

"你走得快嗎？"史高治説。

"御風而行嘛，"鬼回答説。

"這七年裏，你原可以走過許多地方的啊，"史高治説。

那鬼聽了這句話，又發出了一聲號叫，鐺鋃鋃地揮動着它的鏈條，在萬籟俱寂的夜間，聲音怪可怕的，如果治安監護人要控告它擾亂安寧，是很有理由的。

"咳！被綁住手腳並上着雙重桎梏的囚徒啊，"這幽靈叫道，"竟不知道，自古以來有多少不朽的人物為了人間長期不斷地努力，可是在其可感知的好處尚未完全顯露以前，這些努力就要成為泡影！竟不知道，任何具有基督教精神的人，在他那小天地裏善良地工作着，不論這小天地是甚麼，他都會感到，行善之道廣闊無涯，但人生如朝露，無能為力。竟不知道，人生的機緣一旦貽誤，就將從此追悔莫及！然而我正是如此！唉，我正是如此啊！"

"但你向來是一位業務能手嘛，雅各，"史高治結結巴巴地說，他現在開始把這話應用到他自己身上了。

"業務！"那鬼搓搓手，叫道。"人類才是我的業務！大眾的福利才是我的業務；慈悲、仁愛、寬容與和善，這一切才都是我的業務。至於我那一行買賣，在我這浩瀚似海的業務中，只不過是一滴水罷了！"

他伸直手臂，舉起鏈條，彷彿他所有那些徒然的悲傷，都來自這唯一的根源；然後把這根鏈條又重重地摔在地上。

"在這歲月流逝、一年將盡的時候，"這鬼魂說，"我受苦受得最厲害。當我在人群中穿行時，我為甚麼把眼睛向下看，卻從來不朝上望望那顆指引三博士到一個窮人住處去的，神佑的星[7]呢？難道已經沒有窮人的家庭可以讓這顆星的光芒給我領路嗎？"

史高治聽着鬼魂這樣說下去，覺得驚慌失措，不禁渾身發起抖來，抖得非常厲害。

"聽我說！"鬼叫道。"我的時間快要完了。"

"我聽着，"史高治說。"不過可別對我太嚴厲！別咬文嚼字，雅各！懇求你！"

"我怎樣會在你面前，以一種看得見的形態出現，這是我不便告訴你的。我坐在你身邊，而你看不見，這樣已經有很多天了。"

這事叫人聽了可不好受。史高治打了一個寒噤，抹去額上的汗。

"在我補過贖罪的苦行中，這是並不輕鬆的一部份，"這鬼接下去說。"我今夜到這裏來，是要警告你：你還有逃脫我這種命運的一線機會和希望。這是我替你求來的一線機會和希望，埃伯尼澤。"

"你向來是我的好朋友，"史高治說。"謝謝你！"

"有三個幽靈，"那鬼接下去說，"將會來纏着你。"

史高治的臉色立刻沉下來，跟那隻鬼剛才的臉色差不多。

"這就是你剛才提到的機會和希望嗎，雅各？"他聲音顫抖地問。

"正是。"

"我——我想我寧願不要，"史高治說。

"如果沒有他們來找你，"那鬼說，"你就別想能逃避我所走的道路。明天敲一時的時候，你等着第一位到來吧。"

"我能不能讓他們一起來，乾脆了結掉這件事呢，雅各？"史高治透露這個想法說。

"在第二夜的同一個時間，你等着第二位到來吧。第三位，在下一夜剛敲完十二時的時候來。你不必指望再看見我；而且，為了你自己，你必須記住我們之間的這次交談！"

那鬼說完這數句話之後，就把圍巾從桌上拿過來，像先前一樣包在頭上。史高治知道這一點，是因為聽到它的上下顎被圍巾包攏在一起時，牙齒發出清脆的響聲。他壯着膽，舉目又看了一下，只見他這位鬼客筆直地站在他面前，鏈條在手臂上緊緊纏着。

這幽靈從他身邊倒退着走去；它每向後退一步，窗框就自動向上升高一點。等到它退到窗邊時，窗已經敞開了。它叫史高治走過去，史高治聽從了。等他們彼此距離只有兩步路了，馬利的鬼魂舉起手來，警告他不要再走近去。史高治就站住了。

這與其說是服從，不如說是由於驚異和恐懼；因為，當那鬼舉起手來的時候，史高治就聽見空中有一陣嘈雜的聲響：斷斷續續的悲歎聲和悔恨聲；難以形容的悲戚和自我譴責的哭聲。那鬼聽了一會之後，也加入了這悲傷的輓歌聲，並且飄浮到淒冷的黑夜裏去了。

史高治跟到窗邊；他出於好奇心，拼命向窗外望去。

空中充滿了幻影，倉惶不安地東飄西蕩，一面走一面嗚咽着。他們個個都像馬利的鬼魂那樣，鏈條纏身；有數個（它們也許是有罪孽的官僚吧）還給綁在一起；卻沒有一個是自由的。內中有許多在世時是史高治認識的。他很熟悉其中一個年老的鬼，它穿着一件白色的背心，腳踝上掛着一個巨大無比的鐵保險箱，它看見下面一家門口有一個抱着嬰孩的可憐女人，因為自己不能夠去幫助她而傷心地哭着。它們大家的苦惱是很明顯的：為了要行善，都試過問人間的事情，只可惜已經永遠無能為力了。

這些鬼魂究竟是漸漸消失在霧裏，還是被霧籠罩了，他可說不準了。但是它們和它們的幽靈之聲一起消失了；於是黑夜又變得跟他走回家時一樣了。

史高治關上窗，去檢查那鬼從那兒進來的那道門。門還是雙重鎖着，跟他自己親手鎖上的時候一樣，門閂也沒有被人動過。

他想說一聲"胡鬧！"但是說出頭一個字就住口不說了。而且，因為剛才情緒激動了一會，或是因為白天工作得疲乏了，或是因為瞥見了陰間世界，聽到了那鬼的枯燥乏味的談話，以及時間已經很晚了，使他非常需要休息，因此他衣服也不脫，一直走到牀邊，倒在牀上，立刻睡着了。

三幽靈中的第一個

史高治醒來的時候，天還是很黑，他從牀上望出去，簡直無法把那扇透明的窗戶跟他房裏不透明的牆壁分辨出來。他竭力想用他那雙雪貂般銳利的眼睛望穿黑暗，這時，附近一座教堂連敲了報四刻的鐘聲。他便靜聽接着敲何時。

叫他大為驚駭的是，這沉重的鐘聲敲了六下再敲第七下、第八下，這樣有規則地直敲了十二下才停止。十二時了！他上牀的時候已經是二時多。這個鐘一定是出毛病了。一定有一根冰柱攪進它的齒輪之間去了。十二時！

他按按打簧錶的彈簧，來校正一下這個愚蠢的鐘。錶的小脈搏快速地打了十二下，就停止了。

"我竟會睡了整整一個白天，再一直睡到半夜，"史高治說，"這怎麼可能呢！這也不可能是太陽出了甚麼毛病，而現在是中午十二時吧！"

因為這個想法太嚇人了，他就趕快爬下牀來，摸索着走到窗邊去。他非要用晨衣的袖擦掉窗上的霜，才能夠看見東西；可是即使這樣仍然看不大到甚麼。他所能看出的只是：霧還很大，天還非常冷，沒有人跑來跑去的聲音，也沒引起很大的騷動；假如黑夜當真已經趕走了白晝而佔有了世界的話，那就毫無疑問會引起騷動的。這倒是一個莫大的安慰，因為，如果無法計算日子的話，那麼"見此第一聯匯票三日後請付埃伯尼澤·史高治先生或其授權人"等等，就會變得像一張美國債券一樣不值錢了。

史高治回到牀上去，想啊想啊，想了又想，還是想不出甚麼來。而且他越想就越糊塗，他越是竭力不去想它呢，反而越是想得多。馬利的鬼魂使他煩惱得不得了。每當他經過充份思考，斷定這全是一場夢之後，他的心卻老是像一個放鬆了的強力彈簧似的，又彈回到原來的地方去，結果又要從頭研究這同樣的問題："這到底是不是一場夢？"

史高治懷着這種心情躺着，直躺到鐘聲報了三刻，這時候他忽然想起，那鬼警告過他，當鐘報一時的時候就會有訪客。他決定醒着躺在牀上，等候這個時候過去；而這個主意，由於他那時的不能入睡正如他不能入天堂一樣，也許可以説是他所能作出的最聰明的決定了。

這一刻鐘時間真長，以致他不只一次地認為自己一定不知不覺地打起瞌睡，錯過鐘點了。最後，鐘聲傳入他那靜聽着的耳中來了。

"叮！"

"十二時一刻，"史高治數着説。

"叮！"

"十二時半，"史高治説。

"叮！"

"一時差一刻，"史高治説。

"叮！"

"到整點了，"史高治得意地説，"一點事情也沒有發生！"

　　他説話時，報點的那一下還沒有敲響，現在可來了：深沉、滯重、空洞而陰鬱的一聲。房間裏立刻閃起一道亮光，他牀上帳被掀開了。

　　他牀上的帳，我告訴你，是被一隻手掀開的。不是掀他腳邊的帳，也不是他背後的帳，而是他面前的帳。他牀上的帳被掀開到一邊去，於是史高治驚跳起來，成了一個半躺半靠的姿勢，發現自己正面對着那掀開帳的陰間來客：跟它靠攏得就像我現在靠攏你一樣，而我的心神現在正在你的身旁。

　　那是一個稀奇古怪的形體——像一個小孩子；可是，如果説它像一個小孩子，倒不如説更像一個老伯，因為通過某種幽幻的物質看來，它漸漸遠離視線，而縮成一個孩子的大小。它的頭髮披在頸邊，並且下垂到背上，彷彿因為年紀老而變白了；可是臉上卻一絲皺紋也沒有，皮膚上還顯出最嬌嫩的紅色。手臂很長、筋肉發達；一雙手也是這樣，彷彿緊握起來是力大非凡的。它的腿和腳形狀都非常嬌柔，像它的手臂一樣裸露着。它穿着一件最潔白的束腰短袍，腰間紮着一條亮晶晶的帶，光彩奪目。它手裏拿着一根新鮮的冬青樹枝；可是，跟這冬天的標誌特別顯得不調和的是，它的衣服上都綴滿着夏季的鮮花。但是最奇怪的事情是，從它的天靈蓋上射出一道燦爛的光芒，把這一切都照得清清楚楚的；這無疑就是它逢到要使這光較暗的時候，用一頂挺大的熄燈帽來當作睡帽的原因，現在這帽正挾在它腋下。

這情形雖然奇怪，可是史高治越是向它盯着看，就越覺得這還不是它最奇怪的地方。因為，當它那條腰帶一會在這部份，一會在那部份閃爍發光、忽明忽暗的時候，它的形體本身也就一會清晰，一會模糊；有時是一個只有一隻手臂的東西，有時卻是只有一條腿；有時有二十條腿，有時有兩條腿而沒有頭，有時是有頭而沒有身體。那些消失了的肢體都融入了濃黑的夜色裏，一點輪廓也看不出來。接着，就在這樣的奇蹟中，它又會重新恢復原狀，依舊是一清二楚的。

"先生，您就是有人事先通知我要光臨的那位幽靈嗎？"史高治問。

"我就是！"

説話的聲音是輕柔而溫和的。聲音特別小，彷彿不是從他近旁，而是從很遠的地方傳來的。

"你是誰，是做甚麼的？"史高治追問道。

"我是'過去聖誕節之靈'。"

"過去很久嗎？"史高治注意到它那侏儒般的身材，這樣問道。

"不。是你的過去。"

如果有誰來問史高治，史高治也許答不出個所以來，但他懷着一種特別的期望，想看看這幽靈戴上帽的樣子，於是他便請求它把帽戴上。

"怎麼！"這幽靈叫道，"難道你迫不及待地要用你這雙世俗的手來把我發出的光明撲滅嗎？有些人把他們的慾望製成了這頂帽，逼我把它低低地戴在額角上，一直戴了這許多年，而你就是他們中間的一個，難道這還不夠嗎？」

史高治必恭必敬地否認他有絲毫冒犯它的意思，也想不起自己一生中的任何時候曾經故意硬給它"戴上帽"。接着他便大膽地請問它到這兒來有甚麼事。

"為了你的幸福！"幽靈說。

史高治表示十分感激，但是心裏不禁想：沒有人來打擾，讓他安睡一夜，恐怕對於他的幸福更有幫助。這幽靈一定是猜到他的心思了，因為它立刻就說道：

"那麼，就說為了讓你改過自新吧。注意！"

它一邊說，一邊伸出它那隻強壯的手，輕輕地勾住他的胳膊。

"起來！跟我一起走吧！"

史高治即使懇求它，說氣候和時間都不適宜於出去散步；說牀上暖和，溫度計卻降到了零下好幾度；說他只穿着拖鞋和晨衣，戴着睡帽，身上是單薄的；還說他這時正在傷風——即使這樣懇求它，也都是沒有用的。那隻抓住他的手，雖則輕柔得像一隻女人的手，卻是無法抗拒的。他站起來，但是發現那幽靈正向窗口走去，就抓住它的袍，懇求憐憫。

"我是一個凡人，"史高治抗議說，"會摔下去的。"

"只要你經我用手在那裏點一下，"這幽靈說，把手放在他的心口上，"你就會被舉起來，比這還要高！"

話剛說完，他們就穿過了牆壁，站在一條寬闊的鄉村道路上，兩旁都是田野。城市已經完全消失了，連一點影子都看不見了。黑暗和迷霧也跟它一起消失，變成了一個晴朗、寒冷的冬日，地上鋪滿着雪。

「天啊！」史高治向四周看了看，把雙手勾在一起。「我就是在這個地方生長的。我從小就在這兒的！」

那幽靈溫和地盯着他。雖然它那手剛才只是輕微而短促地點了他一下，可是這老伯似乎到現在還帶着這種感覺。他覺得空氣中飄浮着千百種氣味，每一種氣味都使人聯想起很久很久以前就已淡忘的千百種思慮、希望、歡樂和憂愁！

「你的嘴唇在哆嗦，」那幽靈說。「還有，你臉上的那一點是甚麼？」

史高治聲音裏帶點不尋常的哽咽，咕噥了一聲說那是一個粉刺，就懇求這幽靈帶領他到他願去的地方。

「你還記得路嗎？」幽靈問。

「記得！」史高治熱情洋溢地叫道，「我蒙住眼睛也能走到那兒去呢！」

「奇怪的是，你竟把它忘掉那麼多年了，」幽靈說。「我們繼續走吧。」

他們沿着這條路走去，史高治認出了每一道院門，每一根柱和每一棵樹，最後看到遠處出現了一個小小的市鎮，那兒有橋、禮拜堂和一條曲折的河。有幾匹蓬鬆着鬃毛的小馬在向他們快步跑來，馬背上騎着小孩子，他們招呼着坐在農民們駕駛的雙輪小馬車和大車裏的其他孩子們。這些孩子都是興高采烈的，彼此大喊大叫，鬧得這廣闊的田野裏充滿了一片愉快的音樂聲，連那清新的空氣聽了都笑起來！

「這些只是過去事物的影子罷了，」幽靈說。「它們意識不到我們在這兒。"

那些高高興興的旅客走過來了；當他們走來時，史高治認出他們每一個人，並且叫得出每一個人的名字。他為甚麼看見他們就歡喜得不得了呢？為甚麼等他們走過身邊時，他那冷酷的眼睛會發出光亮，他的心會怦怦地跳呢？當他們在十字路口或分岔路上分別，各自回家時，他們彼此祝頌着聖誕快樂，為甚麼他聽見了這種聲音就心中充滿了喜悅呢？聖誕快樂對於史高治算得上甚麼呢？去它的聖誕快樂！它對他哪有過甚麼好處呢？

"學校裏的人還沒有全走掉，"幽靈説。"有一個孤孤單單的孩子，朋友們都不理睬他，還留在那兒。"

史高治説他知道這一回事。接着他就啜泣起來。

他們離開大路，轉過去一條很熟悉的小路，不久就走到一座暗紅色的磚砌大廈跟前。大廈屋頂上有個鐘形小閣，上面放了一個小風信標，裏面掛着一個鐘。這是一幢大屋，不過是一間破落戶的屋；因為那些寬敞的下房已經沒人使用了，牆壁都是潮濕的，生滿着苔蘚，窗都破碎了，院門已經腐爛。家禽在馬廏裏咯咯叫，昂首闊步地走着；馬車房和棚裏都長滿了草。即使房間裏面也沒有比舊觀更舊；因為他們一踏進那凄涼的門廳，從開着的房門望到那許多房間裏，就發現這些房間陳設簡陋，寒冷、空曠。空氣裏有一股泥土氣息，屋裏有一種陰森森的荒涼氣象，這多少使人聯想到是由於常常天不亮就點上蠟燭起牀，同時吃的東西又不充足。

他們，這幽靈和史高治，穿過門廳，走到屋後的一扇門前。門在他們面前開了，展現出一間簡陋凄涼的長形房間，裏面放着數排未油漆的松木長櫈和書桌，使這間房間顯得更加簡陋了。在一張書桌前，有一個孤寂的孩子在暗淡的爐火旁讀着書；史高治看見了自己那被遺忘的、可憐巴巴的小時候的形象，不禁在一張板櫈上坐下，哭了起來。

屋裏潛藏着的回聲，板壁後面老鼠的尖叫和打架聲，陰暗的後院裏雨水管開始解凍的滴滴嗒嗒聲，一棵垂頭喪氣的白楊樹從光禿禿的枝條間發出的嘆息聲，一間空儲藏室的門百無聊賴的搖晃聲，甚至連火爐裏嗶嗶啪啪的響聲，這種種聲音，沒有一種不落在史高治的心上，起軟化的作用，使他淚流不止。

那幽靈碰碰他的手臂，指指小時候正在專心讀書的他。忽然有一個穿外國服裝的人，看起來活靈活現、清清楚楚的，正站在窗戶外面，腰帶裏插着一把斧頭，一手抓住馬勒，牽着一匹馱着木柴的驢。

“唷，那是阿里巴巴呀！”史高治狂喜地叫道。“那是親愛的、誠實的好阿里巴巴！是的，是的，我想起來了！有一年聖誕節，當這個寂寞的孩子孤零零地被撇下在這裏的時候，他真的來了，那是頭一次，就像現在一樣。可憐的孩子！還有范倫坦[8]，”史高治說，“和他那野生的兄弟奧遜；他們從那邊走過去了！還有，那個穿着襯褲睡着了被人放在大馬士革城門口的，他的名字叫甚麼？你看見他沒有？還有那蘇丹的馬夫，妖魔使他倒立，他還在頭朝下地倒立着！他本應如此！我很高興。他有甚麼資格跟公主結婚？”

假使史高治那些在城裏做生意的朋友聽見他把他天性中的滿腔熱誠都發洩在這些事情上，而聲音又像哭又像笑，非常特別；

並且看見他那張又興奮又激動的臉，他們準會大大吃驚的。

「看那隻鸚鵡！」史高治叫道。「綠身體，黃尾巴，頭頂上長着一件像生菜的東西；牠就在那兒！當可憐的魯賓遜環繞全島航行後回家時，鸚鵡就叫他可憐的魯賓遜。『可憐的魯賓遜，你剛才到哪兒去了，魯賓遜？』那人還以為他在做夢呢，其實他並沒有。是那鸚鵡在叫他，你知道。禮拜五跑過去了，他是在往小溪逃命！嗨呀！嗬！嗨呀！」

於是，在一種跟他平時的性格完全不符的迅速轉變下，他痛惜過去的自己，不禁説了聲：「可憐的孩子！」就又哭了起來。

「我希望，」史高治把手伸到口袋裏，嘀咕着説，並且先用袖口擦乾了眼淚，再向周圍看看，「可是如今太遲了！」

「甚麼事？」這幽靈問。

「沒有甚麼，」史高治説。「沒有甚麼。昨天夜晚，有個小孩在我門口唱了一首聖誕頌歌。我當時真該給他一點甚麼。就是這麼一回事。」

那幽靈若有所思地微笑了，一邊擺擺手，一邊説道：「讓我們來看看另外一個聖誕節吧！」

話剛説完，史高治自己小時候的形象馬上長大了，那個房間也變得更暗更髒了。牆上的鑲板蜷縮起來，窗都長裂紋了；天花板上的灰泥一片片地剝落下來，露出了裏面的光板條；但是怎麼會弄成這樣，史高治所知道的也並不比你我多。他只知道這情況是確實的；這一切當初確實是發生過的；他還是獨自一人留在那兒，別的孩子都已經回家歡度節日了。

他這時不在讀書了，而是在絕望地走來走去。史高治對幽靈看看，傷心地搖搖頭，帶着焦急的心情望着門口。

門打開了；一個小女孩，年紀比這男孩子小得多，飛也似地奔進來，用手臂摟住他的脖子，連連地吻着他，稱呼他"親愛的，親愛的哥哥"。

"我是來接你回家去的，親愛的哥哥！"女孩説，拍着她的一雙小手，彎下身體笑着。"來接你回家，回家，回家！"

"回家，小芬？"這男孩應道。

"是的！"女孩子説，充滿了歡喜。"回家去，永遠不再來了。回家去，從此不離開了。父親比從前仁慈得多了，所以家裏就像天堂一樣了！有一個值得紀念的晚上，在我上牀睡覺的時候，他對我説話特別溫和，因此我就壯起膽再問他能不能准許你回家來；他就説，好，你可以回家；還派我坐了馬車來接你。而且你快要成為大人了！"女孩子張大眼睛説。"再也不必回到這裏來了；不過首先，我們要一起過完這個聖誕節假期，享受世界上最愉快的時光。"

"你真像個長大了的女人了，小芬！"這男孩叫道。

她拍着手笑，想去摸他的頭；可是因為個子太小了，就又笑起來，踮起腳尖來摟抱他。接着她帶着她那孩子氣的急不及待的神情，拉着他向門口走去；而他呢，本來很樂意去，就跟着她走了。

門廳裏一把可怕的聲音喊道："把史高治少爺的箱子搬下來！"於是校長本人在門廳裏出現了，他帶着一種惡狠狠的、假作殷勤的樣子盯着史高治少爺，並且跟他握握手，這使他慌張得不得了。校長接着便把他和他妹妹帶到那最好的客廳裏去，那地方簡直像一口從未見過的冷得叫人發抖的古井，在那裏，牆壁上的地圖、窗台上的天體儀和地球儀，都給凍得像蠟一般蒼白了。在這裏，他拿出一細頸玻璃瓶淡得出奇的酒和一大塊重得出奇的餅，並把這些精美的東西分了點給這兩個孩子吃；同時他打發一個挺瘦的僕人送一杯"甚麼東西"去給那車夫喝，車夫回答說，謝謝這位老爺，但是如果這東西就是他上次嚐過的那種桶裝老酒，那麼他情願不要喝。史高治少爺的衣箱這時候已經捆好被放在馬車頂上了，兩個孩子就滿心情願地向校長告別；接着跨上馬車，歡快地沿着花園裏的曲徑駛去；急轉的車輪把常青樹深綠色葉子上的白霜和積雪都震落下來，像水花飛濺一般。

"一向是個體質嬌嫩的人兒，彷彿一口氣就可以把她吹得枯萎的，"那幽靈說。"但是她具有偉大的心胸！"

"她是這樣的一個人，"史高治叫道。"你説得對。我不會否定你這句話，幽靈。上帝也不容許！"

"她死時已經是個婦人了，"幽靈説，"而且，我想，她還生有子女。"

"一個孩子，"史高治回答道。

"不錯，"幽靈説。"就是你的外甥！"

史高治似乎問心有愧，只簡單地回答了一聲"是的"。

他們雖剛剛離開那學校，可是眼前已經到了一個城市的熱鬧的大街上，只見有隱約不清的行人在來來往往，還有隱約不清的運貨車和馬車在爭着路走，凡是一個真正的城市所有的爭吵和喧囂，這裏都有。從店鋪的裝潢上清清楚楚看出，這兒也正好又逢着聖誕節來臨了；但時候是在晚上，街上都已燈火輝煌了。

幽靈在某一所倉庫的門口停下了步，問史高治知不知道這地方。

"知不知道！"史高治說。"我不就是在這兒當過學徒的嗎？"

他們走進去。一位戴着威爾斯假髮的老先生，坐在一張高得可以的寫字枱後面，如果他的身高再多兩英寸的話，他的頭就要碰到天花板了；史高治一看見他，就激動萬分地叫起來：

"哎呀，原來是老費昔威！上天保佑他，費昔威復活了！"

老費昔威放下了筆，抬頭看看鐘，時針正指着七時。他搓搓手，整理他那件寬大的背心，笑得前俯後仰，從他的皮鞋到他那樂善好施的腦袋，都在笑，並且用一種舒暢、圓滑、豐潤、飽滿和喜悅的聲音叫道：

"唷嗬，嗨！埃伯尼澤！迪克！"

史高治從前的自己，這時已經成長為一個青年了，輕快地走進來，他的師兄弟跟他一起進來。

"迪克·威金斯，一點也不錯！"史高治對幽靈說。"天啊，是他。正是他。他跟我很要好的，這個迪克。可憐的迪克！唉，唉！"

"唷嗬，我的孩子們！"費昔威說。"今天晚上不要再工作了。聖誕節前夕嘛，迪克。聖誕節嘛，埃伯尼澤！我們來把百葉窗都上起來，"老費昔威叫道，響亮地拍了一下手，"說做就做吧！"

你簡直不會相信這兩個傢伙怎麼做得這麼快！他們挹起護窗板就衝到街上—— 一，二，三——把窗都上好了——四，五，六——插上窗閂把板扣住了——七，八，九——你還沒有數到十二，他們已經跑了回來，像賽跑的馬那樣直喘氣。

老費昔威異常靈活地從他那張高寫字枱上跳了下來，嘴裏叫道，"唏哩——呵！把東西搬開，孩子們，讓我們這兒多空出些地方！唏哩——呵，迪克！唧、唧、唧，埃伯尼澤！"

把東西全搬開！有老費昔威在旁邊看着，他們還有甚麼東西不高興搬開，或是搬不開的！一眨眼就做好了。每一件可以移動的東西都搬開了，彷彿要把它們永遠摒棄不用似的；地板打掃過了並灑上了水，燈芯都剪好了，木柴都堆在爐火上了；於是這倉庫就變成一個你巴不得在冬天夜晚看見的挺舒服、暖和、乾燥而光明的舞會大廳了。

一位小提琴手夾着樂譜走了進來，跑到那高大的寫字枱上，把它變成一個奏樂台，就調起音來，像胃病患者在連聲地哼叫。費昔威太太走了進來，完全是一副笑逐顏開的樣子。三位費昔威小姐走了進來，笑容可掬，而且令人生愛。六個年輕的追隨者走了進來，他們的心都被她們攪碎了。這個商行所僱用的男女青年們都走了進來。女傭走了進來，帶着她的表兄，一個麵包師傅。廚師走了進來，帶着她哥哥的好朋友，送奶人。街對面的小僕人走了進來，人們懷疑他在他主人家裏是吃不飽的；他想躲在隔壁第二家的女傭的背後，而她是已經證明被她女主人扯過耳朵的。他們都走了進來，一個接着一個；有的害羞，有的大膽，有的優雅，有的笨拙，有的推着，有的拉着；反正以各種各樣的方式，他們大家都走了進來。他們立刻組成了二十對，下去跳舞：手搭着手轉了半圈，然後再從另一方向轉過來；隊伍穿過場中間跳到一端，再回過來；在各個不同的階段中，結成了親密的集體，迴旋再迴旋；原來領頭的那一對總是走錯了地方，後來的第一對跳到領頭的地方就立刻重新開始；最後大家都排成一行，無所謂頭一對了，所以也沒甚麼後面的一對來襯托他們了！等到產生了這樣的結果時，老費昔威就拍拍手叫大家停止了跳舞，大叫一聲"跳得好！"於是那小提琴手把他那張發熱的臉浸到一大罐黑啤酒裏，這罐酒就是特地為他準備的。但是他把頭抬起來之後，雖則這時候還沒有人跳舞，他卻不願意休息，立刻又演奏起來，彷彿先前那個提琴手已經筋疲力盡，被人擱在護窗板上，抬回家去了，而他已成為一個嶄新的人物，決心完全勝過過去的他，寧死也要做到。

接着又跳了數次舞，並玩了數次罰物遊戲，然後又跳了數次舞，還有蛋糕，有尼格斯酒，並且有一大塊冷烤牛肉，一大塊冷燉豬肉，還有百果餡餅以及許多啤酒。但是這一晚的壓軸戲是在上了烤肉和燉肉以後，那時候琴師（是個狡猾的傢伙，注意！他對於業務，比你我所能指點他的要熟悉得多）奏起《羅傑·德·柯維利爵士》舞曲來。於是老費昔威站出來和費昔威太太跳舞，而且是帶頭的一對；這對於他們實在是一件需要有硬功夫的事情，因為舞侶有二十三四對，都是些不可輕視的人，都是些寧願跳舞而絕對不打算散步的人。

但是即使人數增加一倍——哦，甚至四倍於原來的數目吧——老費昔威還是比得過他們的，而費昔威太太也是如此。說到她，她是無論哪一方面都配得上做他的伴侶的。如果這句話還不算是最高的讚美，那麼請你告訴我一句更好的，我就來用這句話。費昔威的兩條小腿似乎當真發出光芒。它們像月亮般在每一個舞步中照耀着。在任何時刻，你都無法預言它們在下一秒鐘內將會怎麼樣。老費昔威和費昔威太太從頭到尾跳着這支舞；你進我退，雙手拉着舞伴，鞠躬和屈膝，來一個螺旋鑽孔，來一個線穿針眼，然後回到原來的位置上，費昔威就來一個"剪式動作"，做得那麼靈活，他似乎把兩條腿像眼睛般眨了眨，就雙腳落地，穩健地站住了。

鐘敲十一下的時候，這個家庭舞會散場了。費昔威先生和太太各就各位，一人站在門口的一邊，等每個人走出去時，和他或她一一握手，並且祝他或她聖誕快樂。等所有的人都走了，只剩下這兩個學徒的時候，他們也同樣跟他們握手祝賀。歡樂的人聲就這樣消散了，這兩個小子留在那兒，回自己牀上去睡覺，牀鋪就在店堂後面的一個櫃檯下面。

在整段時間中，史高治的行動像一個神志失常的人一樣。他全副精神貫注在這一場景中，貫注在他自己從前的形象中。他確證了每一件事，記起了每一件事，享受着每一件事，而且感受到無比奇特的激動。直到這時，當他從前的自己和迪克兩人的快樂臉蛋轉過去的時候，他才記起那幽靈來，並且意識到它正在緊盯着他看，它腦袋上的光芒照耀得非常清楚。

"只不過一件小小的事情，"幽靈說道，"就使那些傻瓜這樣地感激。"

"小小的事情！"史高治重複說。

幽靈向他做了個手勢要他聽那兩個學徒在說的話，他們這時正在竭力稱讚費昔威；等他聽過了，它就說道：

"怎麼！不是嗎？他不過花了你們人世間的數鎊錢，也許不過三四鎊吧。難道這筆錢就那麼了不起，使他這樣值得稱讚？"

“話不是這樣說的，”史高治被這話激惱了，說起話來就不知不覺地像他從前的自己而不像後來的自己了。“話不是這樣說的，幽靈。他有這種權力來使我們快活或不快活，使我們的工作變成輕鬆或是繁重，變成娛樂或是苦工。如果說，他的權力存在於語言和神色之中，存在於一些微不足道得無法匯集起來也無法計算的事情之中，那又怎麼樣呢？他給人的幸福是那樣大，就跟花了極大一筆錢才換來的一樣。”

他覺得幽靈的眼光在看着他，就住口不說了。

“甚麼事不對勁呢？”幽靈問。

“沒有甚麼特別的事，”史高治說。

“總有點甚麼事吧，我想？”幽靈追問着。

“沒有，”史高治說，“沒有。我真想現在就對我的夥伴說一兩句話！就是這麼點事。”

當他說出這個願望時，他從前的自己正在把燈芯捻小；於是史高治和那幽靈又肩並肩地站在戶外了。

“我沒有多少時間可以耽擱了，”幽靈說。“快點！”

這句話不是對史高治說的，也不是對他能看見的任何人說的，但是這話立刻產生了效果。因為史高治又看見他自己了。他現在年紀已經大了一點，是個年富力強的男子。他臉上還沒有後來歲月中出現的那些嚴峻而刻板的紋路，不過已經開始表現出患得患失和貪得無厭的跡象了。那浮躁地轉動着的眼睛裏流露出一種急切的貪婪神氣來，顯示出貪慾已在那兒生了根，在日長夜大地成為一棵大樹，它的陰影將落到甚麼地方。

他不是一個人在那兒，而是坐在一位穿禮服的姣好少女旁邊，她那眼睛裏含着的盈盈淚水，被那"過去聖誕節之靈"所發出的光芒照得亮晶晶的。

"這無關重要，"她輕柔地說。"對你來說，無關緊要。另外一個偶像已經代替了我；如果它在將來能夠像我所想做的那樣，使你得到快樂和安慰，那我就沒有可悲傷的正當理由了。"

"甚麼偶像代替了你？"他接口問。

"一個黃金偶像。"

"難道這就是世上公平合理的待遇！"他說。"世上沒有比貧窮更苦惱的了；但是世上公然加以譴責的也沒有比對追求財富更嚴厲的了！"

"你太害怕世人了，"她溫和地回答說。"你所有的其他希望都匯合成了一個希望，那就是：不至於遭受到世人的苛刻指責。我看見你那些更崇高的志願都一一消失掉了，直到那主要的慾望、貪慾，佔有了你。難道我沒有看到嗎？"

"那又怎麼樣呢？"他反駁道。"即使我變得比從前聰明多了，又怎麼樣呢？我對你一點也沒有變心啊。"

她搖搖頭。

"我沒變心吧？"

"我們的婚約是早就訂下的。訂約的時候我們雙方都是貧窮的，而且是安於貧窮，情願等到適當的時候，能靠着我們堅韌不拔的辛勤勞動，來改善我們在世上的處境。可你現在變了。我們當初訂婚的時候，你可不是這樣一個人啊。"

"我當時還是個乳臭未乾的孩子，"他不耐煩地說。

"你自己的感覺會告訴你，你從前跟現在是大不相同的，"她回答説。"我卻還是老樣子。在我們兩人一條心的時候，本來可以得到幸福，現在我們既然變成了兩顆心，自然是充滿着痛苦的。我對這個問題考慮過多少次，感到怎樣的難過，這些我都不必説了。我只要對你説這一點就夠了：我已經考慮好這件事情，現在可以跟你解婚約了。"

"我曾經要求過解約嗎？"

"在言語中，沒有。從來沒有。"

"那麼，是在甚麼方面呢？"

"是在性情的改變上；在精神的轉移上；在另一種生活氣氛中；你把另外一種希望當作了人生的偉大目標。凡是從前使我的愛情在你眼裏有點身價和價值的一切，現在都改變了。假使我們之間從來沒有發生過這樣的事的話，"這女孩説，溫和而堅定地看着他，"告訴我，你現在會不會來追求我，並且想得到我？唉，不會的！"

他似乎要不由自主地承認這個假設是公正的。但是他勉強地回答道："這是你以為不會。"

"我但願能夠不這樣想，"她回答説，"天知道！等我懂得了這樣一個道理，我知道它必定是非常強有力和不可抗拒的。但是如果你今天、明天或昨天解除了婚約的話，難道我能相信你會選一個沒有嫁妝的女子嗎——你這個人，在你跟她親密無間的時候，也是以財富來衡量一切的；再説，即使你暫時違反了你生平唯一的主導原則而選中了她，難道我不知道你事後一定會後悔莫及的嗎？我知道的，所以我要跟你解約。為了對他——那個從前的你——的愛，我誠心誠意這樣做。"

他正想説話，但是她把頭轉過去不看他，接下去説道：

"這件事也許會使你感到痛苦的——回想起過去的情份，我不免有半點這樣的希望。只要經過一段極短的時間，你就會很高興地把對這件事情的回憶，當作一場無利可圖的夢而撤開，以為你能從這場夢裏醒過來正是再好也沒有的事。願你在你所選擇的生活裏能夠快樂！"

她離開了他，他們就此分手了。

"幽靈！"史高治叫道，"別再顯現給我看了！領我回家去吧。你為甚麼喜歡折磨我？"

"再看一個過去的情境！"幽靈叫道。

"不要再看！"史高治喊道。"不要再看了！我不願意看。不要再顯現甚麼給我看！"

但是這狠心的幽靈用兩臂把他挾住，強迫他再看接着出現的事情。

他們這時到了另外一個場景中，那是一間不很大也不華麗的房間，但是充滿了舒適的陳設。靠近那過冬用的爐火旁，坐着一位美麗的少女，和剛才的那一位非常相像，史高治起初還以為就是同一個人，直到後來才看清她現在已是一位秀麗的主婦了，正坐在她女兒的對面。這房間裏真是聲音嘈雜極了，因為小孩實在太多，史高治心神不寧，所以數也數不清；而且，不像那首詩[9]中的著名的牛群，他們不是四十個孩子行動起來如同一個，卻是每一個孩子行動起來像四十個。結果是吵鬧得令人難以置信，可是似乎沒有一個人覺得討厭；恰恰相反，她們母女倆暢快地大笑着，感到十分有趣；而女兒不久就參加到這些遊戲裏去，受到這幫小強盜毫不留情的騷擾。假使我能夠成為他們中間的一個，要我付出任何代價我都肯！不過我決不會那麼粗魯，決不，決不！不管付出多大代價，我也不願把那結成辮子的頭髮弄散，把它扯下來；還有那隻珍貴的小靴，上帝保佑我，我是無論如何不肯把它脫下來的。至於像他們這一群大膽的小把戲那樣，量她的腰身鬧着玩，這種事情我也決計做不出來；我該料想自己的手臂會遭到天罰，圍着她的腰就此永遠伸不直。然而我承認，我實在巴不得親一親她的嘴唇；想問她一句話，使她張開她的嘴來；想注視她那目光下垂的眼睛上的睫毛，而不致使她臉紅；想解開她那波浪般鬈曲的頭髮──這頭髮，即使得到一英寸，也是無價之寶的紀念品。總而言之，我極願意享受到孩子們的最輕微的放縱自由，同時又像大人似的懂得這種自由的可貴。

但是這時候聽見有人在敲門了，大家立刻都奔過去，她帶着笑臉，穿着被扯亂的衣服，給擁在這一群臉蛋通紅的、吵吵嚷嚷的孩子中間，一直被推到門口去，剛好及時地迎接回家來的父親。父親背後跟隨着一個捧着不少聖誕節玩具和禮物的人。接着是一片大嚷大鬧，爭先恐後地對這毫無防備的門房展開猛烈的攻擊！拿椅子當作梯子，爬到他身上去，伸手到他口袋裏去挖，把那些牛皮紙包從他手裏搶奪過來，緊緊地抓住他的領結，摟住他的脖子，用拳頭捶着他的背脊，以樂不可支的親熱之情踢他的腿！每個包裹打開時引起了一大陣驚奇和欣喜的喊叫聲！接着有人駭人聽聞地聲稱：那嬰孩正要把一個玩具煎鍋塞進嘴去，而且好像已經把一隻膠在木頭碟上的假火雞吞到肚裏去了！後來發現這是一場虛驚，大家又是多麼的快慰啊！那份歡欣、感激和狂喜啊！他們的行動都是言語所無法形容地相似。只要說這一句就夠了：這些孩子們帶着他們的歡樂情緒逐漸地離開了客廳，一步跨一級樓梯，一直走到屋的頂層，上牀睡覺了，這一場喧鬧才平靜下來。

這時史高治比以前更用心地看了，只見這一家的主人，把女兒拉過來親熱地偎在身上，然後跟她和她的母親在自己的爐旁一起坐下來；史高治想到另一個這樣的孩子，同樣的俊秀和富有前途，滿可能稱他為父親，並且成為他蕭瑟的暮年中的一段春日的，這時候，他的眼睛不禁被淚水沾得十分模糊了。

"貝兒，"那丈夫回過頭來，笑着對他的妻子說，"今天下午我看見了你的一個老朋友。"

"誰呢？"

"猜猜看！"

"我怎麼猜得到呢？哦，我還會不知道？"她一口氣接下去說，跟他一樣地笑着，"史高治先生。"

"正是史高治先生。我經過他辦公室的窗外，因為窗沒有關上，而且裏面又點着蠟燭，我就看見了他。他的合夥人躺在牀上快死了，我聽人說；他獨個坐在那裏。孤零零地一個人在世上，我相信正是這樣。"

"幽靈！"史高治聲音哽咽地說，"把我從這地方帶走吧。"

"我對你說過，這些都是往事的影子，"幽靈說。"至於它們今天是這副本來面目，那你別責怪我！"

"把我帶走吧！"史高治叫道，"我實在受不了了！"

他轉身面對着幽靈，只見它正在看着他，而它的那張臉，說也奇怪，竟是它剛才指給他看的那些臉的片段拼湊起來的，他就跟它揪打起來。

"放開我！帶我回去。不要再害我了！"

如果這能算是搏鬥的話，那麼，在這場搏鬥中，他用足了氣力，但那幽靈卻顯然一點都不抵抗，也絲毫不感到驚慌；史高治在搏鬥中看見，那幽靈頭上的光照得又高又亮；他迷迷糊糊地認為這幽靈對他的作祟是跟它的光有關係的，就抓住了那頂熄燈帽，出其不意地往下按在它頭上。

那幽靈在帽下面癱倒下去，這樣，這頂熄燈帽就蓋住了它的整個身體；但是儘管史高治用盡平生之力把帽往下撳，卻仍舊遮不住那道光，它從帽下面放射出來，毫不間斷地瀉照在地上。

他感到筋疲力盡，瞌睡難當；而且還發現正在自己的臥室裏。他把那頂帽最後捏了一把，就鬆了手；人剛剛搖搖晃晃地倒在牀上，就立刻陷入酣睡之中。

三幽靈中的第二個

史高治從鼾聲大作中醒過來，在牀上坐起定了定神，根本不用別人來告訴他，就知道鐘又將敲一時了。他覺得自己正好在這緊要關頭醒過來，就是特地為了要和那第二個使者來一次會面，而這個使者正是由於雅各・馬利的干預，才到他這裏來的。但是當他開始猜想這個新幽靈會把他帳的哪一邊拉開時，他覺得自己很不舒服地發起冷來，便用自己的手把每一邊的帳都拉開來，然後再在牀上躺下，對牀的四周保持嚴密的警戒，因為他打算在這幽靈一出現時，就向它挑戰，而不願意遭突襲，弄得驚惶失措。

那些悠閒自在、不拘形跡的先生們，會為自己了解一兩件事而自豪，而且是份外通曉世事，善於審時應變的，為了要表示他們在冒險應變方面神通廣大，就說他們從擲錢遊戲到殺人勾當，任何事情都是擅長的；而在這兩個相反的極端之間，無疑地還有着範圍相當廣泛的許多事情。我固然不敢把史高治說得這麼有能耐，可是我願意請你們相信，他是準備看到範圍相當廣泛的各種稀奇古怪的東西出現的，從一個嬰兒直到一頭大犀牛之間，無論甚麼東西出現都不會使他太驚駭。

如今，正因為他作了會看見任何東西的準備，他才毫無準備會一無所見；因此，當鐘鳴一下，而並無鬼影出現時，他禁不住劇烈地發起抖來。五分鐘，十分鐘，一刻鐘過去了，可是甚麼都沒有出現。在這一段時間裏，他一直躺在牀上，處於一道紅光的核心和中央，這道光是在鐘敲一時的時候就照射在他身上的；而且，由於只是一道光，竟比一二十隻鬼更驚人，因為他既無法了解它的用意是甚麼，也不知道它打算怎麼樣；有些時候他更深怕自己當時會自燃起來，成為一個有趣的事例，事先卻一點也沒有思想準備。然而，到了最後，他開始想到——至於你我，是一開頭就會想到的，因為旁觀者清，只有不置身在困境中的人才知道應該怎樣去應付這種境遇，並且毫無疑問地會這樣去做——到了最後，我剛才說，他才開始想到，這道鬼光的來源和奧秘，可能就在隔壁的那個房間裏，因為他再把這道光的蹤跡追尋了一下，發現它似乎就是從那個房間裏照射出來的。他心裏既然完全存了這個想法，就輕輕地從牀上起來，拖着拖鞋走到門口去。

史高治的手剛碰到鎖上，一把陌生的聲音就叫了一聲他的名字，而且吩咐他進去。他照做了。

那是他自己的房間。這一點是毫無疑問的。但是這個房間已經起了驚人的變化。四壁和天花板上都掛滿了活的綠色植物，看起來完全像是一座小叢林，亮晶晶的漿果在叢林裏的每一個地方閃耀着。冬青、檞寄生和常青藤的鮮嫩葉子把這些亮光反射出來，好像有許多小鏡子散佈在那兒似的；熊熊的火焰直向煙囱裏轟轟地上躥，無論是在史高治的時期、馬利的時期，還是過去許多的冬季裏，這個陰沉的化石般的壁爐裏都從未有過這樣猛烈的火焰。堆在地板上，形成一個寶座似的，是火雞、鵝、野禽、家禽、醃肉、大塊的腿肉、乳豬、一長串的香腸、百果餡餅、葡萄乾布丁、一桶桶的蠔、火熱的栗子、像孩兒臉般紅彤彤的蘋果、多汁的橙、甘美的生梨、龐大的主顯節餅，以及煮沸的一碗碗五味酒，它們冒出來的芬芳熱氣，把這個房間都燻得模糊了。在這裏的榻上坐着一個興高采烈的巨人，氣派堂皇，手裏拿着一根通紅的火把，形狀跟象徵豐饒的羊角不無相似之處，他把它高高地舉起，等史高治走到門口來張望的時候，火把的光正好照在他身上。

"進來！"這幽靈叫道。"進來！跟我多了解一下，朋友！"

史高治畏畏縮縮地走了進去，在這幽靈面前低頭站着。他已經不是從前那個冥頑不靈的史高治了；雖則那幽靈的眼光是明朗和善的，他卻不願意和它接觸。

"我是'現在聖誕節之靈'，"這幽靈說，"看着我！"

史高治就恭而敬之地照辦了。只見它穿着一件樸素的綠色長袍，或是披風，周圍用白的毛皮鑲邊。這件衣服寬鬆地披在它身上，它那寬闊的胸部都露了出來，彷彿不屑被人為的衣飾所衛護或遮掩。從衣服的寬大的褶襇下面，看得見它的一雙腳也是赤露着的；它的頭上不戴別的東西，只戴着一個冬青編的花冠，上面到處點綴着閃閃發光的冰柱。它那深褐色的鬈髮很長，隨便地披着，就像它那和藹的臉、閃亮的眼睛、張開的手掌、愉快的聲音、自在的舉止和快樂的氣氛那樣地隨便、不羈。它的腰間佩着一把古老的劍鞘，可是裏面沒有劍，而且這古老的劍鞘已經長滿了銹。

"你從來沒有見過像我這樣的吧！"幽靈叫道。

"從來沒有，"史高治回答它。

"從來沒有跟我家裏比較年輕的成員們一起走動過吧？我的意思是說，在最近數年裏誕生的我的哥哥們，因為我的年紀是很小的，"幽靈不放鬆地說。

"我想我是沒有這樣做過，"史高治說。"我恐怕是沒有這樣做過。你有許多兄弟嗎，幽靈？"

"有一千八百多個，"這鬼說。

"這可是一個很不容易贍養的大家庭啊！"史高治嘀咕着說。

"現在聖誕節之靈"站起身來。

"幽靈啊，"史高治恭順地說，"帶我到你要帶我去的地方吧。昨天夜晚我是被逼出去的，可是我已經得到了一種教訓，這教訓現在正在起作用了。今天夜晚，如果你有甚麼要教導我的話，那就讓我受益吧。"

"抓住我的袍！"

史高治遵照他的吩咐做了，把袍緊緊抓住。

冬青、檞寄生、紅漿果、常青藤、火雞、鵝、野禽、家禽、醃肉、鮮肉、豬、香腸、蠔、餡餅、布丁、水果和五味酒，立刻全都消失了。那個房間、壁爐、通紅的火光、夜間的鐘聲，也全都消失了，他們已經站在聖誕節早晨的城裏的街道上。因為天氣寒冷得很，人們在把住宅前面人行道上和屋頂上的雪都鏟掉，發出了一種聒噪、輕快但並不難聽的樂聲，而最使孩子們欣喜若狂的是看見雪從屋頂上沉重地落到下面路上，碎裂成人造的小暴風雪。

跟屋頂上那一片平滑潔白的積雪以及地面上稍微骯髒些的雪對照之下，屋的正面就顯得相當黝黑，而窗戶也顯得更黑了。街上的積雪都已經被那些大車和貨車的沉重的車輪犁成深深的溝；在那幾條大街分岔出去的地方，這些溝重複交叉了不知有幾百次，造成了許多縱橫交錯的水渠，在那很稠的黃泥漿和冰冷的水裏，簡直找不出它們通往哪裏。天空是陰鬱的，那些最短的街道上都充塞着一片半融解半凍結的骯髒霧氣，其中較重的微粒就成為一種煤灰，像陣雨般落下來，彷彿大不列顛所有的煙囪都一起着起火來，正在稱心如意地燃燒着。拿氣候或是這城市來說，這兒並沒有甚麼令人感到十分快樂的地方，然而卻佈滿着一種快樂的氣氛，即使最清淨的夏季空氣和最晴朗的夏季太陽，也一定散發不出來。

因為，那些在屋頂上鏟雪的人，都是興高采烈、滿懷快樂的；他們從矮護牆邊大着嗓子你叫我喚，有時候還互相逗着玩，把雪球拋來拋去——這是一種比口頭的玩笑更富友好意味的飛彈——如果打中了的話就哈哈大笑，如果打偏了的話也笑得同樣起勁。家禽鋪的門剛開了一半，水果鋪則是五光十色。又大又圓、肚皮鼓出的栗子籃——模樣就像快活的老先生們所穿的背心——在門口斜靠着，它們身體肥胖，易患中風，就這麼摔倒在街上。褐色的臉色泛着紅的、圍長很寬的西班牙球葱，像西班牙修道士般長得肥肥胖胖，油光鋥亮；當女孩們走過去時，它們就從架上對她們擠眉弄眼，一派調皮放肆的樣子，並且假裝正經地瞟瞟掛在上面的槲寄生[10]。梨啊，蘋果啊，都疊得高高的，堆成了壯麗的金字塔；一串串的葡萄，由於水果鋪老闆的好心腸，懸掛在特別觸目的鉤上，使人們在經過的時候嘴裏禁不住垂涎；一堆堆帶着苔蘚的褐色榛子，它們所發出的香氣，使人回憶起森林中的古老道路，以及在深可沒踝的枯葉堆裏，愉快地蹣跚行走的情景；還有烹調用的諾福克蘋果，矮胖胖、黑黝黝的，把橙和檸檬的黃色襯托得格外鮮明，而且因為它們那多汁的身體長得非常結實，它們迫切地懇求人們把它們裝在紙袋裏帶回家去，在飯後把它們吃掉。那些金色和銀色的魚，盛在一個缸裏，安置在這些精美的水果中間，它們雖然屬於一個呆笨遲鈍的族類，似乎也知道現今正有甚麼事情在發生着；而且，所有的魚都一樣，全在它們那小天地裏，帶着平淡的興奮之情，喘着氣繞着大圈。

雜貨鋪呢——哦，雜貨鋪！——差不多已經關門了，大概已經上了兩扇或者一扇護窗板，但是從那些窗縫裏可真有看頭呢！不僅僅是磅秤落到櫃檯上發出的悅耳聲音，或者麻線與滾軸很爽快地分開，或者罐子一種有蓋的金屬小罐，裝茶葉、咖啡或香料。給拿上拿下，砰砰作響，像變戲法似的，或者甚至茶葉和咖啡的混合香氣聞在鼻子裏是那麼舒服，或者甚至葡萄乾是那麼豐富和珍貴，杏仁又是那麼異常地潔白，肉桂枝那麼長而且直，其餘的那些香料那麼味美，蜜餞糖果做成圓餅，沾上了糖漿，使最冷淡的旁觀者看了都要覺得頭暈嘴饞，而且事後大發胃氣脹。也不僅僅是因為無花果都是濕潤而柔軟的；法蘭西李子帶着些微的酸澀，在它們那些裝潢得很漂亮的盒裏，紅着臉害羞，或是，一切的東西都是好吃的，並且都穿着它們的聖誕節盛裝；實在是因為顧客們在這充滿希望的大好日子裏，大家都是那麼匆忙和那麼急切，以致在門口彼此碰撞，魯莽地撞壞了他們的籐籃，把他們買的東西遺忘在櫃檯上，再奔回來拿，此外，還懷着好得不能再好的心情，犯下了許多諸如此類的錯誤；而雜貨鋪老闆和他的店員，又都是那麼真誠坦白和精神抖擻，使他們用來把圍裙紮在背後的那些閃閃發亮的心形東西，就像是他們自己的心，露出在外面讓大家來檢查，並且讓聖誕節的穴鳥想來啄的時候就可以來啄。

但是不久，禮拜堂屋頂尖塔上的鐘聲召喚善良的人們都到禮拜堂和小教堂去，他們便都去了，穿着他們最好的衣服，帶着最愉快的面容，成群結隊從街上走過去。同時，從數十條小街、狹巷和無名的角落裏，湧出了無數的人，把他們的膳食帶到麵包店去。幽靈看到這些尋歡作樂的貧苦人，似乎非常感興趣，因為它站在一家麵包店的門口（史高治就站在它身旁），等到他們經過時，把那些飯盒蓋揭開，從它的火把裏灑下一點香料到他們的膳食裏。而這火把又是一個極不平凡的火把，因為有一兩次，數個帶膳食的人由於互相碰撞而發生口角的時候，它從火把裏灑了點水在他們身上，他們那愉快的心情就立刻恢復了。因為他們說，在聖誕節爭吵是一件可恥的事情！這的確是一件可恥的事情！上帝保佑，的確是這樣的！

後來鐘聲停止了，麵包店關上了門；可是在每個麵包店爐灶上面那一片融解了的潮濕斑跡上，親切地隱約顯示出所有這些膳食，和它們進行燒煮的過程，連灶面上鋪着的石頭也冒着煙，彷彿它們也在燒煮着。

"你從你火把上灑出來的東西有一種特別味道嗎？"史高治

問。

"有啊。我自己的味道。"

"是不是今天隨便哪種飯食上都灑上它呢？"史高治問。

"友好地灑給每一種飯食。大都是給一種窮苦的膳食。"

"為甚麼大都是給窮苦的膳食呢？"

"因為窮苦的膳食最需要它。"

"幽靈啊，"史高治想了想後說，"我覺得奇怪的是：在我們周圍這大千世界的芸芸眾生中，對這些人的清白無辜的享受機會橫加阻礙的，偏偏是你。"

"我！"幽靈叫起來。

"他們每逢第七天進正餐一次，而這一天往往就是它們能夠稱為進正餐的唯一日子，你卻要把他們這點點機會都剝奪掉，"史高治說。"你不就是這樣嗎？"

"我！"幽靈叫道。

"你要在第七天把這些地方都關掉，"史高治說。"這事實上還不是一樣。"

"我要這樣！"幽靈驚叫道。

"如果我說錯了，那就請你寬恕我。這事情是利用你的名義來做的，或者至少是利用你家族的名義的，"史高治說。

"在你們這塵世上，"幽靈說，"是有這樣的一批人，他們自稱認識我們，他們利用了我們的名義，來做他們那些縱慾、驕傲、惡意、憎恨、嫉妒、頑固和自私的勾當。他們跟我們，以及我們所有的親戚朋友們，都是素不相識的，就好像他們從來沒有在這世上生活過一樣。記住這一點，並且叫他們做過的勾當由他們自己來負責，不要由我們來負責吧。"

　　史高治答應一定記住；於是他們繼續向前走，而人們看不見他們，就像先前那樣，一直走到了城市的郊區。這幽靈有一種特別的長處（這是史高治在麵包店裏就看出來的），那就是：他的身材雖則龐大無比，但能輕鬆自如地適應任何場所；他站在一個低矮屋簷下的優雅氣度，正如一位超自然的人物，就跟他站在任何一座高大的廳堂裏一樣。

　　也許是由於這位善良的幽靈樂於施展自己的這種法力，或是出於他自己那仁慈、慷慨、熱誠的性格，以及他對於所有窮苦人的同情，才使他一直走到史高治的僱員家裏去；因為他正在往那裏走，而且帶了史高治一同去，史高治拉着他的袍；到了大門的門檻前，幽靈笑了，就停下來拿火把灑一灑法水，祝福鮑伯·奇勒哲的這所住宅。你想想看！鮑伯自己一個禮拜只掙十五個"鮑伯"[11]，他每逢禮拜六裝進口袋的只有十五個和他大名相同的東西；可是這"現在聖誕節之靈"卻祝福了他這四間房的屋！

　　那時只見奇勒哲夫人，奇勒哲的妻子，站起身來，她穿着一件翻製過兩次的長大衣，樣子很寒傖，但是結着色彩鮮豔的絲帶，絲帶價錢便宜，花六個便士就打扮得很好看了；她在鋪着桌布。她的第二個女兒，貝琳達·奇勒哲也紮着很鮮豔的緞帶，正在幫她的忙；同時彼得·奇勒哲少爺正把一隻叉插進一鍋馬鈴薯，並且把他那奇大無比的襯衫領（這是鮑伯的私人財產，為了慶祝節日特地授給他的兒子和繼承人的）的尖角弄到自己的嘴巴裏去，他發現自己穿得這麼華麗，感到十分快活，便急於要到那些時髦的公園裏去把這件亞麻布襯衫出出風頭。這時，那兩個年紀最小的奇勒哲，一男一女，飛快地奔進來，一邊尖聲叫着，說他們在麵包店外面聞到了鵝的香氣，就知道這是為他們家烤的；這兩個小奇勒哲，把洋蘇葉和球葱想得其味無窮，就繞着桌跳起舞來，並且把那位彼得·奇勒哲少爺吹捧得上了天，而他（雖然衣領幾乎叫他透不過氣來，卻並不驕傲）卻在吹着火，直到那些煮起來很慢的馬鈴薯都沸騰起來，響亮地撞着鍋蓋，要求把它們放出來剝皮。

"怎麼，你們那寶貝的父親碰上甚麼了，"奇勒哲夫人說，"還有你們的哥哥小添？還有瑪莎，上次聖誕日她沒有遲到半個小時那麼久呢！"

"瑪莎來了，媽媽！"一位女孩邊說邊走進來。

"瑪莎來了，媽媽！"那兩個小奇勒哲叫道。"好哇！有這麼大的一隻鵝呢，瑪莎。"

"哎，主保佑你，親愛的，你來得多麼晚啊！"奇勒哲夫人說，吻了她一二十遍，格外殷勤地替她把圍巾、帽都拿下來。

"昨天夜晚我們有許多事情要做，"這女孩回答說，"今天早晨又必須收拾乾淨，媽媽！"

"好吧！你已經來了，我們就不談這些吧，"奇勒哲夫人說。"親愛的，你在火爐前面坐下來取取暖吧，主保佑你！"

"不，不！父親快來了，"這兩個小奇勒哲叫道，他們到處蹦跳着。"躲起來，瑪莎，躲起來！"

瑪莎就躲了起來，果然那矮小的父親鮑伯走進來了，他胸前掛着一條圍巾，至少有三英尺長，流蘇還不算在內；他那穿得舊的衣服，已經打好補釘，刷個乾淨，以便像個過節的樣子；肩頭上還縫着一個小添。可憐的小添啊，他拿着一根小拐杖，他的四肢都用鐵架撐着！

"怎麼，我們的瑪莎在哪兒？"鮑伯·奇勒哲看看周圍，叫道。

"沒有來，"奇勒哲夫人說。

"沒有來！"鮑伯說，他的一團高興立刻低落下來；因為他從禮拜堂一路給添當駿馬，馱着他跳跳蹦蹦地奔回來。"聖誕節的時候不來！"

瑪莎不願意看見他失望，即使只是鬧着玩；因此時機雖然還沒到，她已經從壁櫥門的背後走了出來，撲到他懷裏；另外那兩個小奇勒哲卻擁住了小添，把他帶到洗衣間去，讓他可以聽聽布丁在銅鍋裏唱歌的聲音。

"還有，小添乖嗎？"奇勒哲夫人問，這時候她已經把鮑伯上當的事取笑了一番，而鮑伯也已經把他女兒稱心如意地摟抱了一番。

"乖得很呢，"鮑伯說，"簡直十二萬分地乖。不知怎的，他獨個坐太久了，就想起心事來，他想的才是你聽都沒有聽見過的怪事呢。在我們回家來的時候，他告訴我說，因為他是一個跛子，他希望大家在禮拜堂裏都看見他，這樣就會使他們想起，在聖誕節這一天，是誰使瘸子走路、瞎子復明。

當鮑伯把這話告訴大家的時候，他的聲音激動得都發抖了，而當他說到小添已經長得越來越壯健的時候，他的聲音激動得更厲害了。

還沒來得及再說一句話，已經聽得見小添那活躍的拐杖在地板上篤篤地響着回來了，他的哥哥姐姐都護着他，把他送到壁爐邊的小櫈上；同時鮑伯呢，翻起了袖口──這可憐的人，彷彿生怕袖口還會給弄得更破舊似的──在一隻大口杯裏，把杜松子燒酒和檸檬混成一種熱的混合飲料，攪了又攪，然後放在爐旁的保溫鐵架上去慢慢地燉着；彼得少爺和那兩位滿天飛的小奇勒哲出去取鵝，一會就聲勢浩大地列隊回來了。

接下來的那一陣忙亂，使你也許會以為一隻鵝是一切鳥類中最珍貴的，是一種長着羽毛的奇物，即使黑天鵝跟它比起來，也不過是件很平常的東西罷了──而事實上，它在這個家庭的確很像這樣的一件珍品。奇勒哲太太把肉汁（已經預先在一個小鍋裏燒好）燉得滾燙，嘶嘶地響着；彼得少爺把馬鈴薯搗碎，那股力度真大得令人難以相信；貝琳達小姐在蘋果醬裏加糖；瑪莎把熱的盤都擦乾淨；鮑伯把小添帶在身邊，坐在桌旁一個小角落裏；還有那兩個小奇勒哲在給大家擺着座椅，也不忘記給他們自己擺好，然後坐在他們的崗位上守望着，一邊用湯匙塞住嘴巴，生怕分菜還沒有輪到他們的時候，就叫着要吃鵝。最後，盤都擺好了，餐前的感恩禱告也做過了。接着便是一陣屏氣凝神的停頓，這時候奇勒哲太太對那把切肉刀從頭至尾慢慢地端詳了一會，準備把它插進鵝的胸部去；等她把刀插進去，大家盼望已久的鵝肚子裏塞的東西都湧出來時，桌四周就一齊發出了喜悅的聲音，甚至小添，被這兩個小奇勒哲弄得激動起來，也用餐刀的柄在桌上敲着，有氣無力地喊着"好哇！"

從來還不曾有過這樣的一隻鵝。鮑伯説他不相信有人燒過這樣好的鵝來。它又嫩又鮮，肥大而便宜，成為大家一致讚美的話題。加上蘋果醬和薯蓉，它足夠讓全家飽餐一頓；的確，正像奇

勒哲太太興高采烈地説的（眼睛衡量着碟裏的一小粒骨頭），他們
到底沒有把它全吃掉呢！可是每一個人都已經吃得很夠了，尤其
是那兩個最年輕的奇勒哲，都沉浸在洋蘇葉和球葱裏，一直浸到
眉毛邊！可是這時貝琳達小姐已經換過碟，奇勒哲太太就獨自一
個人離開這房間——她實在太緊張了，不願讓旁人看到——去拿
起布丁，送進房來。

　　萬一它還沒有煮透了呢！萬一在翻出來時它裂開來呢！萬一
他們在前面吃鵝吃得很開心的時候，有甚麼人翻過後院的牆頭把
它偷走了呢——想到這裏，那兩個小奇勒哲急得臉都發青了！總
之，擔心着各樣可怕的事情。

　　嗬！那麼多的蒸氣！布丁已經從銅鍋裏拿出來了。一股像洗
衣日的氣味！就是那塊布！就像食店的隔壁開了一家甜品店，
甜品店隔壁開了一家洗衣店，才有這麼一股香味！這就是那個布
丁！半分鐘之後，奇勒哲太太進來了，臉漲得通紅，可是得意地
笑着，手上捧着那個布丁，像一個顏色斑駁的炮彈似的，又堅硬
又結實，周圍燃燒着四分之一品脱的白蘭地，頂上裝飾着一根聖
誕節的冬青樹枝。

　　啊，多了不起的布丁！鮑伯・奇勒哲説（而且是平心靜氣地
説的）他認為這是他們結婚以來奇勒哲太太所獲得的最大成就。
奇勒哲太太就説，既然她心裏的一塊石頭現在總算放下了，她要
承認，這次做布丁所用的麵粉數量，她有點不放心。大家對這個
問題都發表了一點意見，但是沒有一個人説到或是想到，對一個
大家庭來説，這布丁未免太小了。如果這樣説或這樣想的話，那
簡直是離經叛道之談了。奇勒哲家裏的任何一個人，哪怕露出一

點點這種意思，也會羞得面紅耳赤的。

最後，飯吃完了，枱布收拾好了，壁爐打掃乾淨了，爐火也添旺了。壺裏的五味酒已經嚐過了，被認為完美，蘋果和橙都放到了桌上，一滿鏟的栗子放到了爐火上。於是奇勒哲全家的人都圍着火爐坐下，成為鮑伯‧奇勒哲所説的團團一圈，意思其實是指的半個圈；在鮑伯‧奇勒哲的手肘邊陳列着他那套家藏的玻璃器皿，兩隻大口酒杯和一隻沒有柄的牛奶蛋糕杯。

然而，這兩三隻杯裏卻盛着壺裏的熱酒，真不亞於黃金鑄成的酒盅。鮑伯笑容滿面地把酒一杯一杯斟出來，火上的栗子正在畢畢剝剝地響着，爆裂着。於是鮑伯舉杯祝頌道：

"我的親人們，祝我們大家聖誕快樂。上帝保佑我們！"

全家都重複説了這句話。

"上帝保佑我們每一個人！"小添最後一個説。

他坐在他父親身邊的小櫈上，靠得很近。鮑伯把他那隻枯萎的小手握在自己手裏，彷彿他疼愛這個孩子，只想把他留在自己身邊，而唯恐被人從他那裏奪走。

"幽靈啊，"史高治帶着一種他以前從未有過的關懷説，"告訴我，小添將來能不能活下去？"

"我看見一個空的座位，"幽靈回答説，"放在那可憐的煙囪角落裏，還有一根沒有了主人的拐杖，鄭重地保存着。如果'將來'不把這些陰暗的東西改變的話，這孩子是要死的。"

"不，不，"史高治説。"哦，仁慈的幽靈啊，不要這樣！説他會得到倖免吧。"

"如果'將來'不把這些陰暗的東西改變的話，我的同類沒有一個人會在那裏找到他，"幽靈說道。"那又怎麼樣呢？如果他寧願死的話，他還是死掉的好，而且也可以減少過剩的人口。"

史高治聽見幽靈所引用的正是他自己從前說過的話，不禁低下了頭，不勝其愧悔和傷心。

"人啊，"幽靈說，"如果你心腸裏有的是人性，而不是頑石，你就應該放棄你那種惡毒的高調，先弄清楚，所謂過剩的人口究竟是些甚麼人，在甚麼地方？甚麼樣的人該活，甚麼樣的人該死，是不是都要由你來決定呢？也許，在上帝的眼裏看來，你比千百萬個像這窮人的孩子那樣的人更沒有價值，更不配活下去呢。上帝啊！聽聽看：一隻在樹葉上飽餐的蟲竟然宣稱，他那些在塵埃裏捱餓的同類不如多死掉幾個來得好呢！"

史高治受到幽靈的責備，低下了頭，一邊發抖，一邊望着地面。但是他聽見有人在叫他的姓氏，就趕緊往上看。

"史高治先生！"鮑伯說。"我向你們介紹史高治先生，這宴會的創辦人！"

"宴會的創辦人，真是！"奇勒哲太太叫道，臉都氣紅了。"我但願他本人在這兒。那時我倒要教訓教訓他，讓他好好聽一頓，希望他有這種好胃口。"

"親愛的，"鮑伯說。"孩子們在聽着！今天是聖誕節啊。"

"只有在聖誕節這一天，我相信，"她說，"別人才會為一個像史高治先生那樣叫人討厭、小氣刻薄、無情無義的人舉杯祝他健康。你知道他就是這樣的人，羅拔！沒有人比你知道得更清楚的了，可憐的人！"

"親愛的！"鮑伯還是溫和地回答說，"這是聖誕節啊。"

"我要為了你和這個節日的緣故來為他祝酒，"奇勒哲太太說，"但不是為了他本人！祝他長壽！聖誕快樂，新年快樂！他一定會很愉快，很歡樂的，我相信！"

孩子們跟着她舉杯祝酒。今晚這還是第一次，他們對所做的事情毫不起勁。小添最後一個舉杯，可是他才不高興做這種事情。史高治是他們這一家的厲鬼剋星。只要一提到他的名字，就會使這個宴會蒙上一層陰影，足足有五分鐘還消除不掉。

等這件事過去後，他們比原來快活十倍了，僅僅是因為應酬完不吉利的史高治，大家才都輕鬆起來，鮑伯·奇勒哲告訴他們，說他怎樣已經替彼得少爺物色了一個職位，這個職位如果成功應聘的話，每個星期就會有足足五先令半的收入。那兩個小奇勒哲一聽到彼得要做生意了，就笑得不可開交；彼得自己呢，從他衣領中間沉思地看着爐火，彷彿正在深思熟慮，一旦收到那一筆令人張惶失措的進款時，他該向甚麼地方投資。接着，瑪莎——她是一家女帽鋪的可憐的學徒——就告訴他們，她必須做甚麼樣的工作，她一口氣要工作多久，以及她怎樣打算明天早晨在牀上睡個夠，好好地休息，因為明天是她可以在家裏度過的一個例假日。她還說她怎樣在數天前看見一位伯爵夫人和一位爵爺，那位爵爺"跟彼得差不多高"；彼得一聽見這話，便把衣領拉得高高，高得你都看不見他的頭了，如果你在那兒的話。在這整段時間裏，栗子和酒壺都不斷地遞來遞去。一會，他們就聽見小添唱起歌來，這歌唱的是一個迷路的小孩怎樣在雪地跋涉；小添的嗓音弱而悽涼，確實唱得極好。

這兒並不是甚麼高質素的地方。他們不是一個小康之家；他們穿得並不講究；他們的皮鞋都遠不是不漏水的；他們的衣服都很單薄；而且彼得可能知道——很可能知道——當鋪的裏面是甚麼樣子的。但是他們全都快樂、感激，彼此很親切，並且對目前的景況心滿意足。當他們在那幽靈臨別所灑的明亮的法水中逐漸消逝時，他們顯得更快樂了；史高治一直看着他們，尤其看着小添，一直看到最後。

這時候天色已經暗起來了，雪下得很大；史高治和幽靈沿着街上走過去時，家家的廚房、客廳以及各種各樣的房間裏，都是爐火熊熊，亮得不得了。這兒，火光的閃耀中顯出一家人正在準備一頓舒適的晚餐，熱的盤在火爐前面烘了又烘；還有深紅色的窗帷，隨時可以拉攏，把寒冷和黑暗擋在外面。在那邊，這家人所有的孩子都跑到雪地裏去迎接他們那些已經結婚的姐姐、哥哥、堂兄、叔伯和嬸嬸，搶着要做頭一個迎接他們的人。在這兒，還有客人們歡聚的影子照在窗簾上；在那兒，有一群漂亮的女孩，都包着頭巾，穿着毛靴，大家吱吱喳喳地同時在説話，輕盈地走到附近某一個鄰居的家裏去，而在那裏，苦惱的是那個獨身漢，眼看她們容光煥發地走進去——這些機靈的女子，她們很清楚自己的魅力！

但是，出去參加友好集會的人是那麼多，你如果從人數上來判斷，那你就會認為：等他們到了親友們家裏，不會有人來歡迎他們，不是每家人都期待着接待賓客，並且把壁爐裏的火添得旺旺的，有煙囱的一半那麼高。祝福這一切，那幽靈是多麼的欣喜若狂啊！它裸露出它那寬闊的胸部，張開它那闊大的手掌，向前飄盪而去，用它慷慨的手把它那歡快而無害的喜悦，傾瀉給它所接觸到的一切東西！那個點路燈的人，跑在前面，把那些幽暗的街道點綴上星星點點的燈光，他身上已穿着好，準備到甚麼地方去消磨這個晚上。當幽靈經過他身邊的時候，這點燈夫高聲大笑起來，一點也不知道他自己除了聖誕節之外，一個伴侶也沒有。

這時候，那幽靈沒有事先提醒，他們倆已經站在一片陰暗荒涼的原野上了，在那兒，奇形怪狀的粗石塊到處亂丟，彷彿這地方就是巨人們的葬身之處；水喜歡往哪兒流就往哪兒流；或者本來想流過去，可是結冰了，流不動了；那兒長着的全是苔蘚和荊豆，以及亂生的草。在西方落山的太陽留下了一道火辣辣的紅光，這紅光對那片荒地耀眼地照了一會，就像一隻陰沉的眼睛似的，皺緊了眉頭，越沉越下，越沉越下，終於消失在黑夜的濃影中。

"這是甚麼地方？"史高治問。

"這是礦工們居住的地方，他們在地下深處勞動着，"幽靈回答說。"可是他們都認得我。看！"

一間茅屋的窗裏射出一道亮光，他們就趕快向那裏跑去。經過了一座泥土和石頭所築的牆，他們發現有一群興高采烈的人圍着一爐很旺的火坐着。一對很老很老的男女，跟他們的兒女，以及兒女的兒女，和再下一代，都快樂地穿着他們的節日盛裝。風在這貧瘠的荒原上怒號着，那老人家正在給他們大家唱一首聖誕節的歌，聲音難得高過風聲；這是一首他孩提時唱慣的很老的歌；他們時常大家加入合唱。一到他們提高了嗓門的時候，這老人家就唱得相當輕快而響亮；一到他們停下來時，他的精力便又減退了。

幽靈並不在這兒耽擱，卻吩咐史高治抓緊他的袍，在荒原上空繼續前進，趕到哪兒去呢？不是到海裏去吧？正是到海裏去。使史高治大為驚慌的是，他回頭一望，只見那最後一部份陸地，一個可怕的山嶺，已經被撇下在後面了；海浪洶湧怒號，他的耳朵都被雷鳴般的水聲震聾了；海水在那些久被沖蝕的可怕洞窟裏激盪個不住，兇猛地想把陸地沖塌。

　　在一個陷入水中的岩石形成的陰森森的暗礁上，離海岸大約三海里，屹立着一座孤零零的燈塔，海水一年到尾擦洗衝擊着它。一大堆的海藻盤結在暗礁的底部，那些暴風鳥——人們可以猜想，它是在風中誕生的，正如海藻是在水中誕生的一樣——在礁上飛起飛落，像它們飛掠過的海浪那樣。

　　可是，即使在這樣一個地方，兩個看守這燈塔的人也生了一爐火，因此從那厚石牆的窗眼裏，有一道明亮的光線射出來，照在這可怕的海上。他們坐在一張粗糙的桌邊，伸出了他們長滿老繭的手，彼此緊握着，舉起罐頭裏的加水燒酒，互相祝賀聖誕快樂；而且其中的一個——年紀大些的那一個，臉上佈滿了種種飽經風霜的創傷，正像一條舊船的船頭雕像似的——唱起一首雄壯的歌曲，這歌聲就像是颳起了一陣大風。

　　這幽靈又奔向前去，在那漆黑的、洶湧起伏的海面上空——奔啊，奔啊——直到它告訴史高治說，離其他海岸都很遠了，他們才在一艘船上停下來。他們站在操縱着舵輪的舵手旁邊，站在船頭守望者的旁邊，站在值班的高級船員們旁邊；黑黝黝的幽靈般的身影站在他們各自的崗位上；但是他們中間的每一個人都在哼着一首聖誕節的曲，或者懷着一個聖誕節的思念，或者低聲地對他的夥伴談到某一個過去了的聖誕節，言談之中帶着重返家園的希望。船上的每一個人，不管是醒着還是睡着，是好人還是壞人，在這一天的互相交談中，都比一年之中的任何一天更友好；在某種程度上，共同分享着這個節日的歡樂，同時記起了他所懷念的在遠方的人們，並且知道他們是樂於記得他的。

史高治靜聽着風的呻吟聲，想到要在那寂寞的黑暗中，越過一道陌生的深淵（它的深處藏着一些機密，正如死亡那麼深不可測）向前行進，真是一件多麼嚴峻的事情啊。使史高治大吃一驚的是，當他正在這樣想着的時候，忽然聽見一陣哈哈大笑的聲音。使他格外吃驚的是，他聽出這笑聲竟是他自己的外甥的聲音，並且發現他現在正在一間明淨、乾燥的房間裏，而那幽靈正微笑地站在他的身旁，帶着一種表示讚許的親切神情看着這位外甥！

"哈哈！"史高治的外甥笑道，"哈哈哈！"

如果你碰巧——這種機會很微——知道有人笑得比史高治的外甥更愉快，那我只想說，我也很願意認識他。把他介紹給我，我要想法跟他交個朋友。

世事的安排，真可以算是公正、不偏不倚和高尚的了：疾病和憂愁固然是要傳染人的，可是世界上再也沒有比歡笑和快樂更能傳染、更無法抗拒的了。當史高治的外甥笑成這個樣子——捧着他的肚皮，左右轉動他的頭，扭曲着他的臉，做出許多最古怪的模樣時——史高治的外甥媳婦也笑得跟他一樣起勁。而他們那批聚會在一起的朋友們，也都不甘落後，響亮地笑着。

"哈哈！哈哈，哈哈！"

"他説聖誕節是胡鬧，真的！"史高治的外甥叫道。"而且他的確這樣相信。"

"那他更應該羞愧了，弗里！"史高治的外甥媳婦怒氣沖沖地叫道。為這些女士祝福吧！她們做起事來從來不會不徹底的。她們總是很認真的。

她長得非常漂亮，出奇的漂亮。一張有酒窩的、帶着驚詫神情的絕妙的臉；一個圓熟的小嘴，似乎生來是給人親吻的——它無疑正是如此；她下頜上有各種各樣好看的小酒窩，當她笑的時候就互相融合起來，而那一雙眼睛是你在任何小傢伙的臉上都從未看見過的，是最令人愉快的。總而言之，她是一個你會稱之為吸引人的女性，你知道；但也是一個令人滿意的女性。哦，十足地令人滿意！

"他真是一個滑稽的老伯，"史高治的外甥説，"這是千真萬確的；他本來是可以更友好的。不過，他已經是自作自受的了，所以我也不想説甚麼話來指責他。"

"我相信他是很有錢的，弗里，"史高治的外甥媳婦説。"至少，你常常對我這樣説的。"

"那又有甚麼意思呢，親愛的！"史高治的外甥説。"他的財富對他一無好處。他沒有拿自己的錢財來做一點好事。他沒有用它來使自己生活得舒服些。他本來可以想到——哈哈哈！——他將來或許能用自己的錢財來使我們得到好處，但是他連這樣想一下的樂趣都沒有。"

"我容忍不了他，"史高治的外甥媳婦説。她的姐妹，以及所有其餘的女士們，都表示同樣的意見。

"嘿，我容忍得了他的！"史高治的外甥説。"我替他難過；我即使想對他生氣，也生氣不起來。他這種惡劣的脾氣究竟使誰吃虧呢？總還是他自己吧。現在他忽然想到不喜歡我們，不肯來跟我們一起吃飯了。後果是甚麼呢？他不吃這頓飯也不見得有多大損失。"

"其實，我想他是損失了一頓很好的飯，"史高治的外甥媳婦插嘴説。其他的人都這麼説，我們必須承認他們是有資格的裁判員，因為他們剛剛吃過這頓飯。這時，飯後甜品放在桌上，他們都在燈光下圍爐而坐。

"噢！我聽到這句話很高興，"史高治的外甥説。"因為我對這些年輕的主婦們是不大有信心的。你怎麼看，陶泊？"

陶泊顯然正緊盯着史高治外甥媳婦的一個妹妹，因為他回答説，一個獨身的男人是一個可憐的化外之民，無權對這種話題發表意見。於是史高治外甥媳婦的妹妹——圍着花邊領紗的胖胖的那一個，不是戴玫瑰花的那一個——臉就紅起來了。

"説下去，弗里，"史高治的外甥媳婦拍拍手説。"他向來是把話開了頭不説完的！他這人真太可笑！"

史高治的外甥又發出一陣哈哈大笑，而且因為沒法可以制住這笑的影響（雖然那位胖妹妹竭力在聞着香醋，想忍笑），大家也就一起跟着大笑了。

"我只是想説，"史高治的外甥説道，"他不喜歡我們，不肯跟我們一起尋歡作樂，其結果是，照我看來，只會使他自己喪失了一些愉快的時刻，而這種時刻對他是不會有害處的。我相信，他喪失了能使他更加愉快的同伴，比他在自己的冥想中——不管在他那發霉的老寫字間裏，還是他那滿是灰塵的房間裏——所能找到的，都要愉快得多。我正是因為可憐他，才特意每年給他這樣一個機會，不管他喜歡不喜歡。他可以辱罵聖誕節，一直罵到他死為止，但是，如果他發現我高高興興的，一年又一年地到他那兒去，對他説，'史高治舅舅，您好嗎？'——我敢向他挑戰——他總有一天會禁不住覺得聖誕節還不錯的。只要這一來能夠使他心情愉快地留下五十鎊給他那個窮員工，那就很了不起了；我覺得我昨天是觸動了他的。"

現在輪到他們笑了，想到他竟然能觸動史高治。但因為他是一個好脾氣的人，而且不大在乎別人在取笑甚麼人，所以不管大家怎樣在笑，他還是鼓勵他們笑個暢快，並且很快活地把酒瓶遞過去。

喝過茶以後，他們聽了些樂曲。因為他們是一個愛音樂的家庭，而且我能向你保證，當他們唱一首無伴奏的三重唱、四重唱或是一首輪唱曲時，他們都是挺內行的，特別是陶泊，他能夠深沉地唱着低音，像一個歌手似的，而且從來不會唱得額角上青筋暴起，或者為之臉漲得通紅。史高治的外甥媳婦彈豎琴彈得很好，除了奏其他各種曲調之外，還彈了一首簡單的小曲（一首算不了甚麼的曲，你能在兩分鐘內就學會用口哨把它吹出來），而這曲正是一個女孩子所熟悉的，她就是"過去聖誕節之靈"曾經使史高治回憶起來的那個把他從寄宿學校裏接回去的女孩子。當這一節樂曲響起來時，那幽靈顯示給他看過的所有事情，都一齊湧上了他的心頭；他的心腸越變越軟了；他想到：如果他在許多年以前就能夠常常聽到這樣的曲，那他也許已經用自己的手培養起有利於自己幸福的人生的仁愛，而不必去請教那位教堂司事埋葬過雅各‧馬利的鐵鍬了。

但他們沒有把整個夜晚都花在音樂上。過了一會，他們玩起罰物遊戲來，因為有時候再做做小孩子是很有意思的，而且在聖誕節這樣做是再好也沒有了，因為在那一天，它的偉大的創始者本身就是一個小孩子。且慢！他們先玩起捉迷藏來了。自然是要玩這個的。可是我不相信陶泊真的蒙着眼睛裝瞎子，正如我不相信他腳上長着眼睛一樣。我的看法是，這是他跟史高治的外甥預先串通的一齣把戲；而且"現在聖誕節之靈"也曉得的。他追着披花邊領紗的胖妹妹時的那個樣子，簡直是對人性易於相信人的莫大侮辱。他打落了火鉗，絆倒了椅子，撞到了鋼琴，給捲住在窗簾裏，不管她走到哪兒，他就跟到哪裏！他始終知道胖妹妹正在哪兒。他硬是不捉旁人。如果你故意向他身上倒去（他們中有些人就這樣試過），而且站着擋住，他就會假裝竭力要來抓住你——這簡直是公然侮辱你的理解力——然後立刻側過身來，向胖妹妹那邊走去。她常常嚷着說，這樣太不公平了；這也確實是不公平。但是最後他終於捉住她了；她雖則渾身穿着綢，窸窣作響，拍着翅膀似的急忙飛過他身旁，他還是把她逼到一個走投無路的角落裏，到了這時候，他的舉動真是惡劣到極點了。因為他假裝不知道就是她；假裝必須摸一摸她的頭飾，並且為了要證明確實是她，還要把一隻戒指硬戴在她手指上，一條項鏈硬套在她頸上；這種種行徑真是下流可恥、荒唐透頂！難怪等到另外一個蒙眼人上場的時候，他們走到窗簾後面很隱秘地躲在一起之後，她就把她對這件事的意見向他提出。

史高治的外甥媳婦並沒有參加這個捉迷藏遊戲，卻在一個溫暖舒適的角落裏，舒舒服服地坐在一張大椅子上，踏着一張腳櫈，幽靈和史高治就在她的背後附近。但是她參加了罰物遊戲[12]，而且愛她的愛人到了十足崇拜的程度，每個字母為首的字都用上了。在玩"何故、何時、何地"的問答遊戲時，她也是個了不起的好手，她的妹妹們雖然也都是些精明的女孩（陶泊會這樣告訴你），可是都被她徹底擊敗了，這使史高治的外甥心裏暗暗高興。那兒也許有二十個人吧，老的少的都有，但是他們都在玩，史高治也參加在內了；因為他對於眼前所發生的事情太感興趣了，他竟然完全忘掉他的聲音是他們的耳朵聽不見的，有時候也把他自己的猜想相當響亮地喊出來，而且他常常猜中；這就是說，即使是最尖銳的縫衣針，針眼保證不壞的那種最好的"白教堂牌"針，也不會比史高治更銳利，可是他還以為自己是遲鈍的呢。

那幽靈發現他興致這樣好，覺得很高興，就對他表現出那麼寵愛的態度，以致史高治居然像一個小孩子似的懇求它，准許他逗留到客人散去以後。但幽靈說，這是辦不到的。

"這兒又有一種新遊戲，"史高治說。"再留半小時吧，幽靈，只要半小時！"

這是一種叫做"是與否"的遊戲，史高治的外甥要在心裏想好一樣東西，讓其餘的人把它猜出來，而他對於他們提出的問題只是看情況回答一聲是或否。他暴露在像迅猛的炮火般的盤問下，結果吐露出他所想到的東西是一種動物，一種活的動物，而且是一種討厭的動物，野蠻的動物；這種動物有時候咆哮，有時候嘀咕,有時候説話,就住在倫敦,在街道上走來走去,沒有被人拿去展覽,也沒有被人牽着,而且不住在一個動物園裏,也從來沒有在市場上被屠宰;它既不是馬,也不是驢,既不是母牛,也不是公牛,也不是老虎、狗、豬、貓、熊。當每一個新的問題向他提出時,這位外甥總要重新哈哈大笑一番,他被逗得那麼樂不可支,只好從沙發上跳起來,在地上跺着腳。最後那個胖妹妹,也笑成同一個樣子,叫起來道:

"我猜到了!我知道它是甚麼,弗里!我知道它是甚麼!"

"是甚麼?"弗里問。

"就是你的舅舅史高——高——高——高——高治。"

的確就是他。大家都表示佩服,不過有人抗議説,弗里對"是不是熊[13]呢?"這句問話,應當回答"是";因為如果是個否定的回答,那麼假如他們曾經想到這方面去的話,這個回答就足以使他們聯想不到史高治先生身上去了。

"説真的,他給了我們許多樂趣,"弗里説,"我們如果不喝酒祝他健康,那就未免太忘恩負義了。這兒有一杯燙熱的酒,就在我們手邊;因此我説,'為史高治舅舅乾杯!'"

"好啊!為史高治舅舅乾杯!"他們叫道。

"祝他老人家聖誕快樂,新年快樂,不管他是甚麼樣的人!"史高治的外甥説。"他不肯接受我的祝頌,然而我還是希望他能夠得到快樂。為史高治舅舅乾杯!"

史高治舅舅心裏已經不知不覺地變得那麼高興和輕鬆,因此如果那幽靈給他充份時間的話,他一定會對這一群毫未覺察他在旁的人舉杯祝賀作答,而且用他們聽不見的説話來感謝他們。但是他外甥那句話的最後一個字剛剛説出口,這幕景象就全部消逝了;他與那幽靈又開始他們的旅行了。

他們看見了許多,他們跑得很遠,而且探訪了許多人;但結果都是快樂的。那幽靈在一張張病人的牀邊站一下,他們就都快活起來了;它一到他鄉異地,人們就覺得家鄉近在咫尺了;一靠近掙扎着的人,他們便懷有更大的希望而變得忍耐起來了;一站在貧窮的旁邊,富有就跟着來了。在濟貧院、醫院和監獄裏,在貧困所寄身的每一個地方,只要那些自命不凡的人,在他渺小而短促的掌權期間,並沒有把門關緊,並把這幽靈關在門外面,那麼它總是留下它的祝福,並且把它的一些箴言教導史高治。

如果這只是一個夜晚的話,那麼這該是很長的一夜;但是史高治對這是有他的懷疑的,因為似乎聖誕節假期中的那些日子,都壓縮到他們一起度過的這段時間裏了。而且,奇怪的是,史高治在外形上固然絲毫沒有改變,那幽靈卻變得老起來了,清清楚楚地老起來了。史高治已經看出這種改變,但對此卻一句也不提,直到他們離開了一個兒童們參加的第十二夜[14]聯歡會之後,兩人一起站在一個空曠的地方,史高治對這幽靈看看,他才看出它的頭髮都變白了。

"幽靈們的生命難道這樣短暫嗎?"史高治問。

"我在這地球上的生命是很短暫的,"幽靈回答説。"今天夜晚就要完結了。"

"今天夜晚!"史高治叫道。

"今天夜晚,在半夜的時候。聽!快到了。"

這時候,鐘聲正在敲着十一時三刻。

史高治全神貫注地看着幽靈的那件袍，説道："如果我要問的話是不應該問的，那麼請你原諒我。這是因為我看見有一件奇怪的東西，不是屬於你身上的東西，從你袍的下擺裏伸出到外面來。這是一隻腳還是一隻爪？"

"這也許是一隻爪吧，因為它上面還有皮肉，"幽靈哀傷地回答説。"你看！"

它從袍的褶襉裏拿出兩個可憐、卑賤、醜惡、可厭、悲慘的小孩來。他們跪在它的腳下，緊緊地抓住它衣服的外面。

"噢！你看這裏！看看下面！"幽靈叫道。

是一個男孩和一個女孩。面黃肌瘦，衣衫襤褸，怒容滿面，形如惡狼，可又是卑躬屈膝，俯首帖耳。優美的青春本來應當使他們的形體豐滿，而且給他們以最鮮豔的面色的，如今卻好像有一隻陳腐和乾癟的手，像老年人的手似的，在擰他們、扭他們，並且把他們撕成碎片。本來是天使們在寶座上受人膜拜的地方，如今卻潛伏着魔鬼們，他們正用威脅的眼光在瞪人。自從神奇的開天闢地創造萬物以來，不知有過多少不可思議的事情，然而人類不論變化、墮落或反常到甚麼程度，都從來不曾有過任何怪物，有一半這樣恐怖可怕。

史高治嚇得直向後退。看見他們這樣顯露在他眼前，他嘴裏想説他們都是正常的孩子，可是這句話寧願卡住在他的喉嚨裏，也不願撒這樣一個彌天大謊。

"幽靈！他們是你的兒女嗎？"史高治再也沒有別的話可説了。

"他們是人類的兒女，"這幽靈説，低頭看着他們。"可是他們纏住了我，從他們的父親那裏前來申訴。這個男孩名叫'無知'。這個女孩名叫'貧婪'。你要提防他們倆，以及所有他們的同類，但最要緊的是提防這個男孩，因為他的額角上我看見寫着'厄運'這個詞，除非寫下的字跡被消除了。拒絕承認這個！"幽靈叫道，把他的手伸出來指着城市的方向。"誰跟你說這些東西，你就痛罵他！如果你為了黨同伐異的目的而承認它，那就會使事情更糟！你等着將來的後果吧！"

"他們難道沒有避難的地方或者辦法嗎？"史高治叫道。

"難道沒有監獄嗎？"幽靈說，最後一次用史高治自己的話來回答他。"難道沒有聯合救濟院嗎？"

鐘敲了十二下。

史高治周圍看看，要找那幽靈，可是它已經不見了。當最後一下鐘聲停止顫動時，他想起了老雅各・馬利的預告，於是舉目一望，就看見一個莊重嚴肅的幻象，披着衣服，戴着頭巾，像一陣霧似的沿着地面，向他過來。

第四節歌

最後一個幽靈

那幻象緩慢、莊重而沉默地走近來。當它走近他身邊的時候，史高治就雙膝跪下了，因為這幽靈穿過空氣而來，似乎一路在散佈陰鬱和神秘的氣氛。

它全身都裹在一件深黑色的衣服裏，把頭、臉和身體都包住了，甚麼都看不見，露出的只有一隻伸出來的手。要不是有這隻伸在外面的手，那就難以把它的形體跟黑夜分開，並且使它脫離那包圍着它的黑暗了。

等它走到了他的身旁，他發覺它是高大而威嚴的，並且它那神秘的出現，使他充滿了一種嚴肅的畏懼。除此之外，他便甚麼也不知道了，因為這幽靈既不說話也不動彈。

"你是'未來聖誕節之靈'嗎？"史高治說。

幽靈並不回答，只把它的手向前指着。

"你是將要給我看那些還沒有發生、但是在不久的將來就要在我們面前發生的事情吧，"史高治接下去說。"是不是這樣，幽靈？"

　　那衣服上部的皺褶縮了一下，彷彿這幽靈把頭低了一下。這便是史高治得到的唯一答覆。

　　史高治雖則到這時跟鬼打交道已經習以為常了，可是對於這個沉默的形象卻是害怕得不得了，他下邊的兩條腿發着抖，等到發現自己正準備跟它走時，人幾乎站立不住了。那幽靈看見他這種情況，便停頓了片刻，給他時間來定一下神。

　　但是這樣一來，史高治反而更糟糕了。他產生了一種不可名狀的恐怖感，覺得在那陰森森的裹屍衣後面正有一對鬼眼全神貫注地盯着他，而他自己雖然把眼睛睜到最大，卻是除了一隻鬼手和一大堆漆黑的東西之外，甚麼都看不見。

　　"'未來之靈'啊！"他叫道，"我見了你，比過去見過的隨便甚麼鬼都更加害怕。但是因為現在我知道你來的目的是為了讓我得到好處，同時因為我希望今後痛改前非，重新做人，我準備跟你做伴，並懷着感激的心情這樣做。你不願跟我說說話嗎？"

　　它沒有回答他。那隻手一直指向前面。

　　"引路吧！"史高治說。"引路吧！夜晚消逝得很快，時間對於我正是最寶貴的，我知道。引路吧，幽靈！"

　　這幻象像先前向他走過來時那樣，現在向前走了。史高治就跟隨着它衣服的影子，他覺得這影子把他托起來，一路帶往前去。

　　他們似乎並沒有進城去，倒好像是這城市在他們四周湧現出來，主動地把他們包圍在裏面。總之，他們這時已到了城中心；到了交易所裏，在商人們中間，那些商人都在匆忙地跑來跑去，把口袋裏的錢弄得叮噹作響，聚成一群群在談着話，看看他們的錶，或者若有所思地撥弄着他們的金質大圖章，以及諸如此類的事情，而這種情形正是史高治看慣了的。

這幽靈在一小撮生意人的旁邊停了步。史高治看見它的手指點着他們，他便走上前去聽他們在説些甚麼。

"不，"一個下巴碩大無比的大胖子説道，"這件事我也知道得不多。我只知道他已經死了。"

"他是甚麼時候死的？"另外一個問。

"昨天夜晚吧，我相信。"

"怎麼，出了甚麼毛病了？"第三個人問，從一隻很大的鼻煙盒裏拿出一大撮鼻煙。"我還以為他永遠不會死呢。"

"那只有天曉得，"頭一個説，打了個哈欠。

"他把他的錢怎樣安排？"一個紅面孔的紳士問，他鼻尖上掛着一個瘤，搖動起來像是雄火雞下巴邊的垂肉。

"我還沒聽人提過，"那個大下巴的人説，又打了一個呵欠。"把它留下給他的公司吧，也許。他並沒有把它留下來給我。這就是我所知道的一切。"

這句逗人的話引起了大家的笑聲。

"這次喪事大概會是便宜得很的，"同一個人説，"因為，我可以打賭，我不知道有誰會去送葬。我們大家來湊數個人，自告奮勇地去一下怎麼樣？"

"如果有免費午餐的話，我去一趟也無所謂，"鼻上掛着瘤的那位先生説。"如果要我湊個數的話，那就要請我吃一頓。"

又是一陣笑聲。

"話可要這樣説，在你們這些人裏頭，我是最沒有利害關係的一個，"頭一個説話的人説，"因為我向來不戴黑手套，我也向來不吃午餐。但是如果別人願意去的話，我也願意去。説到這裏我卻想起來了：我恐怕不能説，我不是他唯一的朋友吧；因為我們每次碰見的時候，總要站住了攀談一兩句的。再見，再見！"

那些説話的人和聽的人都走開去，混到別的人堆裏去了。史高治是認識這些人的，就對那幽靈看看，希望它作一個解釋。

這幻象卻飄到一條街上去。它的手指點着兩個在碰頭的人。史高治就又聽着他們説話，心想可能聽到解釋。

這兩個人他也是十分熟悉的。他們都是生意人：很有錢，而且地位很高。他一直有意贏得他們的尊重，那就是説，從生意出發，完全是從生意出發。

"你好嗎？"一個説。

"你好嗎？"另一個應道。

"嗯，"頭一個説，"'老刮皮'終於也壽終正寢了，是不是？"

"我聽人這樣説過，"第二個回答。"冷吧，是不是？"

"正合聖誕節的時令。我看你不是個愛溜冰的人吧？"

"不是。不是。我還有別的事情要考慮呢。早安！"

再沒有別的話了。他們的會面、他們的交談和他們的分別就是這樣。

史高治先是感到有些驚奇，怎麼這幽靈居然會對這樣顯然很瑣碎的交談加以重視；但是覺得這裏頭一定隱藏着甚麼用意，他便開始思量這用意可能是甚麼。這些話不可能與他的老合夥人雅各·馬利之死有關，因為那已經是過去的事情，而這隻鬼的活動範圍卻是未來。他也想不出有哪一個跟他自己有直接關係的人，可以用得上這些話。但是他絕不懷疑，不管這些話是關於誰的，他相信對於自己的改過自新都包含着某種教訓，因此他決計把他所聽見的每一句話，所看見的每一件事情，都牢牢記在心裏；特別是等到自己的陰魂出現的時候，要看個清楚。因為他有一種期望，他未來的自己的行為會把他現在所沒有找到的線索提供給他，這樣他要解答這些啞謎就容易得多了。

他就在那個地方找他自己的形象，但是在那個他慣常逗留的角落裏，現在站着的卻是另外一個人了；儘管鐘上所指的時間已經是他通常到那裏的時間，可是他在那許多從門廊裏湧進來的人群中，卻看不見一個像他自己的人。然而，這種情形也不大使他驚異；因為他在心裏已經反覆思考過，要重新做人了，他正料想並希望能夠看見他這新誕生的決心在這裏成為事實。

那幻象站在他身旁，靜默而且陰暗，伸出了一隻手。當他從深思的探索中驚醒過來的時候，他從那隻手的轉動，以及它站在自己身旁的位置，似乎感覺到那雙看不見的眼睛正在銳利地望着他。這情況使他發起抖來，而且覺得渾身發冷。

他們離開了那個熙熙攘攘的地方，來到這城市中一個偏僻的地段，那裏是史高治以前從沒到過的，不過他認識這個去處和它的壞名聲。道路全是污穢而狹隘的，店舖和住宅都很破敗；人們衣衫不全，嗜飲酗酒，邋裏邋遢，面目可憎。一些小巷和拱門，像不計其數的污水坑那樣把惡臭、垃圾和生活中的種種氣味，都傾吐到這些蔓延曲折的街道上；這整個地區散發着罪惡、污穢和窮困的臭味。

在這個藏垢納污之所的巢穴深處，在一個屋簷斜伸出去的屋頂下面，有一家低矮的、門面凸出的鋪，那裏收購廢鐵、破布、瓶子、骨頭和油膩的動物內臟。裏面的地板上放着一堆堆的生了銹的鑰匙、釘、鏈條、鉸鏈、銼刀、磅秤、秤砣以及各種各樣的廢鐵。一座座像山一樣的不成體統的破布、一團團發臭的油脂以及那些骨頭疊成的石墓，不知孕育並藏匿着多少，很少有人高興去仔細探究的秘密。有一個頭髮花白，年近七十歲的壞人，坐在他買賣的貨物中間，靠近一個用舊磚頭砌成的炭爐；他把許多各種各樣的破布掛在一條繩上，做成一個又臭又髒的門簾，來給自己擋住外面的冷空氣，他在這安靜的隱居地，其樂無窮地抽着煙斗。

史高治跟那幻象來到這人面前的時候，恰巧有個女人夾着一個沉重的包裹，偷偷地走進鋪。但是她人剛到，就有另外一個女人，同樣地帶着東西，也走了進來；而她後面緊跟着一個穿褐色黑衣服的男子，他看見她們時吃驚的程度，正和她們認出了她們彼此時一樣。經過了一個短暫的目瞪口呆的時間（那吸煙斗的老伯也和他們一樣）之後，他們三人都禁不住大笑起來。

"讓那打雜女工做頭一個吧！"第一個進來的那女人叫嚷道。"讓那洗衣婆做第二個吧；讓那殯儀館的員工做第三個吧。你看這裏，老喬，這可真是碰巧啊！我們三個人，本來不打算在這裏碰頭的，竟然都來了！"

"你們再也找不到比這裏更好的碰頭地方了，"老喬說，把他的煙斗從嘴裏拿出來。"到客廳裏來吧。你在這裏早就是熟門熟路的了，你知道；至於另外那兩個，也都不是陌生人。等一會，讓我把鋪的門關上。哎喲，這門吱吱地叫得多響啊！這屋裏沒有比它自己的鉸鏈銹得更厲害的鐵器了，我相信；我還肯定這屋裏的骨頭沒有比我這副骨頭更老的了。哈哈！我們都是最配做這一行的，我們都棋逢敵手。到客廳裏來吧。"

這個所謂客廳，就是破布門簾後面的那塊地方。老伯用一根舊的地毯棍撥撥爐裏的火，用他的煙斗柄把冒煙的燈剔剔亮（因為這時候已經是夜晚了），然後又把煙斗塞進嘴去。

在他忙着這些的時候，那個已經說過話的女人把她那包東西丟在地板上，大模大樣地在一張橙上坐了下來，兩臂交叉，手臂肘擱在膝頭上，用一種大膽的挑釁姿態，看着另外那兩個人。

"這又有甚麼關係呢？狄伯太太，這有甚麼關係呢？"那女人說。"每個人都有權利照料他自己。他向來就是這樣的！"

"真的，這話挺對！"那洗衣婦說。"沒有人比他更會照料自己的了。"

"那麼，女人，別站在那裏呆瞪着，好像害怕似的！誰會知曉呢？我想我們總不會互相挑剔吧？"

"不，那才不會呢！"狄伯太太和那男子齊聲說。"我們希望不會。"

"這就很好！"這女人叫道。"這樣就夠了。少了數件像這樣的東西，誰會受損失呢？一個死人是不會的，我猜想？"

"當然不會，"狄伯太太說，大笑起來。

"如果他死了以後，還想保留這些東西，這個刻薄的老死刮皮，"那女人接下去說，"那麼他在世的時候，為甚麼那樣不近人情呢？如果他做人合情合理一些的話，那麼在死神來侵襲他的時候，總會有人來照顧他，不會一個人孤零零地躺在牀上，喘氣直喘到斷氣。"

"這句話真是說得再確切也沒有了，"狄伯太太說。"這就是老天對他的報應。"

"我但願這報應能夠多一點，"這女人回答說。"你可以完全相信，如果我的手能夠弄到任何別的甚麼的話，那麼這種報應一定會更重一點的。把那個包裹打開來，老喬，讓我知道它能值多少錢。爽爽快快地說。我不怕做頭一個，也不怕給他們看見這件事情。我相信，在我們在這裏碰頭之前，我們大家就已經很明白各人是在自己動手了。這不是甚麼犯罪。把包裹打開來，喬。"

但是她的朋友們都很有義氣，不肯讓她先打開包裹；於是那個穿着褪色黑衣服的男子一馬當先，拿出了他掠獲的東西。東西並不豐富。一兩個圖章、一個鉛筆盒、一雙袖扣以及一個不值錢的別針，就這些而已。老喬把它們一件件的仔細檢驗過，估一估價錢，然後把他對每件東西打算付的數目，用粉筆寫在牆壁上，等到他發現已經沒有東西再拿出來時，就加成一個總數。

"這是你的賬，"喬說，"我不能再多給六個便士，哪怕你要把我活活煮死也辦不到。第二個是誰？"

狄伯太太是第二名。數張被單和毛巾、數件破舊的衣服、兩把老式的銀茶匙、一副方糖夾以及數隻靴。她的賬也同樣寫在牆壁上。

"我向來對女士們出手太鬆。這是我的一個弱點，也是我毀掉自己的原因，"老喬說。"那是你的賬。如果你再向我多要一個便士，而且公開提出來，那我就要懊悔自己太慷慨，非削減你半個克朗不可。"

"現在把我的包裹打開來吧，喬，"頭一個女人說。

喬為了打開包裹更方便起見，就跪在地上；他解開了許多繩結，才拉出一大卷挺重的深色東西。

"你叫這東西做甚麼？"喬問。"牀帳嗎？"

"啊！"女人回答說，哈哈大笑，叉着兩臂，身體朝前傾。"帳嘛！"

"難道說，他人還躺在牀上，你就把這些東西，連同銅圈等等，一起都拿了下來？"喬問。

"不錯，我正是這樣，"女人回答說。"為甚麼不可以？"

"你真是生來要發財的，"喬說，"你將來一定會發財。"

"我向你保證，喬，對於像他這樣的一個人，凡是我只要伸出手去就能夠拿到的東西，我是決不會把手縮回來的，"女人冷冷地回答。"喂，你不要把油滴在那被子上。"

"他的被子嗎？"喬問。

"你以為不是他的，那是誰的？"女人回答說。"沒有了這兩張被子，他總不至於傷風感冒吧，我敢說。"

"我希望他不是生了甚麼傳染病死的吧？呃？"老喬停了一下他的工作，朝上面望望，這樣說。

"你不用害怕這個，"那女人應道。"如果他有甚麼傳染病的話，我決不會那麼喜歡跟他做伴，為了這點東西在他身邊多逗留的。啊！你儘管看那件襯衫，把你的眼睛都看痛了，你也不會在上面找到一個破洞，或是一個磨爛的地方的。這是他襯衫中最好的一件，也的確是件好襯衫。要不是有我在，別人早就把它糟蹋掉了。"

"你説糟蹋掉是甚麼意思？"老喬問。

"當然，這是説把它穿在他身上葬掉，"女人笑了一聲，回答説。"有人就蠢得這麼做了，可是我把它又脱了下來。如果白棉布派這種用場不夠好的話，那它還能派甚麼用場呢？蓋在他的身上，還是一樣很得體。他不會比穿上這一件顯得更難看了。"

史高治驚心動魄地聽着這一段話。當他們圍着贓物，在老伯那盞燈的黯淡光線之下，坐在一起的時候，他用一種無以復加的厭惡和痛恨看着他們，即使他們是出賣死人屍體的下流惡魔，也不過如此了。

當老喬拿出一個裝着錢的法蘭絨袋來，把給他們的那數筆錢數了出來擺在地上時，又是那個女人笑道，"哈哈！你們看，這個就是他的下場！他活着的時候，把每個人都嚇得從他身邊跑開，他死掉之後，倒使我們得到了好處！哈哈哈！"

"幽靈，"史高治從頭到腳發着抖説。"我明白了，我明白了。這個不幸的人的遭遇，可能就是我自己的遭遇。我的生活現在正向這個方向走去。慈悲的上帝，這是甚麼？"

他懷着恐懼直向後退，因為眼前的場景又變了，這時他的身體差不多碰到了一張牀，一張光溜溜的、沒有帳的牀，在這牀上，一張破被單的下面，躺着一件被遮蓋住的東西。這東西雖然不會開口，卻用一種可怕的語言宣佈它是甚麼了。

這個房間很黑暗，黑暗得無法看得真切；可是史高治因為私下裏懷着一種衝動，就向房間裏四處張望，急於想知道它究竟是怎樣的一種房間。從外面的空中升起一道黯淡的光線，一直照到這張牀上；而躺在這張牀上的正是這個被人洗劫、被人遺棄、沒人守靈、沒人哭泣、沒人照料的屍體。

史高治朝那幻象望望。它那堅定的手，正指着那人的頭。那條遮體的布是那麼隨便地蓋在上面，史高治只消動一個手指頭，稍微把它掀起一點點，就可以使那張臉露出來。他想到這一層，覺得這件事真是容易做得很，因此巴不得這樣做；只可惜他沒有力量來把這蒙在臉上的布揭開，正如他沒有力量使他身旁這幽靈走開一樣。

如此無情、嚴酷而可畏的死神啊，您在這裏築起了您的神壇，並且調動了那麼多的恐怖手段來把它裝潢起來，因為這兒本來是您的領域啊！但是對於那被人尊敬、受人愛戴並博得榮譽的人，您卻是既無法碰他一根毫髮來達到您那可怕的目的，也無法使他五官中的哪一處變得可憎。這並不是因為他那隻手現在是沉重的，一放鬆就會垂落下去；也不是因為他的心臟和脈搏已經停止了；恰恰是因為那隻手從前是光明正大、慷慨而忠實的；那顆心是勇敢、熱烈和溫柔的；那脈搏是一個大丈夫的。打擊吧，陰靈，打擊吧！您就會看見他的那些善行從傷口裏湧出來，把不朽的生命散播到全世界！

並沒有人在史高治耳邊說這些話，然而當他望着牀上時，他聽到了這些話。他想，如果這個人現在能夠起死回生的話，他最先想到的將會是甚麼呢？難填的慾壑，苛刻的交易，還是不斷的操心呢？說實話，它們不是已經使他落到一個富有成果的下場了嗎？

他躺在那黑暗的空屋裏，沒有一個男人，女人或小孩會說：他曾經在這件事或那件事上對我很好，為了紀念他的一句好心話，我要好好地對待他。一隻貓正在門上抓着，爐邊石頭下面有老鼠在啃咬的聲音。牠們在這個死人的房間裏究竟想要得到甚麼，牠們為甚麼那麼不安靜而蠢蠢欲動，史高治簡直想都不敢想。

「幽靈啊！」他說，「這是一個可怕的地方。在離開這個房間的時候，我決不會把它的教訓丟開的，請相信我。我們走吧！」

然而這幽靈還是用一個毫不移動的手指，指着那死人的頭。

「我明白你的意思，」史高治回答說，「假如我做得到的話，我一定會這樣做的。但是我沒有這個能力，幽靈。我沒有這個能力。」

幽靈似乎又在望着他。

「幽靈，我求求你，」史高治說，感到很痛苦，「如果這城裏有哪一個人，因為這個人的死而心情激動，請你把那個人指給我看看！」

幻象把他的黑袍在他面前張開了一會，好像一隻翅膀似的；等到收攏的時候，顯出了一個陽光照耀下的房間，裏面有一位母親和她的孩子們。

她正在等着甚麼人來，而且是帶着焦急迫切的心情；因為她在房間裏走來走去，聽見每一把聲音就要驚跳起來；一會從窗口向外張望，一會又看看鐘；她想做一點針線工作，可是總做不成；甚至她孩子在玩耍時的聲音她都簡直受不了。

最後，響起了那期待已久的敲門聲。她急忙跑到門口，迎着了她的丈夫；他雖然還年輕，可是他的臉已經是飽經憂患，愁苦不堪的了。這時他臉上帶有一種特殊的表情，一種為自己真正喜悅而覺得不好意思，並竭力想抑制的表情。

他坐下來吃飯，那是早已給他留在爐邊熱着的；而當她（經過了一段長時間的沉默之後）膽怯地問他有甚麼消息時，他似乎窘得不知道該怎樣回答才好。

“是好消息呢，還是壞消息？”她問，幫助他說出來。

“壞消息，”他回答說。

“那麼我們全毀了嗎？”

“不。還有點希望，卡洛琳。”

“如果他變寬容的話，”她驚異地說，“那就有希望了！如果這樣的奇蹟已經出現了的話，那就隨便甚麼都還是有希望的。”

“他已經沒法變寬容了，”她丈夫說，“他已經死了。”

如果她臉上的表情並不騙人的話，她是一個溫和而富有耐心的人；但是她聽見了這句話，心裏實在覺得欣慰，就緊握着雙手，說出了這個意思。她接着就禱告上帝請求恕罪，而且覺得難過；但是她那頭一個舉動是表現她內心的情緒的。

“我想去見他要他答應寬限一星期，那個昨天夜晚我對你提起過的酒喝得半醉的女人跟我說了，我起初還以為只是避不見我的一種藉口，但結果卻的確是如此。那時候，他不僅是病得很厲害，而且是快要死了。”

“我們欠的債將來轉交給誰呢？”

“我不知道。不過，不消等到那時候，我們的錢就可以準備好了；而且，即使我們還沒有準備好，卻碰到了他的繼承人偏偏也是一個這樣狠心的債主，那也就只好說是命該如此了。今天我們總可以心情輕鬆地睡一夜了，卡洛琳。”

的確。他們雖然竭力想使心腸軟一些，但他們的心情到底是輕鬆些了。孩子們都默不作聲，圍繞在他們父母身邊，聽着那些他們很難聽懂的話，他們現在也都變得更容光煥發了。這個人一死，這間屋變成快樂得多了！這隻鬼所能顯現給他看的由此人之死所引起的唯一情感，是一種快樂的情感。

"讓我看到一點對一個人死亡的惻隱之情吧，"史高治說，"不然的話，幽靈啊，我們方才離開的那個黑暗的房間，就會永遠顯現在我眼前了。"

那幽靈帶領他穿過幾條他的腳步所熟悉的街道；他們一路走去時，史高治東張西望，想找到他自己，但是隨便在哪裏都看不到自己。他們走進可憐的鮑伯·奇勒哲的家裏；這個住處是他以前去過的；他們看到那做母親的和她的兒女們都圍爐而坐。

沉靜。非常沉靜。那些愛吵鬧的小奇勒哲，都在一個角落裏沉靜得像是雕像似的；他們坐在那裏望着彼得，彼得面前放着一本書。母親和她的女兒們正在做着針線。但是他們的確都靜默得很！

"他便叫一個小孩子來，使他站在他們當中。[15]"

史高治是在甚麼地方聽見過這句話的呢？他並不是在夢裏聽見的。當他和幽靈跨進門檻的時候，彼得一定是在高聲讀着這句話。他為甚麼不讀下去呢？

母親把她所做的放在桌上，伸手掩住臉。

"這種顏色[16]傷我的眼睛，"她說。

這種顏色？唉，可憐的小添！

"眼睛現在好點了，"奇勒哲的妻子說。"在蠟燭光底下把眼睛都弄模糊了；等你們父親回來了，我隨便怎樣也不能讓他看見我這雙模糊的眼睛。現在一定是快要到他回家的時候了。"

"其實是已經過了時候，"彼得合上書說。"但是我想，母親，在最近這數個晚上，他總是走得比平時稍微慢一點吧。"

他們又變得非常沉靜了。最後，她用一種穩定而愉快的聲音說，只有一次頓了一會：

"我知道他曾把——我知道他曾把小添背在背上走的，還走得很快呢。"

"我也知道是這樣，"彼得叫道。"常常這樣。"

"我也知道是這樣，"另外一個叫道。大家都知道。

"但他背起來是很輕的，"她接下去說，用心工作着，"他的父親又是那樣愛他，所以更覺得不費事，不費事了。現在你們父親到了門口了！"

她趕快出去迎接他；於是鮑伯披着他的圍巾——他實在需要這東西，可憐的人——走進來了。他的茶已經給他準備好了，擱在爐旁的保溫架上，他們都想比比看誰侍候他最好。接着那兩個小奇勒哲爬到他的膝頭上，每個孩子都把自己的一片小臉頰貼在他的臉上，彷彿在說，"父親，不要把這事情掛在心上。不要傷心！"

鮑伯跟他們玩得很快活，並且高高興興地和全家的人談話。他看看桌上面，就稱讚奇勒哲太太和女孩們做事辛勤迅速。不消到禮拜天，這些工作就能做好，他說。

"星期天！那你今天去過了，羅拔？"他妻子問道。

"是的，親愛的，"鮑伯回答說。"我真希望你也能夠去就好了。你如果能夠看見那裏是個多麼蒼翠的地方，對你一定有好處的。可是你今後會常常看見那地方的。我已經答應他，每逢到了禮拜天，我一定要上那裏去走走。我的小小孩子啊！"鮑伯哭了起來。"我的小孩子啊！"

他禁不住一下子痛哭起來。他實在忍不住了。他要是忍得住的話，他和他的孩子恐怕就會比過去離得更遠了。

他離開了這個房間，跑上樓去，走進上面的那個房間，那裏燈火照耀得很歡樂，掛着聖誕節的裝飾。靠近那孩子的身旁，擺着一張椅子，還留着不久前曾有人在那裏坐過的痕跡。可憐的鮑伯就坐了在這張椅上，他想了一會，使自己鎮靜下來之後，吻吻那張小臉。他如今已接受了那已經發生的事實，便又相當高興地走下樓來。

他們圍爐坐着，談着，女孩們跟母親都在工作。鮑伯跟他們說，史高治先生的外甥真是特別厚道，他只不過跟他見過一次面，可是那天史高治的外甥在街上碰見他，看見他的神情有一點——"只不過有一點不開心，你知道，"鮑伯説——他便問發生了甚麼事情使他這樣苦惱。"聽見了這句話，"鮑伯説，"因為他是你所能碰到的，説話最親切動聽的人，我便告訴了他。他就説，'奇勒哲先生，我對此事感到十分難過；而且是替你的好太太十分難過。'順便提一句，我真不懂，他怎麼會知道這個的。"

"知道甚麼，親愛的？"

"噢，知道你是一位好太太，"鮑伯説。

"哪個不知道！"彼得説。

"這話説得好，我的孩子！"鮑伯叫道。"我希望他們都知道。他説，'我真替你的好太太十分難過。假如我有任何地方可以為您效勞的話，'他說，把他的名片遞給我，'這上面就是我的住址。請來找我吧。'啊，這件事情使人覺得很高興，倒不是因為他可能對我們有甚麼幫助，而是因為他那種仁愛的態度。看起來真好像他老早就認識我們的小添，而且很同情我們。"

"我深信他是一個好心腸的人！"奇勒哲夫人說。

"親愛的，"鮑伯回答說，"如果你看見過他，跟他說過話，那你就會更相信他是這樣的了。如果他能給彼得弄到一個更好的職位——你們注意我說的話！——我一點不會覺得驚奇。"

"你聽聽這句話，彼得，"奇勒哲夫人說。

"到了那時候，"女孩們中間的一個叫道，"彼得就會跟甚麼人訂婚，並且自立門戶了。"

"去你的！"彼得回答說，咧嘴笑着。

"這倒多半是可能的，"鮑伯說，"反正總有這麼一天吧；好在往後的日子長得很，來得及，親愛的。但是，不管我們大家將來怎樣分離，在甚麼時候分離，我相信我們沒有一個人會忘掉可憐的小添的——我們總不會吧——也不會忘掉我們中間這頭一次分離吧？"

"決不會的，父親！"他們大家都叫道。

"我們只要一回憶到他是多麼有耐性、多麼溫和，雖然他還是一個小小的、小小的孩子，我就知道，"鮑伯說，"我就知道，我的親人們，我們自己中間決不會輕易爭吵起來，吵得忘掉了可憐的小添的。"

"對，決不會的，父親！"他們大家又都叫道。

"我高興極了，"鮑伯說，"我高興極了！"

奇勒哲夫人吻他，他的女兒們吻他，那兩個小奇勒哲吻他，彼得和他握握手。小添的英靈呵，你那童稚的善良本質就是來自上帝的！

"幽靈啊，"史高治說，"有甚麼東西在通知我，我們分離的時候就要到了。我知道這個，但是我不知道究竟要怎樣分離。告訴我，我們看見的那個死去了躺在牀上的人到底是誰？"

那"未來聖誕節之靈"跟之前一樣——然而史高治認為是在不同的時候；的確，在最後的那些幻景中，時間上的次序似乎是混亂的，只知道這些都是將來的事情——把他運送到一個生意人聚集的地方，但是始終沒有把史高治自己顯現給他看。實在是，這幽靈一點也沒有停留，只顧一直往前去，彷彿正向剛才心目中想去的那個目的地奔去，直到史高治懇求它停留片刻才止。

"我們現在急急忙忙穿過的這個院子，"史高治說，"就是我辦公的地方，而且工作了很長一個時期。我看見那幢屋了。讓我看看我在將來的日子裏究竟會是甚麼樣子！"

那幽靈停下來，可是手卻指着別處。

"屋就在那邊，"史高治叫道。"你為甚麼指着別處呢？"

那隻無情的手指一點也不動。

史高治趕快跑到他辦公室的窗邊，向裏面望去。這裏還是一間辦公室，但已經不是他的了。像具已經不是原來的了，坐在椅子裏的人也不是他自己。那幻象還是跟之前一樣地在指着。

他回到它的身邊，一邊不明白自己為甚麼要這樣和要到哪裏去，他一邊跟隨着它，直至他們到達一個鐵門邊。他進去之前，先停下來望望四周。

一個教堂的墳場。這麼説，這裏就是那個倒霉的人的葬身之地，這個人的姓名他眼看就要知道了。這是一個令人蕭然起敬的地方。四周被房屋包圍住；遍地的良草和雜草，而植物是正在不斷枯死，卻不是正在生長；埋葬了太多的人，塞得滿滿的；由於它的胃口得到滿足，顯出很發福的樣子。好一個令人蕭然起敬的地方！

幽靈站在那些墳墓中間，朝下指着其中的一座。史高治哆嗦着向那座墳走過去。那幻象還是完全跟先前一個模樣，可是他生怕從它那嚴肅的形體上看出新的含意來。

"在我更走近你指點着的那塊石碑之前，"史高治説，"請你回答我一個問題。這些究竟是將要發生的事情的影像呢，還是只不過是或許會發生的事情的影像？"

那鬼依然手指向下，指着它身旁的那個墳。

"人們所走的道路會預示某種結局，這就是説，如果他們堅持走他們的道路，他們就一定會達到那種結局，"史高治説。"但是，假如他們離開了這種道路，那麼結局也會改變的。你説，你顯現給我看的那些事物就是這樣的吧！"

那幽靈還是跟以前一樣絲毫不動。

史高治向這座墳走去，邊走邊發着抖；於是，隨着那個指頭，他在這荒墳的石碑上讀到他自己的姓名：**埃伯尼澤·史高治**。

"難道我就是躺在牀上的那個人嗎？"他叫道，雙膝跪下。

那隻手指從墳指向他，再從他指向墳。

"不，幽靈！啊，不，不！"

那隻手指仍然伸着。

"好幽靈啊！"他叫道，緊緊地抓住它的袍。"聽我說！我現在已經不是從前那樣的人了。要不是因為這次經歷，我不會變成現在這樣。假如我已經是毫無希望的話，那又為甚麼把這個顯現給我看呢？"

那隻手似乎頭一次在顫動起來。

"好幽靈啊，"他接下去說，一邊跪倒在它面前的地上，"你的天性在代我說情，並且可憐我。請你使我相信：如果我今後重新做人，我還能把你顯現給我看的那些影像改變過來！"

那隻仁慈的手抖動起來。

"我以後一定從心底裏尊重聖誕節，並且要一年到頭努力過節。我以後要生活在'過去'、'現在'和'將來'之中。這三位幽靈以後永遠都要在我心裏激勵着我。我決不把它們啟導我的教訓置之腦後。啊，告訴我，我還有可能擦掉這塊石頭上的字跡！"

他在痛苦中抓住了那幽靈的手。它想把手掙脫出來，但是他苦苦祈求着，用力抓住這隻手不放。然而那幽靈比他更強更有力，終於擺脫了他。

他舉起手來作一次最後的禱告，祈求他的命運轉變過來，這時候他看見幽靈的兜帽和衣服都發生了變化。它縮小，塌下去，逐漸縮成一條牀柱。

結局

對啊！這牀柱是他自己的。牀是他自己的，房間是他自己的。而一切之中最好和最幸福的是：他將來的時間是屬於他自己的，使他可以改過自新！

"我以後要生活在'過去'、'現在'和'將來'之中！"史高治從牀上爬下來，又這樣說了一句。"這三位幽靈以後都要在我心裏激勵着我。雅各·馬利啊！為此，讚美上天和聖誕節吧！我現在跪着說這話，老馬利啊，我正跪着！"

他心裏充滿了善良的心願，變得那麼激動和熱誠，使他那哽咽的聲音幾乎難以表達他的呼喚。他剛才與幽靈爭執的時候，曾經痛哭過，因此臉上還沾着淚痕。

史高治把帳的一邊摺攏來抱在自己懷裏，叫道，"它並沒有被人扯下來，它並沒有被人扯下來，連銅圈等等。它們現在都在這裏——我現在也在這裏——那些本來要實現的事情的影像，還有被驅散的可能。它們一定會的。我知道一定會的！"

在這段時間裏，他的雙手一直忙着擺弄自己的衣服：把衣服翻到外面，把它們顛倒了穿上身，或者把它們扯來扯去，把它們放錯了位置，以及對它們加以各種各樣的蹂躪。

"我不知道該怎樣做才好！"史高治叫道，又是笑又是哭，而且把他的長筒襪纏在自己身上，弄得活像拉奧孔[17]似的。"我現在是輕鬆得像一根羽毛，快活得像一個天使，高興得像一個小學生，頭暈得像一個醉漢。祝大家聖誕快樂！祝全世界的人新年愉快！喂喂！呵呵！喂！"

他已經跳跳蹦蹦進入了客廳，這時正站在那裏，簡直喘不過氣來。

"那是盛着粥的鍋！"史高治叫道，又走動起來，在壁爐前跳來蹦去。"那裏是雅各·馬利的鬼魂進來時所走的門！那裏是'現在聖誕節之靈'坐過的角落！那裏是我看見那些遊魂的窗！一切都是不錯的，一切都是真實的，一切都是發生過的。哈哈哈！"

真的，對於一個許多年來在這方面荒疏已久的人，這真是一陣奇妙無比的大笑，一陣精彩萬分的大笑。這是長長一連串的出色笑聲之父！

"我不知道今天是這個月的甚麼日子，"史高治說。"我不知道我在幽靈們之中度過了多久時光。我甚麼事情都不知道。我完全是個小嬰孩。這沒關係。我不管這些。我寧願做個小嬰孩！喂！呵呵！喂喂！"

他正手舞足蹈地欣喜若狂，被禮拜堂的鐘聲止住了：那樣歡樂的鐘聲是他生平從來沒有聽見過的。鏜，鋃，鐘錘敲着；叮，噹，大鐘響着。鐘聲，噹，叮；鐘錘，鋃，鏜！哦，真堂皇啊，真堂皇啊！

他跑到窗邊，打開了窗，把頭伸出去。沒有濃霧、沒有煙靄；晴朗、明亮、歡欣、活躍、寒冷；寒冷，號召血液去跟着跳舞；金黃色的陽光；美妙無比的天空；新鮮清新的空氣；歡樂的鐘聲。哦，真堂皇啊，真堂皇啊！

"今天是甚麼日子？"史高治叫道，他向樓下叫喚着一個穿着星期天衣服[18]的孩子，這孩子大概是走進來看看情況的。

"甚麼？"那孩子問，驚奇得不得了。

"今天是甚麼日子，我的好孩子？"史高治説。

"今天！"孩子回答説。"喲，聖誕節！"

"果然是聖誕節！"史高治自言自語道。"我還沒有錯過這個節日。幽靈們把所有的事情在一夜裏都做完了。他們能做他們喜歡做的任何事情。他們當然能夠的。他們當然能夠的。嗨，我的好孩子！"

"嗨！"那孩子回答説。

"你認得過去第二條街上的那家雞鴨鋪嗎，在轉角的？"史高治問。

"我想我應該認得吧，"這小子回答説。

"真是個聰明的孩子！"史高治説。"真是個了不起的孩子！你知不知道他們有沒有賣掉那隻掛在那裏的好火雞，不是那隻小的好火雞，是那隻大的？"

"甚麼，那隻像我這樣大的嗎？"孩子回答説。

"真是個討人喜歡的孩子！"史高治説，"跟他説話真有趣。是的，我的好孩子！"

"它現在還掛在那裏呢，"孩子説。

"是嗎？"史高治説，"去把它買來。"

"騙人！"孩子驚叫道。

"不，不，"史高治説，"我這話是當真的。你去把它買下了，叫他們送到這裏來，讓我好吩咐他們把這東西送到哪裏去。你跟鋪裏的人一起回來，我給你一個先令。如果不到五分鐘就跟他一起回來，我給你半個克朗！"

那孩子像一發子彈似的飛奔而去了。如果有人放槍能放得一半這麼快，那他已經可以算是一位射擊能手了。

"我要把它送到鮑伯·奇勒哲家去，"史高治小聲説，搓搓雙手，笑得捧着肚子。"不讓他知道是誰送給他的。這隻火雞有兩個小添那麼大。把它送給鮑伯真是開一個大玩笑，連喬·密勒[19]也要自愧不如呢。"

他寫地址時，手都有點抖了；但是不管怎樣，他到底把它寫出來了，而且走到樓下去把臨街的大門打開，等候那雞鴨鋪的人來。當他站在那裏等着的時候，他的眼睛忽然看到了那個門環。

"我活一天就要愛它一天，"史高治説，用手拍拍它。"我以前簡直從來不看它一眼。它那臉上的表情是多麼誠實啊！這真是個奇妙的門環！——火雞來了。嗨！呵呵！你好嗎！聖誕快樂！"

這才真是一隻火雞！它絕對不可能靠着自己的腿站立起來，這隻火雞。它會在一分鐘裏就把它的腿都折斷，像兩根封口的火漆棒似的。

"要把它拿到卡姆登鎮去是辦不到的，"史高治説。"你要租一輛馬車去才行。"

他說這句話時的格格笑聲，和他付火雞錢時的格格笑聲，付馬車費時的格格笑聲，以及他酬謝那小孩時的格格笑聲，都及不上他氣喘咻咻地，重新在他椅子裏坐下時的那一陣格格笑聲，而且直笑得淌出眼淚來。

刮鬍子不是一件容易的事情，這是因為他的手還繼續抖得很厲害；而且刮鬍子是需要全神貫注的，即使你在做這件事時並不歡欣雀躍。但是如果他把鼻子尖剃掉了的話，他會貼一塊橡皮膠布在上面，而仍舊感到心滿意足的。

他穿上了一身"最好的衣服"，終於走到了街上。這時候人們都在湧出來了，這情景正跟他跟着"現在聖誕節之靈"時看見的一樣。於是，史高治反背着雙手，臉帶快活的笑容，看看每一個人。總之，他的神氣看起來是那麼樂不可支，因此有三四個心情愉快的人對他說道，"早安，先生！祝你聖誕快樂！"後來史高治常常說，在他生平所聽到的愉快的聲音中，這數個字聽在耳朵裏要算是最愉快的了。

他還沒有走多遠，就看見那位胖胖的紳士迎面走來——就是昨天走進他的賬房，對他說"史高治與馬利商行，是不是？"的那個人。他一想到這位老先生遇到他時會怎樣看他，心裏就貫穿着一陣痛楚之感；但是他知道擺在他面前的康莊大道是哪一條，他就選擇了這條路。

"親愛的先生，"史高治説，一面加快步伐，抓住了這位老先生的一雙手，"您好嗎？我希望您昨天獲得成功。您真是仁慈得很。祝您聖誕快樂，先生！"

"史高治先生嗎？"

"正是，"史高治説。"這就是在下的姓氏，我怕這名字您聽起來不大愉快。請准許我懇求您的寬恕。而且還要請求您——"説到這裏，史高治便湊在他的耳邊輕輕地説了數句話。

"上帝保佑我！"這位紳士説，簡直氣都喘不過來了。"我親愛的史高治先生，您這話當真嗎？"

"別見笑，"史高治説，"一個法尋[20]都不會少。老實説，這裏頭還包括了許多過期未付的在內。您肯幫我這個忙嗎？"

"我親愛的先生，"對方説，跟他握握手。"我簡直不知道該怎麼説才好，對於您這種慷——"

"請您不要提了，"史高治回答説。"請光臨敝舍。您肯光臨敝舍嗎？"

"我一定來！"那位老先生叫道。很明顯，他是決心要去的。

"謝謝您了，"史高治説。"我真感激您。我對您無限感謝。祝福您！"

他上教堂去，然後在街上逛來逛去，看着人們匆匆來往奔波，拍拍孩子們的頭，對乞丐們問問話，低下頭去看看別人屋裏的廚房，抬起頭來望望別人的窗戶，覺得隨便哪一件事情都使他得到樂趣。他從來做夢也沒有想到任何散步——任何事情——能給他這麼多的幸福。到了下午，他調轉腳步，向他外甥的家走去。

他在門外走來走去，走了十數遍，才鼓起勇氣來上前去敲門。最後他一個衝刺，終於敲起門來。

"你的主人在家嗎，親愛的？"史高治對那女孩説。一位好女孩！好得很。

"在家，先生。"

"他在哪裏，我的好女孩？"史高治問。

"先生，他在客廳裏，跟太太在一起。我領您上樓去，好不好？"

"謝謝你。他認得我的，"史高治説，他的手已經放在餐廳的門把手上了。"我這就進去了，親愛的。"

他輕輕旋着把手，把他的臉從門邊側着伸進去。他們正在望着桌子（桌上這時已經擺滿飯菜了）；因為這些年輕主婦們在這種問題上老是很緊張，喜歡看見一切都安排得好好的。

"弗里！"史高治説。

天啊，他的外甥媳婦真是嚇了一大跳！史高治這時忘掉了她是坐在角落裏，腳擱在一張腳櫈上，否則他隨便怎樣也不會這樣叫的。

"啊呀，上帝保佑我！"弗里叫道，"這是哪一位呢？"

"是我。你的舅舅史高治。我是來吃飯的。你肯讓我進來嗎，弗里？"

讓他進來，那還用説！他握手時沒有把他的手臂搖斷已經算是走運了。五分鐘之後，他就感到舒適自在了。沒有比這更熱誠的接待了。他的外甥媳婦看起來完全是同樣的熱情。陶泊，他走過來的時候也是這樣熱情。那個胖妹妹走過來的時候，她也是這樣熱情。每個人走過來的時候，他們也都是這樣熱情。好得不得了的宴會，好得不得了的遊戲，好得不得了的親密融洽，好——得——不——得——了的幸福快樂！

但是第二天早晨，他老早就到辦公室了。哦，他是特地早去的！他只要能夠先到那裏，撞見鮑伯・奇勒哲遲到就好了！這便是他一心想看見的事情。

　　果然給他看到了；是的，他看到了！鐘敲了九時。鮑伯沒來。九時一刻了。鮑伯沒來。他足足遲到了十八分半鐘。史高治坐在那裏，把他的房門開得大大的，以便能看見鮑伯走進那個"水槽"。

　　鮑伯在推開門之前，已經先把帽脫掉，圍巾也除下來了。他一眨眼就坐到了他的小櫈上，拿起筆來飛快地寫着，彷彿他想追上九時似的。

　　"嗨！"史高治盡可能地裝出他慣常的聲音，咆哮道。"你今天到這個時候才來，究竟是甚麼意思？"

　　"我真抱歉得很，先生，"鮑伯說。"我是遲到了。"

　　"你是遲到了？"史高治重複說一遍。"是啊。我想你是遲到了。對不起，先生，請你到這裏來一下。"

　　"這不過是一年一次啊，先生，"鮑伯從"水槽"裏鑽出來，懇求道。"下次決不會再這樣了。昨天晚上，我玩得太快活了，先生。"

　　"噢，我來說給你聽，我的朋友，"史高治說，"我再也容忍不了這種事情了。所以，"他接下去說，從櫈上跳下來，對着鮑伯身上的背心，那麼用力地一戳，戳得他跌跌撞撞地一直退回到"水槽"裏。——"所以呢，我就要給你加薪金了！"

　　鮑伯發起抖來，朝放着尺的地方走近了一點。有那麼一剎那，他想用這根尺把史高治擊倒，挾住了他的身體，叫院子裏的人大家來幫忙，給他穿上一件緊身衣[21]！

　　"祝你聖誕快樂，鮑伯！"史高治說，輕輕地拍拍他的背脊，他那一副誠懇的樣子，誰看了都不會誤解的。"祝你過一個更加快樂的聖誕節，鮑伯，我的好夥伴，比我許多年來給過你的聖誕節都要快樂得多！我要加你的薪金，並且要盡力幫助你那艱苦奮鬥的家庭，讓我們就在今天下午，邊喝着一碗聖誕節的熱氣騰騰的香甜葡萄酒，邊談你的事，鮑伯！快把爐裏的火加加旺，趕快先去買一桶煤來再動筆寫吧，鮑伯‧奇勒哲！"

史高治不但實現了自己的諾言，而且超過了諾言。他做了所有這些事情，而且還做了不知多少別的事情；至於小添呢，他並沒有死，史高治還做了他的乾爸。他成為這個又好又老的城市所知道的，或者這個又好又老的世界上，任何一個別的又老又好的都市、城鎮和自治市鎮所知道的再好也沒有的朋友，再好也沒有的主人和再好也沒有的人。有些人看見他這種轉變，覺得好笑，但是他讓他們笑，一點也不理會他們；因為他已相當聰明，知道在這個地球上的任何一件事情，在開頭的時候總是有人大笑特笑的；而且知道，這種人無論如何都是盲目的，因此他覺得，與其讓他們犯別種樣子不大雅觀的毛病，倒不如讓他們笑得眯起了眼睛。他自己打從心底在笑，而這對他來說，已經是很足夠的了。

從此以後，他跟幽靈們[22]不再有往來，而是根據"滴酒不沾"的原則生活。後來人們常常談到他，說如果現在世上有甚麼人懂得怎樣過好聖誕節的話，那就要算是他了。但願人們說我們也正是這樣，我們大家都是這樣！因此，正如小添說的：上帝保佑我們，每一個人！

完

註解：

1 踏車：一種梯級形、圓桶形或長帶形的木輪踏車，設在監獄內，令犯人
  終日踏着，旋轉不停，作為刑罰。

2 濟貧法：英國救濟貧民的法律，其經費來自納稅人所繳濟貧稅。史高治
  這裏的意思是説，既然已經交過税，還要再拿出甚麼錢呢？

3 聖鄧斯丹：英國傳説中十世紀的一名修道士，用一把燒得通紅的火鉗鉗
  住魔鬼的鼻子，使它號叫着討饒。

4 當時每逢聖誕節，常有小孩們穿街走巷，唱着聖誕歌討錢。

5 穿制服的人：十九世紀時倫敦七十六家公司和同業公會的榮譽市民、
  會員等，都穿特製的制服，故有此稱。

6 "駕一部六匹馬（或四匹馬）的大馬車衝破新法案" 是一句英國諺語，意
  思是像駕着一部大馬車似的橫衝直撞，把國會剛通過的法案加以破壞。
  意指新法案往往不夠完善，有很大空間可鑽。

7 據《聖經·馬太福音》第 2 章第 1 節，東方有三位博士觀星象而發現耶
  穌基督降生，這顆星在他們前面引路，使他們尋到伯利恆，在約瑟的貧
  苦的家裏，拜見新生的嬰兒。

8 范倫坦和奧遜是法國中世紀騎士故事中的主人公，他們是一對孿生兄
  弟。

9 指英國詩人威廉·華茲華斯（1770 – 1850）的《寫於三月》，其中有名
  句："四十頭牛食草，靜如一頭。"

10 按照英國古老的風俗，男子可以吻凡是站在一串懸着的檞寄生下面的女
   子。

11 "鮑伯"：英國俚語，意為一先令。

12 這裏指的是罰物遊戲中的一種，名叫 "我愛我愛人有個 A 字"，由參加
   的人輪流説出自己所愛的人是怎樣的，要求在這句話的末尾用一個以 A
   或 B、C 等字母開頭的詞。説不出者受罰。

13 原文 bear 一詞亦可指卑鄙粗野之人。

14 第十二夜指主顯節前夕，一月五日的晚上。主顯節為聖誕節假期的最後一天，所以"現在聖誕節之靈"的生命即將結束。

15 引自《聖經・馬太福音》第 18 章第 2 節。當耶穌的門徒問他："天國裏誰是最大的？"他就叫孩子來，説凡是謙卑得像這孩子的，在天國裏就是最大的。"

16 這種顏色指她正在做的喪服的黑色。

17 拉奧孔為希臘神話中特洛伊城的一個祭司，因在特洛伊之戰中，勸市民不要把敵人留下的木馬拉進城而招女神雅典娜之怒，使他們父子三人被海中的兩條大蛇纏繞而死。

18 星期天衣服為英國老百姓在星期天才穿的最好的衣服，不同於平時勞動所穿的服裝。

19 喬・密勒為英國民間傳説中的笑話作者，有一本《喬・密勒笑話集》的古老的書，內容主要是十六、十七世紀時的笑話，據説收集的就是他説過的笑話。

20 法尋：英國舊硬幣，值 1/4 舊便士。

21 緊身衣：一種厚帆布製成的長袖衣服，給發瘋的人穿上，束住手腳，使他無法動彈。這裏是説鮑伯以為史高治發瘋了。

22 "幽靈們"的原文 spirits 另有一種含義：烈酒，酒精。狄更斯在這裏用了雙關語，是説史高治改過自新，不僅戒酒，而且從此以後不再跟鬼打交道了。